Hannah Murray

The Devil and Mrs. Johnson

ELLORA'S CAVE
ROMANTICA PUBLISHING

*W*hat the critics are saying...

ઔ

"Hannah Murray brings us a story of action, adventure and hot sex that jumps off the pages." ~*Ecataromance Reviews*

"Hannah Murray's The Devil and Ms. Johnson starts off with a bang and keeps on delivering one misadventure after the next in this playful and erotic spy story...Ms. Murray really has a way with words." ~*Love Romances*

"The Devil and Ms. Johnson is fun, exciting, sexy and laced with humor. I really enjoyed this book and highly recommend it." ~*Joyfully Reviewed*

"This book was a pleasure to read." ~*Fallen Angel Reviews*

"The Devil and Ms. Johnson is fun from start to finish. Ms. Murray has written a great afternoon read!" ~*Romance Divas*

"Hannah Murray's The Devil and Ms. Johnson is a snappy, laugh-out-loud funny romance, filled with witty dialogue and fast-paced action...a Gold Star Award read." ~*Just Erotic Romance Reviews*

"One of the best erotic action books that I've read, The Devil and Ms. Johnson will appeal to anyone who loves a book with a great adventure, an outstanding story, sensual love, and wonderful characters." ~*Romance Reviews Today*

"The Devil and Ms. Johnson is an exciting love story...Hannah Murray gives her readers a story that is action packed, full of surprises, and at times funny." ~*Romance Junkies Reviews*

An Ellora's Cave Romantica Publication

www.ellorascave.com

The Devil and Ms. Johnson

ISBN 9781419955297
ALL RIGHTS RESERVED.
The Devil and Ms. Johnson Copyright © 2005 Hannah Murray
Edited by Mary Moran
Cover art by Willo

Electronic book Publication November 2005
Trade paperback Publication May 2007

Excerpt from *Grounded* Copyright © Rose Middleton, 2007

Content Advisory:

S – ENSUOUS
E – ROTIC
X – TREME

Ellora's Cave Publishing offers three levels of Romantica® reading entertainment: S (S-ensuous), E (E-rotic), and X (X-treme).

The following material contains graphic sexual content meant for mature readers. This story has been rated S-ensuous.

S-*ensuous* love scenes are explicit and leave nothing to the imagination.

E-*rotic* love scenes are explicit, leave nothing to the imagination, and are high in volume per the overall word count. E-rated titles might contain material that some readers find objectionable—in other words, almost anything goes, sexually. E-rated titles are the most graphic titles we carry in terms of both sexual language and descriptiveness in these works of literature.

X-*treme* titles differ from E-rated titles only in plot premise and storyline execution. Stories designated with the letter X tend to contain difficult or controversial subject matter not for the faint of heart.

Also by Hannah Murray

৯০

Jane and the Sneaky Dom
Knockout
Tooth and Nailed

About the Author

৯০

Hannah Murray started reading romances in junior high, hoarding her allowance to buy them and hiding them from her mother. She's been dreaming up stories of her own for years and finally decided to write them down. Being published is a lifelong dream come true, and even her mother is thrilled for her—she knew about the romances all along. Hannah lives in southern Texas in a very small house with a very large dog, where the battle for supremacy rages daily. The dog usually wins. When not catering to his needs, she can usually be found writing, reading, or doing anything else that allows her to put off the housework for one more day.

Hannah welcomes comments from readers. You can find her website and email address on her author bio page at www.ellorascave.com.

THE DEVIL AND MS. JOHNSON

Dedication

&

*Thanks as always to my friends and family for
believing in me, especially my mom, who has turned into
my biggest fan and a one-woman PR dynamo. Thanks
also to Mary Moran, my tireless and always cheerful
editor who never yells at me, even when she should. And
a special shout out to Kim, who owns the real Raul, and
Amy, who thought he should have a name.*

Trademarks Acknowledgement

Chapter One
Washington, DC

ഇ

Devon Bannion checked his watch for the fourth time in as many minutes and mentally cursed a blue streak. He was going to miss his plane.

He sat outside the office of the man who was currently making him miss his flight, comfortable in the deep leather club chair. Outwardly, he appeared calm, even bored, with one booted foot casually propped on the opposite knee, his battered New York Mets fielder's cap in his lap. His eyes were shaded by mirrored sunglasses, his jaw was covered with three days' worth of stubble and he was at least six weeks past due for a haircut.

To the office workers who buzzed around him like busy little bees in a cubicle-crowded hive, he looked like a rumpled, drowsy, bored man who maybe had just traveled a great distance. They glanced at him as they hustled by with their manila folders and documents and snacks from the commissary, then looked away and went about their business. A few of the women gave him a second glance, and one even tripped over her own shoe when he stretched in the chair, but other than the adoring female glances and stares, which were pretty much a hazard wherever he was, the office drones largely ignored him.

Which was fine with Devon. The fact that no one was looking at him with suspicion or calculation was a refreshing change. No bullets to duck, no jungles to escape, no smugglers or murderers or arms dealers to catch. He could just kick back, relax and go with the flow.

Old habits, however, die hard. Without even realizing it, he was automatically scanning the crowd for potential threats, and he'd chosen the only chair in the reception area that put his back to the wall and offered an unobstructed path to the exit. He sighed in resignation. It was probably going to take several years for the paranoid habits Uncle Sam had taught him so well to fade away.

The door behind the reception desk opened, snapping him out of his thoughts and putting him on automatic alert. A dark-haired man stood in the doorway. "Devon."

Devon rolled his eyes behind the aviator shades at the stiff formality of the greeting. He'd known the man for fifteen years, and he still sounded more like a butler at a dinner party than someone who'd once mopped up his blood after a mission. "Preston," he drawled.

Preston Smythe-White's expression didn't so much as flicker. "Please, come in."

Devon unfolded his legs, scooped up his cap and came slowly to his feet. He strode past the receptionist who'd been eyeing him covertly since he'd first come in and was now watching him with her tongue all but hanging out. Unable to resist, he inched the shades down the bridge of his nose so he could look at her over the tops of them. He gave her a wink and a slow grin, chuckling to himself when she dropped her pen in her coffee cup.

He walked past Preston and his disapproving look into perhaps the dullest, drabbest office on the planet. The gunmetal gray filing cabinets, the pressboard and veneer bookcases, and chairs covered in cracked vinyl stood in stark contrast to the casually modern and expensively appointed reception area.

"Jesus, Pres." He turned to his old friend. "Don't you have seniority?"

"Yes." Preston walked around his desk—gunmetal gray to match the filing cabinets—unbuttoned his suit coat, hitched

14

his trousers with precise, economical movements, and sat in the burgundy vinyl desk chair that had probably been around when J. Edgar Hoover was running the feebs.

"Well then, don't you think you could get some decent furniture?"

"What's wrong with my furniture?"

Devon snorted out a laugh. "You're wearing an eight-hundred-dollar suit and sitting in a chair worth about fifty cents."

Preston blinked and folded his hands neatly on the desk. "My wife picked out the suit."

Devon chuckled, shaking his head. "You don't change, do you?"

"Why would I?" He gestured to the other cracked vinyl chair in the room. "Sit, Devon."

With a sigh, he sat. "Why do I not think this is going to be good news?"

"A certain situation has come to our attention," Preston began.

Devon's eyes narrowed. "No."

"This situation involves certain members of a well-known Eastern European crime syndicate."

"No."

"Our intelligence tells us they're preparing to enter the United States and, once they have, they'll be attempting to—"

"Dammit, Preston!" Devon slammed his fist down on the desk. Preston didn't even blink. "What part of *no* do you not understand?"

"It isn't a request, Agent Bannion."

Devon leaned back in the chair. "I'm not an agent anymore—I'm retiring, remember? The Ukraine was my last job."

"It *was* your last job. Now this is your last job."

15

"Uh-uh."

"Yes-huh."

Devon would've been amused at the incongruity of a guy with the last name Smythe-White using teenage slang if he wasn't so pissed off. "I'm retired, Preston."

"Not yet."

"Why?" He dragged his fingers through his hair in an effort to keep from strangling one of the highest-ranking officials in the international intelligence community. "You've got dozens of well-qualified agents who can handle it, most of them are younger than me and I'm sure all of them have a better attitude."

"That certainly goes without saying. However, we feel your particular skills and expertise would be an asset in this operation."

Devon's opinion of that was short, succinct and anatomically impossible.

"In addition," Preston continued, unfazed, "you have experience in dealing with these particular individuals. Now, the FBI will coordinate and Treasury has given us a full budget for this operation—"

"Wait a minute." Devon sat up straight in the chair. "What does Treasury have to do with this?"

"This is a counterfeiting case and therefore falls under the jurisdiction of the Treasury Department."

"So why not let them handle it?"

"Treasury doesn't have the intel to handle this particular situation. We do. Or more specifically, you do."

"Treasury is going to let us handle it?"

"They are."

"Do they know you want me on it?"

"They do."

"And they're okay with that?"

"They're resigned to it."

Devon snorted. "That's bullshit. Treasury hates me."

"While certain members of the Treasury Department are less than thrilled with both your track record and your involvement in this operation—"

"How was I supposed to know she was his niece?"

"—they have, after careful consideration, decided to defer to our greater knowledge in this matter. And since you're our operative with the most experience in this area, they're willing to use you. Even if you are the 'Devil'."

Devon winced—he hated that nickname—even as he snorted in disbelief. Then he got a good look at Preston's face. "You're serious, aren't you?"

"Perfectly."

"Oh, Christ, Preston," Devon said impatiently. "Take the stick out of your ass for one minute and just tell me."

"There's no stick in my ass, and I am telling you. You're to go undercover, with a partner from the local FBI field office as support, to stop an international arms smuggler from becoming an international counterfeiter."

"Aw, fuck." Devon groaned. "I'm supposed to be in a wedding in—" he glanced at his watch "—six and a half hours. I'm supposed to be on a plane in forty-five minutes."

Preston reached into his desk drawer and hauled out a manila folder so crammed with papers it had a rubber band around it to hold it together. He slid it across the table to Devon. "This is the data you'll need to be briefed on for this operation."

"What are the chances of my getting out of this?"

Preston simply stared at him, unblinking. Devon cursed under his breath. "Give me a minute," he muttered with ill grace, and dug in his pocket for his cell phone.

He punched in the number. While he waited for his friend to answer, he slipped the rubber band from the folder and began to leaf through the pages.

"Domino's Pizza."

Devon grinned at Ian's cheerful greeting. "I'll take a ham and pineapple with jalapeño peppers and extra cheese."

"Man, that's disgusting."

"Hey, to each his own, my friend."

Ian's response to that was a derisive snort. "So you on the plane yet?"

Devon winced. "Not exactly. I'm in Preston's office, being coerced into one last job."

"Thought your retirement went into effect after you got done with the Ukraine."

Devon's mouth twisted into a sour smile. "Yeah, so did I. But Smythe-White here, he's got other ideas."

"Typical of him. What's the job?"

"Don't know yet." Devon continued to absently thumb through the pages of the file as he spoke. "But they've got a file here with enough paper to give a tree hugger a heart attack." He turned the page, absently skimmed the slightly fuzzy copy of a fax. He was in the midst of turning to the next when he froze and quickly flipped back. "Holy shit."

"Well, that doesn't sound good."

Devon ignored Ian and stared at Preston. "Are you sure about this?"

Preston's expression became slightly haughtier. "We don't make mistakes, Agent Bannion."

"Yes, you do."

"Okay, we do. But I don't, and not about this."

"Dev?" Ian's voice sounded sharply in his ear, jerking him back the conversation. "What is it?"

"It's Devereaux."

"You're kidding." Ian's voice went low and hard as flint. "What's he doing back in circulation? After the debacle in Prague a while back, I thought he was laying low."

"Yeah, he was." Devon was turning the pages faster, skimming quickly for information. "Looks like Interpol kept tabs on him for a bit, a few sightings here and there."

"Agent Bannion," Preston began, "that's classified information, and subject to—"

Devon spared him a glance. "Fuck off." He grinned briefly at Ian's chuckle and turned his attention back to the pages in front of him. "Then it looks like he went under."

"Shit," Ian swore.

"Yeah. That was eighteen months ago. The good news is," Devon said as he read the pages of a CIA brief, "he's not running arms anymore."

"What's the bad news?"

"He's moved on to counterfeiting."

"Oh, nice. And with his roster of contacts, I'm sure he'd have no trouble finding a market."

"Yeah. I'm sorry, Ian, but it doesn't look like I'm going to make the wedding."

"I figured that, man. Don't worry about it, we'll figure something out."

"You sure? Your bride might be pretty pissed. I hear women get all weird about things like weddings and a missing best man might be seen as a problem."

Ian laughed. "Jane's just happy it'll be over and done with. Her mother's driving her crazy. And I'm sure her older brother can stand in as best man."

"Great. I'd hate to think I ruined your big day. Too bad, though. I really wanted to see Jane again and I was looking forward to being able to explore Chicago a bit before you got back from your honeymoon and I had to go to work."

"Chicago?"

Devon looked up at Preston. "Yeah, Chicago. That's where I'm moving, where I'm going into business, and where I was headed when you hauled me in here."

"Coincidentally, that's where you'll be rendezvousing with your partner for this assignment." Preston smiled genially.

Devon narrowed his eyes. "Coincidence. Really."

"Dev?"

"Sorry, Ian." Devon turned his attention back to his friend. "I probably won't make the wedding, but I'll be in Chicago. Apparently, the Chicago FBI office is coordinating this little party."

"Huh. Nice coincidence."

Devon smiled fiercely at Preston's blank expression. "Isn't it?"

"How long's it going to take you to get through the briefing?"

Devon eyed the file. "Three, four hours at least."

"Okay, so with the prep work and arrangements, you might hit town by midnight. Sound about right?"

"If I'm lucky," Devon muttered.

"Okay, stay at our place."

"Yeah?"

"Yeah. We're not leaving for Hawaii until tomorrow, but Lacey got us the honeymoon suite at the Drake as a wedding gift, so we won't be at the apartment tonight."

Devon whistled softly. "Nice wedding gift. Wait—you're staying at Jane's apartment? What happened to the house you bought?"

"I'm having some work done while we're out of town. Renovating the bathrooms, new kitchen tile. The contractor screwed up the dates and started a week early, so we're temporarily back at the apartment. Jane's lease wasn't up until the end of next month anyway, so there's a lot still there."

"Is the bed still there?"

Ian chuckled. "Yep."

"Then I'll take you up on it. Where can I get a key?"

"There's no secure place at the apartment to leave one. I'd have Lacey give it to you, but you might beat her there. She'll be at the reception late most likely, doing some maid of honor thing that I'd rather not know about. I assume you're still skilled in certain areas?"

Devon grinned. "You want me to break into your apartment?"

"Beats me having to figure out a way to get a key to you." Ian rattled off the address of Jane's building and apartment number. "Listen, if you make it in early, stop by the wedding."

"Will do."

"Do not, under any circumstances not involving death, dismemberment or government coup, stop by the honeymoon suite."

Devon laughed and clicked off. He looked up at Preston. "Okay, start filling me in."

Chapter Two
Chicago

೧

Lacey yawned so hard she felt her jaw pop then blinked watery eyes as she tried to fit her key into the lock. She wasn't really her best at three a.m.—even when sober—and she was about as far from sober as it was possible to get and still be vertical. She juggled her liberated bottle of champagne as she fought with the lock. Through what she liked to think was sheer force of will, she managed to finally fit key into lock, opened the door and lurched into the hallway.

She swung the door shut behind her, the resounding bang as it connected with a smidge more force than she intended echoing though the hallway. She winced then shrugged. No neighbors to worry about. Mrs. O'Malley was visiting her sister in Gary, Jane and Ian were ensconced in the honeymoon suite at the Drake having fabulous newlywed sex and the fourth apartment in the renovated town home was empty. So there was no one to hear her stomp around.

The thought was so depressing she slumped against the wall and nearly dropped the champagne. She stood there for a moment, wallowing in the self-pity that had been threatening to engulf her all evening. Her best friend was married and was moving away from what they'd always thought of as their little bachelorette pad. From now on, she wouldn't be just upstairs to talk with or eat with or watch bad reality television with—although Jane had sworn a blood oath that they'd keep their standing dates for *The West Wing* and *Survivor*. But afterwards, Jane would be climbing into her car and driving back across town.

Lacey tipped her head back against the wall and blinked back sentimental tears. She knew she was drunk and overly emotional and acting like a bitch. She was really happy for her friend. Ian was a great guy and he certainly loved Jane. Not only that, he genuinely got her, got what she was about and what made her tick and knew how to get around the little defense mechanisms and shields she used to keep people away. No one had really bothered before, and Jane had walked all over every previous boyfriend because they'd been so concerned about doing and saying what they thought she wanted that she got bored and ditched them.

But Ian hadn't done the expected and Jane hadn't ditched him, and now they were off to Hawaii and happily ever after. Lacey was thrilled to death for both of them. And jealous as hell.

She winced and straightened up, looking at herself in the hallway mirror. "You," she said to the blowsy-looking blonde in the pink bridesmaid's dress, "are a hideous bitch. It's not all about you, ya know." She stuck her tongue out at the mirror then tucked the bottle of champagne under her arm, hitched up her dress and started up the stairs to Jane's apartment.

"Gotta water the plants," she muttered. "Feed the fish. Wait, they don't have fish. What'm I s'posed to feed then?" She frowned as she trudged down the hall, thinking. "No cat. They don't have a dog."

She squinted one eye and aimed her key at the lock, hitting it on the first try with sheer dumb luck. "Maybe it's feed the plants. But then, what'm I s'posed to water?" She turned the key and shoved open the door, shutting it behind her and automatically flipping the locks.

She dropped her keys on the table by the door, not bothering to turn on the lights. She knew Jane's apartment just as well as she knew her own and the lights would just hurt her head. She took three steps and tripped over a pile of packing material, falling and twisting at the last second to land on her hip in order to save the champagne.

"Dumb moving stuff," she muttered, and gave a roll of bubble wrap a bad-tempered kick. It sailed across the room and smacked into an African violet. Not hard—it was bubble wrap, for crying out loud—but it made the plant teeter on its already precarious window ledge perch and, after a couple seconds of teetering, it toppled to the floor.

It bounced once in its plastic planter and landed, violets down, on the bubble wrap.

Lacey shrugged. "One less to feed. Or water. Whatever."

She struggled to her hands and knees, cursing like a sailor when she got caught in the damn dress. She ended up having to put down the champagne in order to stand up then had to grab onto the back of the couch when the room spun merrily around her. When the spinning slowed down enough so she could stand on her own, she grabbed the champagne, tucked it under her arm like a football and headed for the kitchen.

Watering the plants took about twice as long as it would have if she'd have put down the bottle, and about four times longer than it would have if she'd been sober. She even watered the African violet, after scooping it back into the pot along with most of the soil, because she felt bad that it had fallen victim to her maid-of-honor depression. She looked for plant food but since there wasn't any, she figured she was just supposed to water and the feeding part of the instructions had just been her imagination.

She couldn't seem to get the watering can to fit in its regular spot under the kitchen sink, so she left it propped against the wall by the sink and started to head down to her own apartment. But the room did that tilt-o-whirl thing again, and this time it didn't seem to want to slow down enough for her to get off. And since she figured stairs would probably not be a great idea, she made her way into the bedroom, one hand on the wall for support, the other for the champagne, of course.

She tripped over another stack of packing boxes that were piled next to the bed. Since it was right there, this time she aimed her fall at the mattress. She landed about half on and half off, her feet dangling off the side and the champagne bottle pinned underneath her. She wriggled around a bit because the cork was digging into the underside of her left breast, and managed to pull it out from under herself after only three tries. She flailed her feet to get rid of the shoes that were already dangling by the toes and curled into a ball on the middle of the mattress. The champagne hugged tight to her breast, she fell into sleep almost immediately.

* * * * *

Devon paid the cabbie and started up the walk, juggling what he considered to be a ridiculous amount of luggage — a carryon and a garment bag. He'd have left the garment bag at home but he'd already had the tuxedo packed for the wedding, and there hadn't been time to drop it off at the apartment before catching the last flight out of DC. The carryon held a change of clothes and his shaving gear, which, in his opinion, was all that was ever needed, except for his gun. He wasn't carrying it now, however, because trying to get through airport security with a firearm after September 11 was way too much trouble, even if he did have all the correct paperwork and authorization. He figured he'd just acquire what he needed from the field agent he was supposed to meet with tomorrow to finalize the arrangements for his assignment.

He set the bags down on the stoop and unzipped the garment bag, taking a slim case from an inside pocket. He eyed the lock for a moment then selected his tools and went to work. He grinned when it popped free in less than fifteen seconds. "I still got the touch, baby," he murmured, and, picking up his bags, stepped inside.

The walls were standard apartment off-white, but the floor was a warm golden pine under a colorful throw rug and there were delicate sconces on the wall that threw soft light into the hall. He took the stairs two at a time, grinning at the framed, autographed photo of Abbot and Costello in their baseball gear, which hung on the landing. He found the door marked 4 and, noting with a raised brow the double deadbolt, dug out his tools again.

It took thirty-seven seconds, but he got it open. He set his bags beside the door and took a look around in the dim wash of light from the hall. He'd only met his friend's fiancée—check that, his friend's wife—once, but from what knew about her from Ian, the apartment fit her personality to a T. Colorful, interesting art competed for space with books, knickknacks and plants. The furniture was modern and looked comfortable, like a guy could prop his feet on the coffee table without anyone throwing a fit. There were packing boxes and rolls of bubble wrap stacked hither and yon throughout the living room, and from what he could see of the kitchen through the open arch, it was in the same half-packed state.

He nudged the door closed with his foot. Leaving his bags by the front door for the time being, he went to the kitchen. A quick search of the refrigerator yielded half a meatball sub and a single bottle of Rolling Rock. He'd have preferred a Guinness, but he figured beggars couldn't be choosers, so he sat down at the kitchen table and assessed the sub. The butcher wrap had yesterday's date on it, so he figured it was still good and made quick work of it, washing it down with the beer.

Devon glanced at the glowing numbers on the stove clock—one in the morning. He was tired, but years of training had conditioned him to ignore the toll that travel and stress took on the body so he didn't need sleep right away. But he had to be at the local FBI field office at ten o'clock in the morning and, for once, he didn't have to stay awake to stay alive so he swung by the living room to pick up his bags and went to check out the bedroom.

More boxes lined the hallway, some filled, taped and labeled clearly for the move, some half filled and more still standing empty in piles. He dodged them with ease, his eyes having grown accustomed to the dark, and looked for the bedroom. He peeked into the first room he came to—bathroom. He noted with relief that he wouldn't have to hunch over in the shower then moved on. The next door yielded a linen closet that smelled faintly of vanilla and held half a dozen fluffy-looking bath sheets. Thankful that his absent hosts hadn't gotten around to packing up the towels yet, he moved on to the room at the end of the hall which he presumed, since it was the only one left, held a bed.

He used two fingers to twist the knob then nudged open the door with his foot. He stood, staring in bemusement at the elfin-looking blonde sleeping curled up on the bed.

"Well." He let his bags drop with a thump. "This ought to be interesting."

Chapter Three

ဢ

Devon rubbed his hands over his eyes but she didn't disappear. Nuts.

He stepped into the room, leaving the door open at his back as an escape route out of habit. He didn't really think she was an international operative sent to seduce him and derail his latest assignment, then kill him while he slept in post-coital bliss, but he wasn't taking any chances.

There was enough moonlight and spill over from the hall light to see by so he didn't bother turning on a light. He toed more packing boxes out of the way and stepped closer, not taking his eyes off the blonde. For such an itty-bitty thing — probably no more than five foot one or two, it was hard to tell by the way she was curled up on the bed — she certainly had a helluva snore. He was surprised he hadn't heard it on his way down the hall. He ignored the window-rattling noise and looked his fill. She was young, maybe mid to late twenties, and delicately built. The thing she was wearing — some sort of pink gown thing, from what he could see — was strapless, leaving slim arms and gently rounded shoulders bare. He could see the gentle ridge of her collarbone and the fine bones of her wrists and hands. Hands that were cradling — was that a bottle of champagne? He grinned. Sleeping Beauty wasn't sleeping — she was passed out cold.

He leaned in, more curious now than cautious. She had a head full of blonde curls, the kind that mothers used to put in their little girl's hair for Sunday church, all fat and sassy and bouncy. Some of those curls had been pinned back — and some still were — but the majority of them had escaped their confines and now fell across her face. He allowed himself a small chuckle when he saw the curtain of hair that blanketed her features lift in concert with her exhale then settle again as she breathed noisily in. He frowned a bit—the enormous champagne bottle and her tucked-up position kept him from seeing most of her figure, which was annoying. He angled his head to the side, but it didn't improve the view any.

Devon shook his head. "Wrong thing to focus on," he muttered. He stopped trying to guess her cup size and concentrated on figuring out who she might be. From what Ian had told him of Jane's best friend and downstairs neighbor, he figured he was looking at Lacey Johnson. If memory served, she was also Jane's maid of honor, which explained the dress. It sure looked like something a maid of honor would wear, at least to his untrained masculine eye, and the champagne made sense if she'd just come from a wedding reception. But what was she doing in Jane's apartment instead of her own?

She certainly looked as though she'd partied a little too hearty, but from what he'd gleaned from Ian's grumpy grumbling over the last few weeks, Jane's mother had spared no expense in the wedding of her only daughter. What Jane and Ian had intended as a low-key, intimate gathering of family and close friends had turned into a Martha Stewart-worthy circus, complete with catered sit-down dinner for four hundred, couture dress and a wedding cake that cost more than he paid in rent all year.

Considering all that, he imagined they'd also had an open bar. Which would explain the maid of honor not only being a tad on the snookered side with a full bottle of bubbly, it might also explain how she'd ended up in the wrong apartment.

However, in his line of work it didn't pay to make assumptions. So he decided to wake her up and find out just what was going on. He ruthlessly quashed any remorse he might feel about doing so—after all, she was snoring away in what was supposed to be his bed for the night—and reached down to shake her awake.

He laid one hand on her shoulder, noting with absent and automatic interest the soft, supple texture of her skin, and brushed the hair off her face with the other. Her features were relaxed in sleep. Surprisingly long lashes fanned shadows on flushed cheeks and the bone-rattling snores were coming from a dainty-looking Cupid's bow mouth. He gave her shoulder a quick shake, trying to ignore the fact that she smelled fabulous. "Lacey."

Nothing. Except the snoring did increase in volume slightly.

He shook her again with a little more force, called her name about six inches from her ear—where the warm, gently spicy scent of her was even stronger—and got the same result. He sat down on the edge of the bed, hard, and watched while she bounced under the impact. It didn't even put a hitch in her snore. Jesus, was she in a coma? The thought entered his mind that she might be on something, even though he couldn't see Ian marrying a woman who was best friends with a junkie. Still, he checked her eyes. Doe brown irises surrounding pupils that were equal and reactive.

Well, hell. She wasn't on drugs, she didn't seem to be hurt in any way. She was just sleeping hard. Really, really hard. He sighed, resigning himself to a night on the sofa. No matter that he had an invitation to stay there, his Southern belle grandmother would box his ears if she knew he'd forced a lady out of bed.

He stood, ready to head back to the living room and a sofa that was sure to be too short. He glanced down at her, amused in spite of himself at the way she was curled around the champagne bottle. It couldn't be comfortable, he thought, to sleep like that. No matter that she was out cold—she was sure to wake up cramped and sore and probably a little bruised. She looked like she had delicate skin—she'd definitely bruise. Probably definitely. So, the least he could do would be to take the bottle so she wouldn't bruise. In the interest of protecting her, of course. From the bruising. It had nothing to do with the possibility that without the bottle, he'd be able to see her chest.

And now he felt like a major pervert. What kind of sicko tried to sneak a peek at the chest of a woman who was snoring so hard she was almost sucking her own hair down her throat? The same sicko, he thought with no small amount of self-disgust, who had a semi-erection just thinking about the snoring woman's chest. Devon walked toward the door, disgusted with himself and determined to be a gentleman if it killed him, dammit.

But... He stopped at the door, hands gripping his suitcase handles. There was still the matter of her delicate skin and the very real possibility she would bruise like a peach. He released the bags and turned back around. She was lying exactly as he'd left her, curled around the champagne and snoring like a teamster. He'd just...pluck it from her grip. That was it. Then he'd leave, go back to the living room and sleep on the sofa.

That was the plan. But apparently the universe didn't buy the "because she'll bruise, not because I want to see what her tits are like" argument.

Chapter Four

ॐ

His reflexes saved him from a concussion. He was pretty sure of that, and would likely be grateful for it when the swelling went down.

All he'd done was lean down, lay one hand on her wrist—gently!—and with the other hand on the neck of the bottle, started to slide it out of her slack grip. If he hadn't had his eyes on her face—or rather, what he could see of her face through the mass of hair—he wouldn't have seen her eyes fly open. On the other hand, if he hadn't been watching her face and thus hadn't been mesmerized by the startling beauty of it when she was awake and not snoring like a wounded buffalo, he might have felt her grip shift and tighten on the bottle.

But he didn't. The only warning he got was the flare of awareness in those suddenly open, doe-brown eyes and the sudden flash of green glass out of the corner of his eye. Instinct had him ducking to the side, but the bottom of the magnum glanced off the side of his head then bounced to his shoulder. He grunted under the impact and tried to dodge out of the way, but his feet got tangled in a pile of empty packing boxes and he pitched forward, his balance thrown. Unfortunately, he landed right on top of Lacey.

Experience and training had taught him that most women, while strong and independent and fully capable of taking care of themselves in everyday situations, often panicked in high-danger situations and lost focus. They were products of their society, one which told them that it was impolite to yell, that a lady didn't hit, that it was unseemly to cause a ruckus. So they waited until it was often too late to act. Somehow, he didn't think this girl had gotten that memo.

She started shrieking so loud his ears rang. "Get off me, you sick, twisted son of a bitch!" She punctuated each word with a whack, swinging the champagne bottle like Babe Ruth. He'd landed heavily on her torso with his face tucked into her neck. At that angle, it was impossible for her to reach his head, but his back and shoulders were easy enough to reach, and she didn't waste any time shifting targets.

"Pervert!"

Smack!

"Freak!"

Wham!

"Puppy kicker!"

"Puppy kicker?" He picked his head up at that and glared at her, then swore ripely when she landed a blow to the side of his neck. "Goddammit! Give me that bottle!"

"No!" She stuck her tongue out at him then landed another blow while he simply stared at her in astonishment.

"Jesus!" He levered himself up on one hand and wrapped the other around the champagne bottle. He gave it a hard yank, expecting her to fight him to keep it. Instead, she let go instantly and his own momentum caused his arm to snap back at the lack of resistance, and he smashed himself in the nose with the butt of the bottle.

He rocked back, temporarily blinded by the fresh pain that exploded in his face. He fought to keep his precarious perch on the bed, his arms pinwheeling frantically. Then she planted her foot in the middle of his chest and pushed, and he went flying over the footboard with a roar.

He decided at that point his best course of action was to stay put. If she called the cops, he'd just show them his credentials and get it all straightened out. It would take a while—they'd have to call the local field office and verify his identity, and perhaps even contact Preston's office in DC to make sure, since no one in the local FBI office knew him yet. But at least he wouldn't be arrested.

If she decided to finish him off, he wasn't sure he could stop her.

He tried to blink the spots from his eyes and reached up a cautious hand to see if his nose was broken. He was wiggling it gently, hissing at the resulting pain, when her face suddenly filled his vision.

"Ah!" He couldn't help the flinch.

"Don't you move," she growled at him, jabbing a French-manicured finger dangerously close to his face. "I'm calling the cops, and you can explain to them what you're doing sneaking into people's bedrooms and taking their champagne."

"Okay," he gasped, focused on that pointing finger. It was dangerously close to his already abused face, and he didn't trust her not to bop him one again.

"Okay." She gave a satisfied grunt then peered at him a little closer. "Hey. Do I know you?"

"No, no you don't." He wasn't taking his eyes off that finger.

"You look awfully familiar." She scooted a little farther off the end of the bed, hovering over him like a disheveled Tinkerbell. The finger all but poked him between the eyes.

He shrunk back into the floor, his eyes all but crossing as he tried to keep the finger in focus. "No, really. We've never met. Shouldn't you go call the cops?"

"In a minute." She took her hand out of his face to brace it, along with the other one, on the footboard. He exhaled slowly, relieved to see the finger go. However, she used her grip on the footboard to boost herself forward until they were all but nose to nose.

"No, I think I do. I know you." She frowned. If it wasn't for the fact that the chest he'd been trying to ogle was threatening to spill out of her dress, she'd look about twelve years old. "But why do I remember you with dirt on your face?"

Devon was trying to keep his eyes off her cleavage—which, for such a slight woman, was very impressive. "I don't know. Are you going to call the cops now?"

She ignored him, moving her head around, peering at his face from several angles. "Yeah, I definitely remember you with dirt on your face. And wearing weird clothes. Weird black clothes. Or maybe weird green clothes."

She was making him dizzy, ducking and bobbing around like that. The fact that her dress was losing its battle with gravity wasn't helping his concentration any. "Honestly, we've never met before."

"No, I don't think we have." She stopped bobbing and weaving and all but pushed her face into his. "But I still know you from somewhere."

Devon had just about had it. His body, already battered and bruised from what was supposed to have been his last assignment, was feeling every ache and pain she and her damn champagne bottle had inflicted. He'd be lucky if his nose wasn't broken, and he didn't think that going undercover with a broken nose was the best way to maintain a low profile. The local feebs would probably be annoyed.

Which normally wouldn't bother him, but since he'd been practically blackmailed into this assignment and his retirement appeared to hinge on its successful completion, he'd rather not have it mucked up. Plus, they were bound to ask how his nose was broken and he'd rather not have to tell him that Tinkerbell did it. He'd never live it down.

"Look," he began, "we have never—"

"That's it!" She squealed. "I've got it! You're Ian's friend! You're the Devil!" With that, she flung her arms into the air in victory, lost her balance and fell on him.

Chapter Five

๛

Lacey really didn't think that it was fair for him to blame her for the state of his face and she told him so.

"Honestly," she said from inside the freezer where she was gathering ice for a cold pack, "how do you expect me to react to a man hovering over me in the middle of the night?"

He didn't answer as he was trying to keep his freshly bloodied nose from dripping all over the kitchen floor.

She turned to him, folding the ice into a tea towel. "You're lucky you only ended up with a broken nose."

"I dobt tink ids brwoked."

"Huh?"

He took his fingers from where they'd been pinching his nostrils shut. "I said, I don't think it's broken," he said, then cursed when blood began to flow again.

"Here, sit down and tilt your head back." Lacey dragged a chair over from the table and waited while he eased himself into it, then settled the ice pack onto his nose. She winced when he hissed in pain. "Does it hurt?"

He stared at her over the tea towel. "No, it tickles."

She sniffed. "You don't have to be snide. I said I was sorry about your nose."

"I know," he said, then muttered something under his breath.

"What?"

"I said, you were right."

She blinked. "What was I right about?"

He sighed. "About me being lucky that it's just my nose that's hurt. You could've smashed my balls, I suppose."

"I was going to, but my dress is too tight and I couldn't get the angle," she admitted.

"Thank God for that."

"Besides," she went on, pulling a chair next to his and curling up on it Indian-style, "I had the champagne and it made a dandy weapon."

"It sure did," he ruefully lifted the ice pack and surveyed the bloodstains on the tea towel.

"Put it back on," she directed, and he did, sighing as the ice numbed the sting.

Lacey tugged her knees to her chest, her bare heels on the seat of the chair and her arms wrapped around her legs as she watched him try to get comfortable in the too-small chair. Now that she'd recognized him, she couldn't see how she'd ever mistaken him for a burglar slash rapist. She'd seen his picture countless times, every time she'd been over to Jane and Ian's house. They'd done most of the wedding planning out of Ian's home office, and the only personal photo in the room—in the whole house, actually—was one of Ian and Devon in some jungle somewhere.

She'd actually spent a lot of time looking at that picture. It sat on a bookshelf next to the workstation, and every time Jane and her mother had locked horns over some wedding detail, she'd distracted herself by looking at the handsome warrior in the picture.

They'd been dressed in some sort of combat fatigues, all dark greens and blacks, with their faces smeared with something that turned their skin the same color as their clothes. Both men had impressive-looking weapons—which she couldn't identify if one was pointing at her—slung over their shoulders by some sort of strap, and they each had some sort of fancy utility belt that held all kinds of nasty-looking toys. Knives, extra bullets, and what she thought might have been hand grenades. She couldn't be sure though, having never seen a hand grenade before, at least not outside of an Arnold Swarzenegger movie.

She'd also never seen such a handsome man before. Ian came close, but when she'd met him, he'd already been irrevocably involved with Jane, and the fact that he was spoken for lowered his hottie-factor a few points. Still a hottie, but an unavailable one, and since he was in love with her best friend, he'd almost automatically been relegated to honorary brother status. The tawny-haired Adonis—she almost winced at the analogy, but really, it was so fitting—was another matter entirely.

Since she couldn't tell from a picture if he was involved with anyone, she felt perfectly safe in assuming he wasn't and consequently could fantasize about him as much as she wanted.

And, oh, she'd fantasized. While Jane and her mom went round after round over the flowers, the caterer, the centerpieces, the cake, the canapés—canapés, for sweet Lord's sake!—the dress, the music…Lacey had just focused on the photo. Imagining herself flat on her back in some tent in the jungle, his big, rangy warrior's form looming over her as he devoured her like a decadent desert.

Looking at him now, sprawled in one of Jane's kitchen chairs, blood dripping on a shirt that had already seen better days, he looked more like a bum than a warrior. But he was still a hottie.

She was quiet for so long, Devon started to get nervous. The ice pack she'd made for his battered nose was roughly the size of a bowling ball and he couldn't see her face over it. But he could make out the top of her head—her hair was sticking straight up—and he could see her bare feet out of the corner of his eye. Her big toes were twitching. Not her feet, just her big toes. Like she was tapping her toes independently. Which, frankly, was a little weird.

Finally, the silence got to be too much. "What?"

He saw her hair move and assumed she was shifting position in the chair. "Aren't you supposed to be like, this super-dangerous mercenary or something?"

Not seeing her face while she was talking was making him nuts so he scooted the chair around so he could see her and keep the ice pack on. "A what?"

She shrugged. "A mercenary. The 'Devil'. That's what they call you, right? Devil?"

He tried to scrunch up his face in a scowl, but the swelling made it more of a grimace so he gave up and settled for a glare. "I hate that nickname. And, no, I am not a mercenary."

"No?"

"No. I work for the government."

Lacey blinked big brown eyes at him. "There's a difference?"

He put more effort into the scowl this time. "Yes, there's a difference. A mercenary is a hired gun. They work for anyone with enough money to hire them and they'll do anything they get paid to do."

"And that's different than what you do for the government?"

"Yes."

"How?"

"I don't make any money."

She snorted a laugh. "Right. But you are some kind of agent, right? Law enforcement, stopping bad guys, that kind of thing?"

He sighed and adjusted the ice pack. "Unfortunately, yes."

"Highly skilled, combat-trained, blah, blah, blah, etcetera?" She took his pained mumble as agreement. "So, how come I kicked your ass?"

That got his attention. He sat straight up, the ice pack falling forgotten to the floor. "Come again?"

Lacey blinked, surprised. Well, here was the warrior from the picture. His voice had gone very soft and dangerous-sounding, even with the slight nasal quality she attributed to the swollen nose. She tried and utterly failed to suppress the purely female shiver in the face of all that testosterone. "Ah…I said, how come I kicked your ass?"

"You did not, 'kick my ass'." He practically growled it at her.

"Excuse me, but I think I did." She started counting on her fingers. "I beat you about the neck and shoulders repeatedly—"

"'Beat me about the neck and shoulders'?"

"Repeatedly." She gave him an arched look and continued ticking items off on her fingers. "And I bloodied your nose and kicked you, and landed on you and bloodied your nose again."

He was getting better at the scowl. "You got in a couple of shots with the champagne bottle and you did kick me and fall on me, but I bloodied my own nose."

She frowned thoughtfully. "You kinda did, didn't you?"

"Only because I was defending myself, trying to get the bottle away from you, and you let go too fast."

"You were defending yourself because I was kicking your ass."

She could practically hear his teeth grind. "You were not."

She held up her hands in a gesture of peace. "All right, all right. I didn't kick your ass. You kicked your own ass, I was just there to watch."

He glared at her. "You know, you look like a cream puff, but you're really a barracuda, aren't you?"

She beamed at him. "It's so sweet of you to notice!"

He groaned and picked up the ice pack from the floor. He grimaced at it—the ice had soaked through the towel and made it a sodden, bloody mess. He rose, carrying it over to the sink and dumping it in.

Lacey watched as he began to wash up. "So, why are you sleeping up here?" he asked, keeping his back to her.

"Hmm? Oh, I got a little sloshed at the reception." He really had a fine butt, she decided. It shimmied just the tiniest bit with the movement of his body as he scrubbed his hands with dish soap. She felt her mouth start to water, and it wasn't from the citrus scent of the soap.

"I figured that out from the snoring," he said dryly, still facing the sink. "But if you were drunk, why didn't you just crash at your own place, rather than climb a flight of stairs? Although you seem fairly sober now."

"I wasn't totally blitzed, just a little tipsy. And I don't snore." She said it automatically as her attention was still on his very presentable ass. It looked apple firm. She wondered what would happen if she took a bite out of it. "And how come you know where I live?"

"Darlin', you were sawing logs like Paul Bunyan." He startled her, flashing a quick grin over his shoulder before he turned back again. "And I know where you live because Ian told me."

"Oh." That was a close one. She felt a giddy laugh bubbling up in her chest and squeezed it off before it could escape. He'd just about caught her eyeing his ass like a piece of candy. She took a slow, steady breath and tried to cool her suddenly heated blood.

"So?" he asked, looking over his shoulder again. "How come you crashed here instead of at home?"

Lacey nodded at the watering can that still stood next to the sink. "I promised to water the plants."

He looked at the can, leaning haphazardly against the tile backsplash, and she took the opportunity to eye his ass again. She put her feet back on the floor and fussed with the skirt of her gown, rubbing her thighs together in what she hoped was an imperceptible attempt to ease the sudden ache between them. Just one little bite. Okay, a big bite, with maybe a lick or two—

"Lacey."

Her eyes flew to his and her cheeks flushed guiltily. "What?"

"You were staring at my ass."

To her complete mortification, she felt her cheeks flush. "I don't know what you're talking about."

"You were!" He was grinning at her over his shoulder while he finished rinsing his hands.

"You know, I'm surprised you can walk, what with that ego weighing you down."

He winked at her, eyes twinkling with mirth. "Honey, I don't need an ego when I caught you eyeing my butt like the last cookie in the jar."

"Hah!" Lacey snorted. "You wish."

"Nah, *you* wish." He was clearly enjoying himself now, leaning back against the sink, ankles and arms crossed. "You wish you could take a big bite out of me."

That statement hit a little too close to home. In the absence of any other strategy, she decided to try to brazen her way out of it. "Please," she sniffed. "I may have noticed that you have a slightly better than average tushie—"

"Tushie?"

"—however, that doesn't mean I want to bite it, for Pete's sake." She rolled her eyes. "Jeez."

"You lie worse than anyone I've ever met."

Her mouth fell open and she stared at him. "That is the meanest thing anyone's ever said to me!"

"Well, it's true." Devon started chuckling. "You can't even look at me when you talk, you're staring over my shoulder. That's the biggest tell in the world."

"Fine." Lacey narrowed her eyes, keeping them on his. "Your ass is awful. Flat, narrow and saggy. It's a chicken butt."

Devon snorted a laugh. "You're really bad at this."

"I looked at you!"

"Yeah, but I know I don't have a chicken butt. If you're going to lie, you've got to make it at least marginally believable." He shook his head, still chuckling.

"You are so mean." She glared at him then got up off her chair, tugging her dress back into place as she headed for the door. "See if I ever fantasize about you again," she muttered under her breath.

"What?"

She stopped walking and turned as he straightened from his easy slouch against the sink. "What?" she repeated.

His eyes were dark as he stared at her. "What did you just say?"

She moistened her lips with her tongue and watched his eyes track the movement. "Um...nothing?"

"I don't think it was nothing." He took a step toward her. "You said 'fantasize'."

"Nuh-uh."

His lips twitched. "Yes-huh."

Lacey heaved a sigh. "Okay, fine. I said 'fantasize'. What of it?"

"So, tell me about some of these fantasies."

"No."

"No?"

"That's what I said." She crossed her arms over her chest. "You were mean to me, and you called me a bad liar and I'm not sharing with you."

"I was mean to you? I'm the one who got beat up!"

"Ah-HA!" She pointed at him. "You admit it! I kicked your ass!"

"Jesus." Devon rolled his eyes at the ceiling, clearly trying to get a grip so he wouldn't smack her. Lacey just waited him out—she was used to the reaction.

"It's just as well." He muttered, still looking at the ceiling. "I can't sleep with you."

Lacey blinked. "Huh?"

"You're Jane's best friend," he said, still looking at the ceiling. "So it's just as well you think I have a chicken butt." He paused, his brow furrowing in confusion. "Who painted all the fat babies on the ceiling? They sparkle."

She frowned, annoyed. "Jane did, and they're not fat babies, they're cherubs. Cherubs are supposed to sparkle. And don't change the subject." She paused. "What was the subject?" she asked.

"My chicken butt," he offered, still looking at the sparkling cherubs. "What're they doing?"

"Bowling. And we weren't talking about your chicken butt—which you know very well it isn't. Jesus, I could serve tea on that ass," she said. "We were talking about why you can't sleep with me."

"Uh-huh. Jane painted sparkling, bowling cherubs on her ceiling?"

Lacey shrugged. "She got bored with the motorcycle-riding goats. And what does that mean, 'you can't sleep with me'? Who asked you to sleep with me?"

He shrugged and pulled his gaze from the cherubs and bowling pins. "Nobody. But I couldn't anyway, so it's just as well."

"Because I'm Jane's best friend?" At his nod of assent, Lacey threw her hands up. "What's that got to do with anything?"

"Ian wouldn't like it."

"What the hell's that got to do with anything?" Lacey repeated in a near wail.

"Trust me." He grinned at her again, apparently enjoying her confusion. "He wouldn't like it."

"Maybe not," she allowed grumpily. "So what? Do you always factor his feelings in before you sleep with someone?"

"No. But I think there's some rule about sleeping with your best friend's wife's best friend. So it's a good thing I don't have to worry about it."

"Right." Lacey frowned. "Good thing."

"Although, I have to admit," he said, "I'm curious about these fantasies."

"Alleged fantasies," she corrected.

"Right. Alleged fantasies." He settled himself on a kitchen chair, straddling the seat and crossing his arms over the back. He grinned at her, oozing charm and sex and pheromones, and she felt herself getting a little lightheaded from the combination.

"You shouldn't smile at people like that," she admonished, her voice not nearly as prim or strong as she'd have preferred. "You could cause an accident or something."

"Come on," he cajoled. "Tell me a fantasy. It's the least you can do after kicking my ass."

"Nope, can't do it. Wouldn't be fair to you."

"Oh?" He raised one tawny brow in question.

She sniffed. "I'd just end up taking horrible advantage of you."

"How do you figure that?"

She shrugged. "I'd tell you my fantasies then you'd want to go to bed with me, and you already said you didn't want to."

"Not true." He held up a finger. "I said I can't sleep with you, not that I didn't want to."

She rolled her eyes. "Semantics. The result is the same."

"Besides," he continued, "I'm not that easily seduced. So I really doubt you could do it just by telling me a fantasy."

"Oh, honey—" she looked at him with pity "—you have no idea the power I wield."

He grinned at her, obviously entertained, and she felt herself go lightheaded again. That smile was lethal.

"You a gambling kind of woman, Lacey Johnson?"

She narrowed her eyes slightly. She loved to gamble, it was her favorite recreational activity. But he was up to something. "Depends on the bet."

He nodded, angling his body on the narrow kitchen chair to dig into one of his front pockets. He pulled out a money clip and peeled off a couple of bills, tossing them on the table. "A hundred bucks says you can't seduce me."

Chapter Six

ॐ

Lacey starred at the money on the table and didn't know if she should be amused or offended. She looked at him. "You're nuts."

He shrugged, pure devilment dancing in his eyes. "You're so confident in the 'power that you wield', take the bet. If you don't—" he spread his hands "—I'll have to assume you're all talk."

She crossed her arms and stared at him through narrowed eyes. "Honey, I could make you forget your own name."

"Then prove it. Put your money where your mouth is. Unless, of course…"

Lacey knew she shouldn't ask but she did it anyway. "Unless what, chicken butt?"

He shrugged. "Unless you're scared."

No way could she let a statement like that go unanswered. "Okay, little man, you're on." She dipped into the bodice of her dress.

"Little man?" he asked, watching her hand disappear into her cleavage. "Baby, if you win this bet you'll find out different. What are you doing?"

"Looking for…dammit!" she muttered, and slid her other hand into her dress. After a few seconds of fishing around, she let out a triumphant "Ah-ha!" and held up her hand, displaying a fistful of cash.

"You always keep cash in your cleavage?" he asked, watching her uncrumple the wad of bills.

"I had to tip the caterers," she said absently, counting. "Sixty, eighty, one hundred. There." She strode over to the table and slapped five wilted twenties on top of his two crisp fifties. "Bet."

Devon grinned. "So. Seduce me."

Lacey held up a hand. "Slow down, quick draw. What're the rules?"

He shrugged. "Rules are you have to seduce me."

"Doy. But what constitutes a seduction?"

"Well," he said, "you have to convince me to do what I've already said I don't want to do, which is sleep with you."

"You didn't say you didn't want to sleep with me, you said you couldn't."

"Touché," he grinned at her. "You have to convince me to do what I said I couldn't do."

"Okay." She nodded, bouncing on her toes like a prizefighter stepping into the ring. "Any restrictions?"

"You can't touch me," he decided. "And you have to tell at least one fantasy."

"Doy," she muttered again. "Is that it?"

"That's it." He spread his arms wide, smiling smugly. "Do your worst."

"I have to tell a fantasy?" she asked. When he nodded, she smiled. "Okay. Well, Jane planned the wedding with her mother, you know."

He frowned. "If this is how your fantasies start, you're losing that hundred bucks."

"Bear with me. As maid of honor—" she jerked a thumb at herself "—I had to sit in on most of the wedding plans. Now, I don't know how much you know about mothers and daughters and weddings, but there was bickering. Lots of it. Especially when Mrs. D wanted salmon croquets and Jane wanted asparagus wrapped in prosciutto. Or when Mrs. D wanted herb-roasted squab and Jane wanted prime rib. Or when—"

"I get it." Devon held up a hand to halt the litany. "They butted heads. I think I'll buy tickets to a Blackhawks game with your money."

"I'll loan you my season seats," she said. "So, when they'd start in on the appetizers or what have you, I'd just kind of tune them out and distract myself. And since we did most of these brainstorming sessions in Ian's office, the most distracting thing in the room was the picture of you."

Devon frowned in surprise. "Ian has a picture of me in his office?"

"Yeah, you and he in some jungle setting, all decked out in fatigues and grinning like a couple goobers."

Devon stared at her. "Goobers?"

"Yeah. And you had face paint, I guess to match the outfits or whatever. So whenever Jane and her mom would get into it, I'd get into you."

"Well, now we're getting to the good part," he said, twisting the chair around so he could face her and stretch his legs out. "Took you long enough."

"I'm just getting started. So, I was having all these fantasies and…"

"Yes?"

"I wasn't wearing this much clothing in them." With that, she reached for the hidden seam in the side of the dress, flicked the zipper down and let the dress fall. She smiled as his eyes went blank and his jaw went slack. She gave brief mental thanks to Jane's mother who had insisted on the gravity-defying strapless bra that was currently holding her breasts to her chin and Devon's attention. The skimpy g-string she thanked herself for. "I have this showerhead," she said conversationally.

Devon swallowed audibly. "Showerhead?" he echoed, his eyes riveted to her cleavage.

"Hmmm." She reached behind her and almost nonchalantly unclipped the bra. It slipped free, landing in the puddle of pink satin already on the floor.

"So," she continued. "This showerhead. It's got seven different settings, handheld. I've had it since college. I call it Raul."

"Raul," he said, still starring at her bare breasts. The apartment was comfortably warm, but excitement had her nipples tightening and Devon was all but drooling at the sight. "Um…why?"

"Why do I call him Raul?" She watched him nod, not taking his eyes off her chest. She smiled. "Well, considering what he does for me, not giving him a name would just be so…impersonal."

That got his eyes off her tits for a second. "Yeah? What does Raul do for you?"

"Oh, he's sort of my all-purpose man substitute, if you know what I mean." Lacey hooked her thumbs in the thin strings on her hips, toying with them while he watched.

"So anyway, I'd be tuning Jane and her mother out, concentrating on that picture of you, and then I'd go home to my lonely, empty bed. And I'd be tense. I have trouble sleeping when I'm tense, do you ever have that problem?" She inched the panties down her hips.

"Gnog," he said, completely focused on the descent of that tiny scrap of black silk. She decided to take that as a yes.

"So when I'm tense and can't sleep, I usually take a nice, hot shower to help me relax." She smiled and shimmied the rest of the way out of her panties.

She stood in her best friend's kitchen, naked as a jaybird, knowing she looked pretty damn good. Spinning and weight lifting, while torturous and evil, nevertheless helped her maintain a trim and taut physique, despite her somewhat adolescent eating habits. Sometime around her mid-twenties, she realized her metabolism had started to change and it was either work out regularly or give up potato chips and sticky buns. Since she had no intention of switching to veggies and tofu, she put in enough hours at the gym to keep everything firm and where it was supposed to be.

And from the way he was staring, slack-jawed, she figured it was all worth it. She skimmed her hands over her own skin, up her torso, over the rise of her breasts, and hummed a little sound of desire in the back of her throat.

"But a hot shower usually isn't enough to make all the tension go away." She stroked her palms back down, sliding them over her hips, circling around to her belly. She tickled her fingers against the bare flesh of her pussy, pulling his eyes there like a lodestone. She knew in the harsh light of the kitchen there was no way he could miss the dampness that coated her flesh.

"Uh...so...uh...what makes the tension go away?"

She allowed herself a humming chuckle at the hoarse quality of his voice. "Well, I'm a big believer in natural stress relief. Like endorphins."

"Endorphins."

"Mmmmm," she purred, still idly stroking her fingers along the damp flesh of her pussy. The look in his eyes combined with the thrill of touching herself in front of him was getting her pretty worked up.

He managed to tear his eyes away from the juncture of her thighs to look at her face and the wild light in his eyes kicked her heart rate into high gear. "So how do you get endorphins?"

"Exercise, of course. Although, since I don't have any gym equipment in the apartment and my gym isn't open twenty-four hours, sometimes it's hard to work up a good sweat. But Raul, he's great with endorphins."

She was dragging her fingers back up the sleek plane of her torso, leaving a damp trail of her own juice over her skin. She saw him swallow hard, licking his lips, and couldn't suppress a shudder of her own at the thought of his mouth on her.

With an effort, she pulled her mind back to the task of seduction. "So, Raul. Did I mention he has seven different settings?" He nodded, eyes still glued to her fingers. They were now toying lightly with her breasts, just brushing over the bottom curve and up across the turgid nipple. "And did I mention that my favorite setting is 'pulse'," she whispered.

His eyes were glued to both her hands now as she brought them together over her pussy. "And when I put him right here—" she pointed "—and put the setting on 'pulse'," she fluttered her fingers, mimicking the rapid beat of the showerhead. She moaned slightly, her eyes closing as the little sparks of arousal turned into lightning bolts as she drummed her fingers on her clit.

"When I do that," she continued, her voice thick now with strain and lust, "the tension just seems to drift away."

She panted, slightly out of breath, and opened her eyes to look at him. His eyes were riveted on her hands, his breath coming in harsh pants and tension showed in every line of his body, despite his slouched posture in the chair. She raised one eyebrow at the very definite bulge in his jeans.

"Well," she said in as normal a tone as she could manage, "that ought to do it, I think."

She took two strides and, reaching past him, picked the money up from the table. She was careful not to brush her breasts against him, so as not to violate the rules of the bet. She saw him inhale sharply, picking up the scent of her skin, heated by her arousal. She straightened, bringing her fingers, coated with her own fragrant moisture, within inches of his nose and folded the bills in half. She turned on her bare heel and walked away, feeling his eyes on her like a physical stroke. She stopped at the doorway, casting a look over her shoulder.

"I'm a little tense, Devil-man. Do you have any endorphins you could lend me?" She didn't wait for him to answer but turned and sauntered down the hall to the bedroom. Lacey could feel his eyes boring into her back as she walked and could barely contain her excitement. And when she heard his chair scrape back and his footsteps thundering after her, she smiled in triumph and anticipation.

Chapter Seven

 જી

She reached the bedroom door and nudged it open with her foot. She sauntered into the room, skirting boxes and packing materials to reach the bed. She set the money on the night table then bent down and picked up the champagne bottle from where it lay on the floor. She turned to find him standing in the doorway, watching her with that incredible heat in his eyes. "Don't think I'll need this, do you?"

He managed a saucy grin. "If you like it that rough, honey, I'd better excuse myself right now."

She giggled, surprising herself. She hadn't enjoyed herself this much with a man in a long time. "Oh, don't worry. I might like a little variation from time to time, but my tastes don't run to bruises. And I don't have the submissive fantasies Jane does, either."

She found it immensely amusing that his face went totally and completely expressionless at that. "Submissive fantasies? I don't know anything about that."

She snorted, rolling her eyes. "Please. I know you boys talk like old biddies over the fence." She pointed a finger at him, eyes dancing. "And if you didn't know what I was talking about, then your face wouldn't look like you're facing down interrogation."

He had the grace to look slightly sheepish. "Okay, so Ian told me. But I resent the 'old biddies' comment."

"If the shoe fits," she said. "Anyway, I just wanted you to know that if that's what you're hoping for, it's really not my thing. I prefer to participate."

"Well," he rumbled, reaching out and taking the bottle from her, "it so happens I like a participatory kind of woman."

Lacey watched as he set the bottle on the bedside table, unable to hold off a shiver at the thought of those hands on her. "Well then," she managed, taking a deep breath, "that works out well."

He grinned at her, all predatory male, and she felt her pussy clutch in anticipation. He flicked on the bedside lamp, adding its soft glow to the light spilling in from the hall. He sat on the bed and braced his hands on the mattress. "Now that I'm seduced," he all but growled, "what do you plan on doing with me?"

She smiled, regaining her equilibrium at the lust in his eyes. She took a step toward him. "Well, I think you're a little overdressed, don't you?"

He watched her with hot eyes. "You don't believe in foreplay?"

"Of course I do. I'm female. But I prefer my foreplay naked." She took another step forward, her smile knowing and just a little smug. "And I should warn you that I don't fantasize like most women."

She watched his Adam's apple bob convulsively as he swallowed. "Yeah, I see that," he managed.

"A lot of women fantasize in whole stories. You know, they picture the entire event in their minds, from the first meeting to the sweaty, orgasmic end."

"And you don't?" he asked, his eyes on her hands as she stroked them over her torso.

She shook her head, enjoying the little zing of lust in her blood. "No, I like to just...get right to it, you know?" She slid the fingers of one hand into the damp slit of her sex. "So in most of these fantasies we were already naked. And I'd hate to do this part without you."

She squeaked in surprise as he lurched to his feet. "What're you—" she broke off when he started stripping off his clothes with dazzling speed.

"You're not doing this without me, that's for damn sure." His voice was muffled by the shirt he was trying to pull off over his head. He got it stuck, presumably because he didn't bother to unbutton it first, and she began giggling at the stream of creative profanity coming from his mouth.

He finally got the shirt off, flinging it across the room. It hit a bedside lamp with enough force to topple it from its perch. Luckily, it was off and landed in an open box of blankets and quilts. His hair stood on end, full of static electricity from its bout with the shirt, and he was breathing like he'd just run a marathon, which brought her attention inevitably to his chest.

"Oh, that's nice," she whispered, not even aware she'd spoken. He was better than she'd imagined, with just the most beautiful chest. Muscled, but not overly bulked up like a bodybuilder. No, this was a man who stayed fit doing things besides pumping iron, and it showed. He was hairy too, a fan of dark fuzz spreading over his pectorals and tapering down to a nice little trail that disappeared into the waistband of his jeans. A happy trail, Jane would've called it and, right now, Lacey could concur—she was *very* happy.

She watched his hands go to the button of his jeans, pop it open. "Wait!"

"*Wait?*" he repeated, his voice incredulous.

She laughed. "No, not wait like that. Just—" she dropped to her knees in front of him and gripped his waistband "—wait for me."

He rumbled a moan as she stroked her hand down the hard ridge of his cock through his zipper. She licked her lips, fingering the little metal tab that was all that stood between them.

He cursed under his breath as she took her time, drawing out the simple act of unzipping his pants until he was all but writhing under her hands. The metal teeth parted slowly, revealing tanned skin, tawny hair and no underwear.

She looked up at him from beneath her lashes. "Going commando?"

He bared his teeth in a tight smile. "Didn't get to the laundry this week."

She smiled, flicking her tongue out to wet suddenly dry lips. "One less thing to peel off."

She started to slide his pants down, slowly, when he suddenly stepped back. "Oh, no," he said, shaking his head. "I'm not going through that again." And he shucked them off himself.

She stood and swallowed hard, her mouth suddenly dry. His cock stood fully erect, throbbing in time with the frantic beats of his heart. She felt her pussy throb in time with her own heart, flooding with moisture.

"Jesus," he groaned, and her eyes flew to his.

"What's wrong?"

He shook his head, his dark eyes hooded and fierce on hers. "I could actually *see* your pussy get wet," he growled. His eyes dropped to the juncture of her thighs where moisture glistened in the faint light. "And I can see your clit."

Lacey licked her lips and fought not to whimper. His gaze on her was like a physical touch, sending shivers racing over her skin and winding the knot of desire in her belly tighter. She drew a shuddering breath and straightened her spine, feet slightly apart, and let him look his fill.

"Should be able to see it better now," she purred, sliding one hand down her belly, the tips of her fingers flirting with the bare flesh of her cunt. She could feel the moisture gathered there and such heat she was surprised she didn't see steam.

Devon growled low in his throat and she felt her pussy clutch again at the sound. Desperate to get back on track and regain the upper hand, she blurted out, "Did you want to hear more about those fantasies?"

"Oh, yeah," he rasped. He took a step back and settled on the bed, stretching out full-length and propping himself up on the pillows, hands behind his head. "I definitely want to hear about them. As I recall, they start out with us naked."

She nodded. "Yes, we were definitely always naked. And usually in some kind of tent."

"A tent?"

"The only picture I had ever seen of you was in some jungle, so I always pictured us in a tent in the jungle." She shrugged, smiling. "But I'm flexible, so we'll substitute tent with best friend's bedroom."

He grinned. "Gotcha. Go on."

"Well." She walked around to the foot of the bed, toeing empty boxes out of the way. She bent forward, placing her hands on the footboard. "In my favorite version, I crawl on top of you."

He remained still, but his breathing deepened and his cock twitched tellingly. "Why is that your favorite?"

Lacey climbed onto the bed and crouched on all fours over his lower legs. "Because that way," she whispered, "I get to feel your whole body against mine, inch by inch, until I get close enough to kiss you." She cocked her head to the side. "That sound all right to you?"

He watched with hooded eyes as she bent her arms, lowering her torso far enough to tease his shins with her nipples. "Mmmm," he rumbled. "What're you waiting for?"

She grinned. "What's your hurry, handsome?"

He quirked a brow. "In case you haven't noticed, I'm sporting a baseball bat for a dick here."

She surprised herself by giggling. God, this was fun. "Trust me, I noticed. But ya know, there's something to be said for taking your time." With that, she lowered her head and drew her tongue up the inside of his knee.

He hissed, cursing as his hips arched. He shifted his legs farther apart. "I noticed you like to take these things slow," he groaned.

"Slow and steady wins the race," she murmured, and nipped his leg.

He hissed. "Go as slow as you want to, baby," he muttered, and shifted his thighs farther apart.

She smiled against the hair-roughened skin of his inner thigh. "Thank you, I think I will," she sighed. She closed her eyes, inhaling the musky scent of his skin. Sweat and sex and man—it swirled into her head and made her dizzy with lust.

She worked her way up his legs, alternating back and forth between them with licks and nibbles and little sucking kisses that brought a steady stream of groans and heavy breathing. She wasn't breathing so easily herself, the taste and scent of him going to her head like a half a dozen Jell-O shots.

She finally reached the juncture of his thighs, humming in approving delight as she drew in the scent of him. It was stronger here, darker and more intensely masculine. Unable to help herself, she nuzzled her nose into the skin there and inhaled. "God, you smell like sex on toast," she groaned.

He laughed, the sound strained and sharp. "That's a compliment, I think," he gasped.

She chuckled, smiling when the brush of her breath against the tender skin of his balls had him hissing in pleasure. "Oh, it was meant as one, believe me. I wonder…" she let her words hang in the air, raised herself up. She waited until he lifted his head to look at her. Her own sex clutched with lust at the look of blind need in his eyes and she had to take a shuddering breath.

"I wonder," she continued, her voice raspy and shaky with her own need, "if you'll taste as good as you smell." And with her eyes on his, slowly dipped her head and engulfed the head of his cock in her warm, wet mouth.

His head fell back with a groan at the first touch of her tongue on him then raised it again to watch her with hooded eyes. She moaned, the taste of him exploding in her mouth as she swirled her tongue around the swollen head of his cock, gathering the pre-come already pooling there. She drew away with one last lingering lick. "Mmmm," she murmured. "Oh my, that's nice. Can I have some more?"

"Be my guest," he managed through clenched teeth, and she chuckled again.

"That's very generous of you," she whispered, and bent over him once more. She drew him deep with one stroke, glorying in the thrill of both his taste and his moan of approval.

Lacey had always felt that oral sex was more than just foreplay. She'd never understood a woman who went in for a couple of cursory licks then rolled over on her back and claimed paybacks. Giving pleasure, in Lacey's opinion, was just as much fun—if not more so—than getting it, and she intended to enjoy herself with the Devil.

She settled into a rhythm, using her hands and mouth, teeth and tongue, to bring him to the brink and keep him perched there. He trembled under her hands, his cock leaking pre-come steadily, and she lapped it up like a cat would fresh cream. His hands came up, stroking her hair away from where it had fallen in her face, and she shifted her eyes up to find him watching her. She moaned out loud, feeling her pussy tighten and tingle. Somehow having him watch her suck his cock while she looked into his eyes made the act, already one of the most intimate ones she could think of, almost unbearably intense.

She closed her eyes briefly then forced them open again. She wanted to watch his face when he came.

She'd just begun a deep, tight stroke, taking him all the way to the back of her throat and sucking hard, when she felt his hands suddenly tangle in her hair and tug her back. Surprised—because what guy stops a blow job?—she released him immediately and found herself dragged up his body until her face was even with his.

"Why'd you stop me?" she panted. Her hands were braced on his chest, her face inches from his. She was so close she could see the little flecks of black and green that lived in the golden brown of his irises. "You were close, why didn't you let me finish?"

"Is that your fantasy?" he rumbled. "The one you pictured in your head when you used Raul for tension relief?"

She licked her lips. "One of them."

He looked a little surprised. "Really?"

"Oh yeah," she whispered, panting. "You'd come into the tent, tired and tense and unable to rest. And I'd…relax you."

He let out a rough laugh. "If you did it in your fantasies half as good as you do in reality, I'd have been dead by the time you were finished."

She grinned. "I'd be happy to continue the demonstration."

He shook his head. "Uh-uh. I want to hear a different fantasy. One where we both participate."

"Okay," she breathed, feeling the liquid heat of her own arousal spill out of her. Perched as she was on the flat plane of his stomach she doubted he could miss it.

"God, you're so wet," he said, and she couldn't even feel embarrassment that he'd noticed. She was so turned on, more so than she'd been with anyone else recently, and all she could think of was finding a condom and sliding him deep inside her where she needed him most.

Before she could do more than think it, she found herself twisting in the air, landing flat on her back with him looming over her. She blinked in surprise. "What...?"

He grinned at her with that fierce warrior's grin she remembered so well from the photograph. It was even more powerful now, when she knew the desire in his eyes and the fierce determination in his face was all for her. "Participatory, remember? You got your turn, now I—" he slid down her body "—get mine."

Lacey opened her mouth, to say what, she wasn't sure. But whatever it was slid back down her throat as he clamped his mouth over her breast. She choked back a scream at the suddenness of his mouth on her. She arched hard against him, riding the wave of sensation, her head tossing on the pillow and her fingers clutching at his hair.

"Oh, God, Devon. Oh, please, don't stop, whatever you do, don't stop!"

He growled something against her skin that sounded like, "*not on your nelly*", but the blood in her head was roaring and she couldn't really tell. And didn't really care, as long as his mouth stayed on her.

He treated her breasts like a starving man treats an all-you-can-eat $3.99 Vegas buffet, devouring her in great gulps. He went back and forth between her breasts until they both glistened with the moisture from his mouth and both peaks stood out like pencil erasers—hard and pink. Normally sensitive anyway, the touch of his teeth against her aching flesh had the effect of an electric shock, and soon she was sobbing mindlessly with lust.

He picked up his head, his fingers taking the place of his mouth, twisting and tugging and pulling as he watched her face. "You like that."

It wasn't a question, but she answered anyway. "Yes," she gasped, arching into his touch, her legs shifting restlessly against him as she struggled to get closer. "Please."

"Please what?" he murmured.

"Please what?" she repeated, confused, and forced her eyes to focus on his face.

He was staring down at her with the fierce sensuality that had been so apparent to her in the photograph. She licked her lips. "What do you mean, 'please what'?"

His voice was so low, so rough with lust, she had to concentrate hard to understand him. "These fantasies are participatory, right?" She nodded, panting. "So my part of the fantasy is I want you to tell me what you want. I want that perfect, sexy mouth—" he lowered his face until he was a hair's breadth away from her lips "—to give me the words. Tell me what you want, what you need." He brushed his mouth over her trembling lips once, twice, gentle as a breeze. "Give it to me," he whispered.

Chapter Eight
ᴇᴏ

Lacey thought for a moment her heart would explode. When it didn't, she figured it was God's way of telling her to go for it. So with a sound that was half moan, half squeal, she dragged his head down to hers.

He kissed her like he wanted to eat her whole, and she gave it back to him with equal fervor. When they both needed air, he lifted his head. She only gave them both time for one gulping breath before she was dragging him back down for more.

Lacey whimpered and sucked at his tongue, desperate to hold some part of him inside her. She felt him stiffen above her, felt his groan rumble through his chest and vibrate against her sensitive nipples. He tore his mouth from hers, panting. "Tell me," he rumbled. "Tell me."

"I want your mouth on me," she whispered. "I want your hands on me, I want you inside me."

His eyes blazed, his nostrils flaring. "Where?" he rasped. He chest heaved like a bellows. "Where do you want my mouth?"

"Everywhere," she whispered. Keeping her eyes open, watching him, she pulled her hands from his hair and stroked her palms over her trembling breasts. "I want it on my breasts."

She slid her hands down, over the sweat slick skin of her torso. "On my belly." As her hands moved lower, he raised himself fully on his arms and followed their path with his eyes.

She spread her thighs, her knees bumping into his where they were braced on either side of her. "I want it on my thighs." She drew a shuddering breath when he looked up at her, her belly clenching at the lust there. "I want it on my clit, I want it on my pussy," she whispered. She dipped her fingers into the warm cavern of her sex, feeling the wetness there. She raised damp fingers to his mouth, shakily painted his lips with her own moisture. "I want it everywhere."

Devon growled against her fingertips, his nostrils flaring as he caught the scent of her on her hand. He flicked out his tongue, tasting her, and the tight leash he kept on his self-control snapped clean. He took her mouth hard, thrusting his tongue past her teeth over and over until she was squirming and twisting underneath him. He was fucking her mouth, mimicking the rhythm of sex, and driving her crazy.

Just when she thought she'd go insane, he tore his mouth free. He slid down her body, trailing his mouth down her neck, nipping at her throat, her collarbone. He paused at her breasts, treating each hypersensitive nipple to a quick lick-nip combo that had her hissing in renewed pleasure and her back arching off the bed.

He didn't give her system time to settle but continued down. Her stomach muscles quivered uncontrollably when he dipped his tongue in her belly button. When he trailed his tongue over the sensitive flesh where thigh met torso, her legs started to shake. "Devon," she moaned. "I can't...I can't..."

"Yes you can," he growled. And parting her engorged flesh with his thumbs, buried his tongue in her pussy.

Lacey screamed, the shock of feeling his mouth on her sending her flying over the first peak into orgasm. He gave a low growl of approval, sliding his hands under her buttocks and holding her surging hips tight as the orgasm pumped through her.

She would've sagged to the bed exhausted when the spasms finally faded, but he shifted. Sliding two fingers deep into her still quivering sheath, he fastened his mouth over her clit and incredibly, she found herself climbing back toward orgasm again.

He pushed her to come twice more before he finally moved away. She dimly heard him rustling around in the nightstand, heard with relief the telltale tear of foil that meant he'd be inside her soon. Then he was back, his broad shoulders blocking the light that spilled in from the hall and throwing his face into shadows. She felt him slide his arms under her legs, lifting them high and wide as he moved between her thighs. The brush of his cock against her thigh startled her out of her satiated stupor and she began to struggle feebly.

"Wait," she gasped, pushing her hands against the immovable rock of his chest. "Devon, wait. Please."

He frowned down at her, skin pulled tight across his cheekbones as he fought to keep from driving himself into her cunt. "What?" he rasped.

She didn't answer, just kept pushing against his shoulders until he sat back. She kept pushing at him, rising to her knees, and he finally relented and rolled to his back.

"If you've changed your mind," he growled, "you might as well just shoot me and be done with it. It'd be kinder."

Somewhere she found the energy to emit a shaky laugh as she straddled his hips. "I haven't changed my mind," she panted. She reached between them, grasping his latex-covered cock firmly, holding it in place as she rose up. "I just especially wanted to fulfill this part of my fantasy." She licked her lips. "I like to be on top."

His answering grin was fierce as he settled his hands on her hips, steadying her as she began to lower herself onto his aching cock. "Just do it fast," he groaned.

She laughed again, the sound strained. She lowered herself just far enough to take the sensitive head of his cock within the heated damp of her cunt then stopped. She shivered as the breadth of him stretched her tender opening, her flesh quivering and clutching as she adjusted to the feel of him inside her. She slid down another inch, biting her lip to hold back the gasping moan that threatened to spill out.

"None of that," he said, and her eyes flew to his face. He was watching her, his breath coming hard and fast, his face flushed and eyes glittering. "Don't bite your lip. I want to hear every moan, every whimper."

Compelled, she released her lip and slid down another inch. This time she let the moaning gasp slip out and felt his fingers tighten on her hips reflexively in response. She'd likely have bruises the next morning, but who cared?

She drew out the act of penetration as long as she could, sliding down a scant inch then stopping, savoring the feeling. This was her favorite part about sex, the heat and friction of that first piercing thrust. She could feel his heartbeat pulsing in the turgid flesh of his cock, the sensation wringing another whimper from her swollen lips.

She slid down a little more, gasping at the increasing sensation of fullness. He was big, bigger than she'd realized in the heat of the moment, and she began to worry that she wouldn't be able to take all of him.

"Don't do that," he muttered, and let go of her hips to lever himself up on his elbow. "Don't wreck it by thinking. You can take me, I know you can. Just let yourself go, baby."

She licked her lips and continued to inch down, crying out a little. She felt full, stretched to the limit. "I don't think I can," she gasped.

He hissed, grabbing hold of her hips again. She braced herself, squeezing her eyes shut and tensing in anticipation of being slammed down. Instead, she felt his thumb stroke over her pubic bone and down over her clit. He pressed hard, using a heavy stroke that had her breath strangling in her throat and her cunt clenching convulsively on his cock. She heard him draw a strangled breath of his own through the roaring in her ears, saw his own head go back through the starbursts in her vision.

Then he was looking at her, where his thumb was pushing against her in hard circles, and he groaned. "Lacey, look down." She stared at him, not understanding at first. "Look at us, you and me," he said, and the hoarse command in his voice had her automatically obeying.

She looked down, her body angled slightly backward as she tried to see what he saw. "Oh, God," she gasped. She could see the root of him, barely two inches left outside her body, the skin dusky under the sheen of the condom. She could see herself, spread around him like a clutching flower, pink and wet. She could see her clit throb in time with the beat of her heart and felt the first flutters of yet another orgasm begin to swirl in her belly.

"Oh, God, Devon," she whispered. She never took her eyes off the place where they joined, but held out her hands blindly. She felt him take them, his grip hard enough to grind bone and, hanging onto him, slid herself down the last two inches.

She hung there, clinging to him as she struggled to quiet the riot of her senses. She couldn't focus, couldn't concentrate, there was simply too much going on inside her. Her pussy felt stretched beyond its capacity, the flesh quivering and shivering around the wedge of his cock as her body fought to adjust and relax to the invasion. Her breasts felt heavy, the nipples throbbing in time with the racing of her heart. Dimly she heard him talking, words of lust and encouragement that she didn't really hear. She only heard the tone, the desire so thick in his voice it was a rumble that seemed to vibrate through her. She could feel the tension in him, knew he was giving her time to adjust and relax when every instinct he had was pushing him to move, to thrust, to fuck.

After a few moments the flare of discomfort at his sudden penetration had eased, and she drew a full, shuddering breath of relief. Then moaned as even that slight motion shifted her on his shaft enough to wring a spasm from her hypersensitive flesh.

She shifted her gaze to his face, licked her lips. "This," she managed, her voice hoarse and strained, "is my fantasy." And she began to move.

They both groaned as she rose up, her pussy clinging to his shaft in a wet kiss as she slowly pulled free. She slid up so that his cock barely remained inside her then slowly lowered herself again until she could feel his testicles against her bottom. The sensation was so delicious she barely paused before doing it again, the motion smooth and unhurried. And again, over and over at the same steady, slow pace, keeping her eyes on his face, her hands clutched in his for balance as she savored the feel of him.

Lacey knew he was holding back. His grip on her hands was nearly crushing and the muscles of his neck and shoulders were corded with strain. Every stroke of her cunt over his cock brought strangled moans and whispered curses from his lips, and his hips were surging now to meet her every down stroke. She wasn't sure how long she could continue to torture him with the slow pace—she could feel the force of her own orgasm building in her belly, and the urge to race to the finish was getting harder to ignore.

She let her eyes drift shut and focused on the sensations bombarding her body as she rose and fell on him steadily. The wonderful feeling of fullness as he pushed deep into her body, the luscious friction as she moved back up, the head of his cock catching and scraping along her sensitive inner walls as they clutched instinctively to keep him deep within. She could feel her skin prickle with increased sensitivity—it was almost as if a fine current of electricity ran just under the surface, tingling and sparking deliciously.

Wanting to feel his hands on her again, she leaned forward slightly and pulled his palms to her quivering breasts. Immediately his fingers closed on her sensitive flesh, kneading and stroking. She was so aroused, so tightly wound that a gentle touch would have been annoying, distracting. He seemed to know that, using strong fingers to knead and rub and pluck with enough pressure to add to her already intense arousal, her head falling back and a groan emerging from her throat.

Suddenly the slow and steady pace wasn't enough. "I have to move faster," she gasped, not knowing why she was telling him since she didn't wait for him to acquiesce but began moving faster almost before she finished speaking.

She thought she heard him say something like "Thank Christ", but the words sounded faint, as if spoken from a great distance. She moved even faster, racing now to get to the peak she could feel just beyond her reach. She knew the increased speed and force of her pumping hips would make her come within minutes and suddenly she wanted to be looking at him, connected with him with more than just her body when she did.

Her eyes flew open, unfocused and blind for a moment as she fought to get her bearings. Then his face snapped clear, his cheeks flushed and taut with lust, his eyes blazing. "I'm going to come," she gasped, biting her lip as she felt her orgasm begin to bloom.

He growled, pulling her attention back to his face. "Yes," he hissed. "Yes, come for me. Watch me while you come, Lacey, don't look away." He pumped his hips hard, lifting her clear off the bed. Her eyes all but rolled back into her head. "Don't look away."

She struggled to focus, trying to keep her eyes open and on his. She clamped her hands over his where they still rested over her breasts, holding onto him as an anchor as he thrust up again and again, pushing her high so her knees left the bed, leaving her impaled fully on his cock.

"Oh, oh, Jesus," she cried. She could feel her pussy begin to clamp down, felt the orgasm fluttering as the edges of her vision blurred and her breath began to hitch in her chest.

"I can't...I can't stop it," she gasped, struggling to keep her eyes on his face. She clung to his hands, bracing herself as her body began to arch into the sensation. "I'm going to...oh, God, Devon, I'm coming!" She screamed, the sound thin and high, and shattered around him into a thousand pieces.

She felt herself coming apart, felt her pussy clamp down hard in rhythmic spasms as the orgasm moved through her like a freight train. Her screams tapered off into a keening moan that seemed to go on forever as the orgasm pulsed through her and, through it all, she kept her eyes on his face.

It was a mask of agony, his teeth gritted and his muscles tense as he stroked to his own orgasm. His cock was gripped tight in the clasp of her body and he continued to thrust, pushing through her spasming sheath without mercy. The added friction kicked her orgasm higher, and this time when she screamed and clamped down on him, he let out a roar, thrust so hard she feared for a moment she might be tossed over his head and into the wall, and exploded.

Chapter Nine

ॐ

They lay there like survivors of a shipwreck, limp with exhaustion and battered by the storm. Lacey was sure she'd have bruises in the morning, and she had a vague recollection of digging her nails into Devon's hands hard enough to draw blood. She thought idly that she should look to see if he needed a bandage, but she couldn't find the energy to lift her head. So she lay there and concentrated on making her lungs work, listening to his heart pound under her ear.

After a minute she felt him stir, stretching and groaning beneath her and forcing her to hold on or get tossed off.

"Jesus," he groaned. "I'd like to think that a lesser man would be dead by now."

She chuckled weakly. "Best hundred bucks I ever made."

He went still under her and she winced, cursing the brain-numbing lethargy that allowed her glib tongue to override her common sense. "Sorry," she began, then stopped. "Okay, I'm not really sure what to say next."

She felt him turn his head toward her and made the effort to open her eyes and look at him. His face was very close, close enough for her to see the growth pattern of his stubble. "Actually," he rumbled, "I was thinking I ought to be apologizing to you."

She frowned. "For what?"

"Well," he said, "I made the bet."

She yawned. "And I took the bet, and we both got laid."

"I tricked you into sleeping with me."

She chuckled weakly and settled her head into the curve of his shoulder. "You want to believe that, you go right ahead." She sighed once, loving the boneless lethargy that always seemed to follow great sex, and prepared to drift off to sleep.

She heard him mutter, "Wait just a damn minute," and suddenly found herself dumped off the warm mattress of his chest and onto the bed.

"Hey," she protested, frowning and peering at him through one open eye.

"I did trick you into sleeping with me."

"Of course you did." She patted his arm absently and wondered if she had the energy to pull the comforter out from under their tangled legs.

"I gave you a challenge that I knew you couldn't refuse and you took it."

"Yep." She decided she didn't need the comforter, but instead pulled his arm around her and snuggled into his heat. "You got me, but good. Not sure how I'll live with the shame," she murmured.

"I'm really sorry," he said, and the strained tone of his voice had both of her eyes popping open.

"Hey." She peered up at him in the dim light. "Are you really worried about this?"

He looked distinctly uncomfortable. "I hate that I tricked you."

"You didn't," she insisted.

"I knew you wouldn't be able to not take the bet."

"Oh, sweetie." She laid her hand on his cheek and stared deep into his eyes. "Duh."

He blinked. "What?"

"Duh," she repeated, and smiled gently. "I knew you knew I wouldn't be able to turn down the bet. Why do you think I took it?"

Devon shook his head. "I'm confused."

"It's really quite simple," she explained. "You said you wouldn't sleep with me because I'm Jane's best friend. I wanted to sleep with you anyway. You thought you were tricking me to get laid. And since it's impossible to trick someone who wants to do what you're tricking her into, you didn't. And I knew you were going to cave because you can't seduce the unwilling.

"So you didn't trick me, I slept with you because I wanted to, and you slept with me because you wanted to, and you get to tell Ian it's not your fault because I seduced you, although I really don't see why he'd care one way or another. And I made a hundred bucks besides." She grinned. "Everybody wins."

He stared at her. "So really, you should apologize to me then."

She rolled her eyes and lay back down. "Sure. Sorry about all the fabulous sex." She closed her eyes.

"And you should give me my hundred bucks back."

She snorted, not even bothering to open her eyes. "Yeah, that's going to happen. I'm going shoe shopping with that money."

He grumbled and lay down beside her. She immediately curled into his side, sighing as his body heat warmed her cool skin. "I still think I deserve an apology. You played me."

She snuggled closer. "I'm not apologizing. But maybe I'll seduce you again in the morning."

He was silent for a moment then, "I can live with that."

She chuckled once, feeling his arms come up around her as she drifted off to sleep.

* * * * *

The ringing of a cell phone pulled her out of a deep sleep the next morning. The alarm she could ignore for hours, but a ringing phone in the middle of the night generally meant something was wrong. She came awake with a start, disoriented when she didn't immediately recognize the room. She remembered she was in Jane's apartment a split second before Devon sat up beside her. He spent a frantic few seconds digging in the pocket of his discarded slacks for the phone before flipping it open and barking, "Bannion."

Since the crisis, if there was one, wasn't hers, she snuggled back into her pillow and watched him struggle to wake up.

"Uh-huh. Yeah. Right." He yawned, his jaw popping. "Sure. No, I'll be there. Bye."

He flipped the phone shut, let it drop to the blanket and raised his arms over his head in a long stretch that had the muscles of his back bunching and shifting in a way that made Lacey's mouth water.

"Nice," she murmured, and gave him a sleepy smile as he looked over his shoulder at her.

"Morning," he rumbled, and leaned down to kiss her.

The soft morning kiss turned heated quickly. Lacey was clinging to his ribs and moaning when he pulled abruptly away. "Hey," she protested.

"Sorry," he murmured with a quick nip of her lower lip that did nothing to cool her libido. "That was work. My ten o'clock meeting just got moved up, and I have twenty minutes to shower, shave and get downtown."

She frowned. "That's so inconvenient. I was going to seduce you again."

"And I was going to let you," he said. He pushed himself up, swinging off the bed and heading for the suitcase that still sat just outside the bedroom door. He dug in the bag and pulled out a shaving kit before turning back to look at her.

"You want to have lunch later?"

"Sure," she said, her eyes riveted on his very impressive morning wood. "Um…do you need me to wash your back?" she asked.

He laughed. "If you climb in there with me, I'll never get out of here. Lunch," he repeated. "I'll meet you back here around noon?"

"Sure. Noon." She took a deep breath. "I'm going to go back downstairs, grab a shower. Jerk off."

He winked. "Don't work all of that out," he said, and headed for the bathroom.

Lacey kept her eyes on his very delectable backside until it disappeared down the hall. "Jesus," she muttered to herself. "That is a fine ass."

She got out of bed, stretching sore muscles. Suddenly aware of all the aches and pains that the night's activities had awakened, she scooped up her winnings from the night table and started gingerly toward the kitchen. If she didn't want to stiffen up, she should get in that warm shower soon.

She heard the shower start as she was slipping back into her very wrinkled dress. She gathered her shoes, panties and bra, located her keys on the table by the door and let herself out of the apartment.

The sore muscles were even more apparent as she went down the stairs, wincing and using the handrail for balance. She finally made it down to her landing, pushing her key into the lock just as her phone started ringing.

Wondering who would be calling this early on a Saturday, she moved as fast as she could to the cordless phone in the kitchen. She picked it up, looked at the caller ID display and groaned. She hit the talk button.

"Gordon, it's too early."

"Lacey, good morning!" The resounding cheer in the squeaky little voice made Lacey wince. No one should ever be that cheerful, especially not at the crack of dawn on a weekend.

"Gordon, I sent the paperwork through on the last thing three days ago. It's not my fault if your little drones can't find it." She dropped her underwear and cash on the counter, let her shoes drop to the floor and sat gingerly in the leather armchair next to the refrigerator.

"No, no, no! It's not that—we found the paperwork, just like you said. The courier had put it on the wrong reception desk is all."

She yawned wide. "You know, Gordon, for the FBI, you guys are pretty lax about security."

Gordon chuckled, a sound that somehow managed to be jovial and smarmy at the same time. "Oh, we always keep an eye on things."

Lacey mumbled something Gordon apparently took for agreement, because he kept on talking. "Okay, so what I'm calling about." She could practically hear him rubbing his hands on the seat of his pants like he always did when he was excited. She could never decide if it was cute or creepy.

"Okay, what I'm calling about." He also repeated himself when he got excited. "Okay, it's a new thing, a new assignment. Are you free? I mean, are you available?"

Lacey sighed and stood again. She really needed that shower. "Yeah, Gordon. I cleared my schedule for the wedding, and I don't have anything starting for about two weeks."

"Okay, great. Okay, so here's the deal. I need you to come to the office. I need you to come to the office this morning."

She frowned. "Why? Just email me the details like usual or use the courier if it's upper level."

"No, can't do it this time, can't do it. It's a totally different kind of assignment, just different. You need to come down here, meet the guy in charge."

"Okay, don't blow a fuse." Lacey rolled her eyes at the ceiling as she minced her way down the hall. Gordon was so high-strung. It was amazing he'd ended up in the FBI. One would think that the Bureau would have some kind of personality test to weed out the wackos.

In Gordon's defense, he probably wasn't a wacko—just seriously OCD. But it sure came across as wacko sometimes.

She yawned as she stumbled into the bathroom. "Give me a chance to shower and get dressed, then I'll head in."

"Okay, but hurry, okay. Hurry. This thing, this new thing, it's important."

"I got it, Gordon. I'll be there as soon as I can, okay?"

"Okay. Okay, see you then."

"Right." Lacey clicked the phone off. She stared at it for a second then took a deep, bracing breath and looked in the mirror.

"Oh, ouch." She winced. "That's not pretty."

Her hair was still half out of its maid-of-honor do, pins poking out and hair sticking every which way. She hadn't bothered with washing her face before falling asleep last night so her mascara was half down her cheeks and her eyeliner seemed to have expanded. With the slightly bloodshot eyes, she looked like a hungover raccoon.

Correction, she decided, eyeing the pink dress. A hung-over raccoon the day after prom. She tried to smooth a few of the wrinkles out of the bodice, knowing that Jane's mother would faint dead away if she could see the state of the dress. Spending the night on the kitchen floor was not the recommended care on the label she was sure. Jane, however, would just laugh and ask her whose Chevy she'd been rolling around in. She grinned, thinking that the answer would delight her friend as much as doing it had delighted her.

Deciding to leave the dress to the genius of Mr. Wong at the Quicky Cleaners, Lacey shimmied out of it. She turned on the water, letting it heat up while she tugged the remaining pins out of her hair and tossed them in the trash bin. She wouldn't be needing those anymore. The pins gone, she tried to push her fingers through her hair, grimacing when they got stuck in the layers of styling product.

She pulled the lever to activate the shower then stepped in and let the steam and hot water envelop her. She stood still for a moment, letting the hot water pound on her head and soak into her hair, then reached for the shampoo.

As she scrubbed, her thoughts wandered to the night before. Devon had been sexy enough when he'd just been a grinning image in a photo. Now that she had experienced firsthand the force of the personality behind the smile, sexy didn't even begin to cover it.

And, oh, his body. Broad-shouldered, lean-hipped and solid muscle. When she'd fallen on him, it had felt like landing on concrete. Warm concrete that smelled like musk and man, she amended, shivering slightly at the memory. And a magic cock that tasted better than he smelled. She frowned, looking down at her nipples in disbelief. Despite the scalding water, steamy air, and the fact she'd gotten laid less than six hours earlier, they were suddenly puckered tight.

"God, I'm so easy," she muttered, grabbing a loofah and a bottle of body wash from the shelf. She began scrubbing briskly, shivering a bit as the friction of rough sponge on soft skin only intensified the sudden tingle in her nipples.

She ducked her head under the spray, rinsing the shampoo from her hair then went to work with conditioner. After all that product, she was going to need layers of the stuff. As she worked through the tangles, her mind drifted once again to Devon Bannion, and how she could get him into bed again, preferably not looking like a prom queen on speed. She chuckled as she thought of how she must have looked when he walked into the bedroom and found her there. Dressed in pink evening wear, hugging a bottle of champagne, hair sticking up in every direction, and, yes—she could admit this in the privacy of her own shower—snoring loud enough to wake a hibernating grizzly bear.

She grimaced slightly at the image then shrugged. It hadn't seemed to matter much to him when the dress came off. That was the refreshing thing about men—they could usually be counted on to ignore bad hair days and runny makeup if there was nudity involved.

However, next time it would be nice to look a little bit more like a woman and less like a reject from an art house production of *Carrie*. That was what her vanity demanded. She was female, after all, and vanity was her God-given right. Her humor, on the other hand, was tickled pink. It *was* funny. And she imagined Jane would laugh herself into a hernia when she told her.

She sighed, missing her friend. Normally at this point, when she'd met a guy who she not only had that immediate, physical reaction to but also slept with on a bet, she'd be on the phone to Jane. But Jane was on her way to Hawaii—or maybe already there with the time difference—so it looked like, for the first time since college, Lacey was on her own.

She gave her hair a final rinse, chuckling as she remembered the look on Devon's face when she'd asked him why she'd been able to kick his ass. She'd only said it to fill the silence. He'd been just sitting there bleeding, all grumpy and glowering, and she knew she'd make a fool of herself if someone didn't break the ice, so she'd said the first thing that came to mind. But he'd had such a typically male reaction to having his manly strength called into question, she hadn't been able to resist twisting the knife a little bit.

He hadn't even really taken offense, not like some men would. Some men would've been compelled to lift the refrigerator or something equally ridiculous to restore their virile image. No, he'd just glared at her. And there was something seriously wrong with her, she decided, when remembering it puckered her nipples even more and sent a little trickle of moisture to her cunt.

"Well, there are two ways to handle this," she told herself aloud. "Option one—you can ignore it, hope for a nooner over lunch, and throw yourself into this new little project the FBI has for you. Give the United States government the benefit of your repressed sexual urges in the form of workaholism."

Option one, while patriotic, didn't sound like a heck of a lot of fun.

"Or option two." She eyed the showerhead with consideration. "Raul."

Raul the showerhead had, as she'd told Devon last night, been with her since college and through four different apartments. They didn't make him anymore. He was handheld, with an extra-long reach and seven different settings, and had made her see God more times than a lapsed Catholic should admit to.

"As much as I want to be patriotic," she mused out loud, "it's probably better for my health not to keep all these feelings locked up inside. They could fester. Festering isn't good." She reached for Raul.

She flipped the setting to pulsate, or what Jane had once referred to after a particularly long shower when her own had been broken as "sexual tsunami". Since time was of the essence, she didn't play around with the gentler settings. Gordon was probably even now pacing his office, wondering repeatedly where she was.

She winced, pushing thoughts of Gordon out of her head. Not conducive to feeling sexy. No more Gordon.

Think Devon. "Oh, that's much better," she murmured. She held the showerhead loosely in her hand, letting the water pound and stroke over suddenly sensitive skin as she called Devon's image to mind. Normally when she did this, the image that came to mind was the photo in Ian's office. Military fatigues, those oddly sexual-looking weapons. The camouflage paint smeared on his face that made him look like an exotic stranger.

But this time, the picture that popped into her head was the man from last night. Slightly rumpled from a long day of travel, more than a day's worth of growth shadowing his jaw and golden eyes that had by turns laughed, glared and glittered with heat and lust.

She felt her pussy heat and dampen, heard the little hitch in her own breath, and moved the showerhead lower.

Her eyes drifted closed. She stroked her free hand over her neck, the smooth, wet skin of her shoulders, and recalled the feel of his rougher palms touching her. She held the showerhead aimed just south of her belly button, a particularly sensitive spot. The water pounded her skin, echoing the suddenly unsteady beat of her own heart, and she stroked her fingertips over one achingly sensitive nipple.

She hummed in pleasure, enjoying the little jolt of sensation as she plucked at the tender nub, scraping at it with her fingernail. The slight friction of that set off an unexpected spasm in her cunt, so she did it again.

"That's nice," she whispered, and slid her hand over to her other breast. She pictured Devon, his golden eyes fixed on hers as, in her mind's eye, he took her slowly into his mouth. She gripped her own flesh, twisting slightly as she imagined he would. She could see his hands on her, rough and large and tanned against her pale skin, could picture his mouth closing over her hotly and suckling.

She moaned, her thighs shifting together restlessly as the heat between them built. She imagined his head moving lower, scraping stubble over the tender skin of her torso, her belly. Wanting the rough sensation of that day-old beard on her skin, she reached for the loofah. She whimpered now, stroking her own skin and picturing him going to his knees before her in the shower, his eyes on hers all the while.

Her breathing was coming in little whimpering pants now, her mind spinning as she pictured Devon's strong hands on her thighs, pushing them apart. He would slide one long finger along her damp cleft, feeling the heat and moisture that pooled there to ease his way. He'd smile at her, approving, before gently pulling the swollen flesh of her outer lips apart and blowing.

She gasped, her hips jerking as the imagined sensation was nearly as effective as a real touch. Her arousal had suddenly reached critical mass—she needed the orgasm she could feel hovering just out of reach. She shifted the showerhead lower, lifting one foot to rest on the rim of the bathtub. The position tilted her pelvis up, opening her wide, and she slid the showerhead down, aiming it directly at her clit.

She cried out, hips surging at the jolt of astonishing pleasure. She saw behind closed eyelids Devon on his knees, his strong, agile tongue curling around the inflamed knot of her clit, suckling strongly and swirling his tongue in rapid little flicks. She half screamed, her orgasm building to flash point and hovering there, so close and yet frustratingly out of reach. Sobbing, with the image of his head buried between her thighs in her mind, she scraped the loofah over the swollen, sensitive folds of her spread-open cunt. And exploded into orgasm.

When she came back to reality, the water was turning cold. And as she had a hot water heater that allowed her to indulge in thirty-minute showers, she imagined that meant she'd stood there, slumped against the wall for support, for a good long while.

She pushed herself up on shaky legs and shut off the water, then climbed carefully out onto the bath mat. Between the shaky post-orgasm feeling and the shivering from the cold water, she wasn't too steady. She managed to get a bath sheet around her dripping form after two tries then stood, hands braced on the sink, and grinned into the mirror.

Option two, she decided, was much better.

* * * * *

Half an hour later she walked off the elevator at the local FBI field office and nearly ran straight into Gordon.

"Whoa!" Hands out to both brace herself and to keep Gordon at arm's length—honestly, he must bathe in cheap aftershave—she skidded to halt on the scuffed tile.

"Lacey, you're here! Okay, you're here." Gordon leaned forward, his face flushed with excitement. Since he was shorter than her own less than statuesque five foot four, he would've landed on her throat if she hadn't put out a hand to stop him.

"Yes, Gordon. I'm here." She gave him a gentle shove that sent him rocking back on his wingtips.

"Right, okay, right." He rubbed his palms on the seat of his pants. "Okay, here's the thing, here's what—"

"Gordon." He stopped talking, mouth open, watching her expectantly. "Are you going to tell me about it right here in the hallway?"

"Oh." He looked around, blinking. "Oh, no. We should probably go to my office. Office is better."

He spun on his heel and took off at a hurried trot toward the windowless, artless, colorless little hole he called an office. Lacey followed, shaking her head. She'd met Gordon at career day at a high school near Lincoln Park. She'd been there talking about careers in web design and computers, he'd been the local representative from the FBI, there to talk the teenagers into careers in law enforcement.

The kids had loved him. He'd looked like a penguin, rocking back and forth on his spit-shined wing tips, rubbing his hands on his pants almost constantly. She wouldn't have been surprised to see rug burn on his palms. As a recruiter, he was a total bust. But he was entertaining and he'd obviously been having the time of his life.

After the assembly there'd been coffee and cake for the attendees. He'd approached her there, asking more about her web design business and computer skills. Once he found out she'd been a bit of a hacker in her younger days, his interest had sharpened. She didn't even think about the fact she was telling an agent of the FBI about some of the stunts and tricks she'd pulled—hacking into the school computer to change her grades, bumping herself up the waiting list for Cubs tickets then marking them as paid. He just didn't *act* like an FBI agent.

She didn't think much about it until a few days later when she'd gotten a phone call from him. The FBI, it turned out, was very interested in her computer skills. After she got over the fact they'd done a background check on her—one so extensive that they knew she used to fake a cough so her sugar-hating mother would give her grape-flavored cough syrup—she'd been intrigued. She hadn't had a chance to do much hacking since becoming an adult. Once she turned eighteen and graduated from high school, the threat of prison time had been enough to keep her from straying to the wrong side of the law. The idea of getting back into it—without crossing the line—had lured her like a siren song.

"Okay, um. Okay." Lacey looked up to see Gordon hovering outside his office door. "Okay, you have to stay here, okay? Stay here while I go get the other guy."

"Other guy?"

"Right, the other guy. You'll be working with him, the other guy."

"Okay, Gordon." She smiled at him, mentally wincing as she saw him rub his palms on his backside again. It was a good thing he didn't wear corduroy. "I'll wait here."

"Okay, okay, great." He flashed her a grin of surprising charm then toddled off down the hall.

"He should SO be an Oompa Loompa for Halloween," Lacey muttered to herself, and settled into one of the amazingly uncomfortable chairs in front of Gordon's desk to wait.

Chapter Ten

ဆာ

"So that's pretty much the layout." Special Agent Ronald P. Jacobs, Acting Agent in Charge, settled back in his desk chair. He steepled his hands, tapping his index fingers against the tip of his hawk-like nose in a move Devon was sure he thought was authoritative and intimidating. It was neither.

"You'll go up with another agent, find out who the intended buyer is and alert this office. The Treasury Department will be standing by—the case does fall within their jurisdiction, after all—and they'll move in to make the apprehension and recover the plates. If necessary, you'll assist them, of course. But your role will be mainly to identify and observe."

Devon kept the mild smile on his face, despite the mention of the Treasury Department. His jaw was beginning to ache from maintaining it. "You've briefed the other agent?"

"Not yet. She's just been called in this morning and should be here shortly. We'll get her filled in and brought up to speed while we finalize the details."

"No need. The details seem pretty final to me." The smile turned sharp at the edges. "And I'd prefer to be in for the briefing."

Acting In Charge, as Devon was beginning to think of him, drew his brows together in a fierce frown. "That's not our usual procedure here, Agent Bannion."

"Well, it's how I do things." Devon raised one eyebrow, but otherwise didn't change expression. "And it's my understanding, Acting Agent in Charge Jacobs, that your office's role in this operation is to support and coordinate. And that my role, per orders of the Director, is to run the show."

Jacobs' face flushed a deep red. "Yes, that's correct." He practically bit the words off. "You're in charge of the operation. At least until Treasury steps in."

"Well, since Treasury isn't here now, I guess that means I'm in charge." Devon flipped open the file on his lap. "While we're waiting for the agent to arrive, let's go over the equipment list."

He turned at the sound of approaching footsteps then simply stared. A man wearing a disturbingly ugly brown suit with red suspenders and black wing tips came skidding around the corner and barely kept himself from being cut in half by the doorframe. He was short, balding, pale and had the beadiest eyes Devon had ever seen.

He slipped again, his shiny shoes sliding on the tile before he used his death grip on the doorframe to right himself. "She's here, okay. She's here, she's in my office."

Devon blinked. The guy sounded like he'd been sucking on helium. He turned back to Jacobs. "Who is this?"

Jacobs had gotten to his feet and was fussily smoothing his tie. "Agent Bannion, this is Gordon Aggate. He's been working on some of the background for this case."

"You're Bannion. Hi, I'm Gordon." The little man stumbled into the room, grabbing Devon's hand and pumping vigorously. "Gordon Aggate. Pleased to meet you, very pleased. An honor, really."

"Thank you." Devon wrenched his hand back as discretely as he could. "It's a pleasure to meet you as well."

Gordon beamed. "Thanks, thanks a lot!"

Jacobs cleared his throat. "Excuse me, Agent Aggate." He waited for Gordon's attention to turn to him. "Did you say that our other agent for this assignment has arrived?"

"What? Oh! Oh, yeah! She's in my office. I told her to wait there." He turned back to Devon. "I'll take you there. If you want, I'll take you there."

"I think, Agent Aggate, that we'd all be more comfortable if you brought Ms. Johnson to the conference room." Jacobs gave a curt nod.

Gordon's head bobbed. "Okay, sure. Okay, I'll get her." He turned to leave, bumped solidly into the wall then skidded out the door.

Jacobs smiled genially. "Agent Bannion, if you'll follow me?"

Devon frowned as he followed Jacobs out the door. Something was off here. "Ms. Johnson?"

"I'm sorry?"

"Ms. Johnson," Devon repeated, eyes sharp. "That's the other agent who's been tapped for this?"

"Yes, that's correct." He gestured for Devon to precede him into the conference room. "She's the appropriate age for this assignment and she has considerable technical skills."

"You didn't call her Agent Johnson." Devon leaned a hip on the corner of the table, crossing his arms and pinning the other man with a glare.

"Well, strictly speaking, she isn't an agent."

Devon felt his blood pressure shoot up a few notches. "Strictly speaking, what is she?"

Jacobs swallowed. He may be a pompous suit, Devon noted with a tiny spurt of satisfaction, but he had sense enough to know when he was wading in deep shit. "Strictly speaking, she's a civilian consultant."

"A civilian consultant?" Devon's voice had gone dangerously quiet. Jacobs bobbed his head like a puppet on a string. "And what," Devon went on in the same even, deadly tone, "does she consult on? Arms dealing, counterfeit currency?" Jacobs shook his head. "What then?"

Jacobs looked slightly ill. "Cyber investigations."

"Computers."

"Yes."

"Let me see if I've got this straight. Your first choice for this assignment is a civilian consultant who specializes in computer investigations? I'm curious, Special Agent Acting in Charge. What in the *hell* – " Jacobs flinched visibly " – made you think that a computer geek, much less a civilian computer geek, could handle an assignment as potentially dangerous as this one?"

"Why not?" The amused voice from the door had Devon's head whipping around. "I kicked your ass, didn't I?"

Chapter Eleven

∞

Lacey wasn't sure who was more surprised—Devon, herself or the other agent in the room who looked like he might puke any second.

Devon was staring at her, his mouth slightly open in shock. Just to confuse him, she winked. "I didn't notice this morning, but your nose looks much better today. Hardly any swelling left at all."

Immediately, his brows slammed together over the bridge of said nose. "What," he growled, practically biting the words off, "are you doing here?"

She shrugged casually, even though the butterflies in her stomach were doing a mad tango, and strolled into the room. She made sure to give the other agent a wide berth—he was still looking a little green around the gills. "I got a call from Gordon here—" she gestured to where he still hovered in the doorway, rubbing his pants "—to come straight down. So I did."

She sat in one of the ugly chairs gathered around an even uglier conference table, crossed her legs and fastidiously brushed a speck of lint away from her bare knee where it showed through the hole in her jeans. She looked up and, despite the trepidation and nerves in her belly at his fierce expression, smiled. "What're you doing here?"

He ignored her and turned his attention back to Green Gills. "Jacobs, you better know something I don't know or I'm going to have your ass on a plate."

Jacobs's jaw worked but no words came out and his eyes started to spin back in his head. In disgust, Devon clamped a hand on the back of his head, shoved his butt in a chair and his head between his legs. "Breathe, dammit." While Jacobs took deep, gulping breaths, Devon turned to Gordon. "You. Tell me what's going on."

"Okay! Okay, so here it is. Lacey, she works for us sometimes. Usually just hacker stuff, finding out where the money's hidden. That kind of thing. And this came up so all of a sudden, and she's the best we've got so I picked her for this island thing, and Jacobs said it was okay." Gordon took a deep breath. "He said it was okay."

Devon turned to look at Lacey. "I knew you were going to be trouble."

* * * * *

They left her sitting in the conference room. Devon shoved everyone out the door, barked at her to stay put and slammed the door behind him.

"Boy, he is *pissed*." She supposed she couldn't blame him too much. Whatever Gordon had brought her in for apparently involved Devon and, judging from his reaction, he obviously wasn't expecting to work with a freelancer. Especially not the freelancer who'd bopped him in the nose and fucked his brains out last night.

Since she was alone, she allowed herself a small chuckle at the memory of his face when she'd mentioned kicking his ass. She'd wager not too many people got the upper hand with Devon Bannion, and she couldn't help feeling a little bit smug about the fact she'd been doing it since they met.

Her smile faded. Unfortunately, he wasn't likely to be very happy when he came back. She chewed her lower lip, considering. She was curious as to why Gordon had called her down here in such a frenzy. Curious, hell, she was *dying* to know what was going on. Gordon had said "island". What island? Where? Could she bring her aqua bikini along?

Unfortunately, if the look on Devon's face when he'd slammed the door on his way out was anything to go by, she didn't think she or her bikini would be going anywhere.

* * * * *

Devon wanted to tear his hair out. "Are you telling me she's the only option?"

Jacobs still looked like he was going to puke but he was a bit steadier on his feet. "I'm afraid so." He winced as Devon cursed but resolutely plowed ahead. "Look, all of our field agents that could do this are already committed to other investigations. Even if we were to pull someone out of the field, we'd have to have time to get a replacement, brief her on the situation and put her in place. We already have this set up and if we have to start over, we might well miss our window of opportunity with Deveraux."

"I know, I know." Devon paced, fighting the urge to punch his hand through the wall. "Devereaux already has a buyer in place, we need to be there to see it go down."

"If you're worried that your personal relationship with her will jeopardize the operation—"

"We do not have a personal relationship, Jacobs."

"But she knew you and you seemed to know her, and I thought—"

"Stop thinking," Devon advised curtly, and Jacobs shut his mouth with an audible click of teeth. "We've met once and we have some mutual acquaintances. But it doesn't qualify as a personal relationship. And even if it did, Special Agent In Charge—" he smiled grimly "—it would not affect my ability to run this operation. Understood?"

He got a gulping nod in response and nearly shook his head in despair. Jacobs was a weasel. He was used to commanding a certain amount of respect from the people he worked with—his reputation usually preceded him, and it was well-earned—but Jacobs was all but genuflecting. He made a mental note to talk to the Smythe-White about it. Anyone that easily intimidated, even when it was warranted, shouldn't be running an FBI field office.

He put thoughts of Jacobs and his obvious ineptitude out of his mind and turned back to the problem at hand. He fixed Gordon with a look. "Is she good enough for this?"

"Oh, of course. Of course she is. She's the best tech we've got. She can do this, Mr. Bannion—I mean, Agent Bannion. Yeah, she can totally do it."

Devon sighed. "Not like I have a lot of choice," he muttered. He rolled his shoulders. "Okay, I need to talk to her. Fill her in. Alone," he amended when Gordon popped up like a puppet on a string.

"But I need to brief her," Gordon protested, his beady little eyes gone round as saucers in distress. "I'm her handler, I have to tell her, tell her what she's supposed to do."

Devon barely resisted rolling his eyes. The little guy was a pain, but he was sincere and he was eager, which was more than he could say for Jacobs. "Don't worry about it, Gordon. I'll take care of the briefing this time." He picked up the file from where he'd slammed it on the table. "Thank you, Gordon."

Gordon beamed. "Thank you, sir. Thanks. Tell Lacey I said good luck, okay? Tell her good luck."

Devon nodded. "She'll need it," he muttered.

* * * * *

By the time the door to the conference room opened again, Lacey had all but worked herself into an anxiety attack wondering what was happening. She'd heard nothing, not even one shout, and the walls in this place were thin. She'd even pushed her ear to the wall but all she'd heard was the agent in the next office on his speakerphone telling his wife he was going to be working late. Then he called someone named Cherrie and told her to buy extra whipped cream.

After she'd spent a couple of minutes hoping Cherrie was as dim as she sounded and would buy whipped cream past its expiration date, she'd gone back to worrying about Devon.

She wasn't afraid he'd hurt her. Hell, if he was going to do that, he'd have done it while she was waling on him with a champagne bottle, and he sure could've done it while they were burning up the sheets if that was how he got his kicks. But for a minute back there, when he'd looked like he was going to tear poor Jacobs a new asshole, the warrior from the photo in Ian's office had been standing right in front of her. In living color. And she figured there must be something seriously wrong with her since her panties were wet enough to wring out. Apparently, great sex and a session with Raul just wasn't enough in the face of such unabashed testosterone.

"Maybe I'm a danger junkie," she muttered to herself just as the door swung open.

"What was that?"

"Uh...nothing." God, he looked good. He was still in what she was coming to think of as his Super-Spy Serious Mode. Stern and gruff and unsmiling. All business. She squirmed in her seat and imagined she could feel her thong squish.

He closed the door at his back then simply folded his arms and stared at her.

"What?"

"Why didn't you tell me you worked for the FBI?"

She shrugged with feigned nonchalance and shifted in her seat. Wet panties were not comfortable. "I don't work for the FBI. I do an occasional freelance project for them, that's all."

"That counts as working for the FBI," he informed her. "Ian doesn't know, does he?"

She frowned, confused. "No. Why would he?"

"I don't know." He tossed a thick manila folder on the conference table then tugged out the chair to her left and settled in. "You tell Jane, she tells Ian…"

Lacey rolled her eyes at him, even as the warm male scent of him surrounded her and made her want to climb in his lap. "You don't know much about girlfriends, do you?" At his frown, she elaborated. "If I told Jane something in confidence, she wouldn't tell Ian. She wouldn't tell anyone."

He lifted a brow. "You seem awfully sure of that."

"And you seem awfully cynical." She shook her head. "Look, the only way she'd tell Ian something I told her in confidence would be if she thought I was in some kind of danger and might get hurt."

"And she didn't think you working for the FBI might be dangerous?"

"*Consulting* for the FBI. And she probably would, but I never told her so it's never been an issue."

Both brows went up. "You didn't? Not ever?"

"No."

"Why not?"

She stared at him like there were horns growing out of his head. "Because it's the *FBI*, you dope. They pretty much swear you to secrecy!"

He grinned suddenly. "Right."

She blinked, taken aback by his sudden change of demeanor. The intensity of Super-Spy Serious was tough enough to take but when he switched to Charlie Charm, her system just went all haywire.

She was preoccupied with suppressing her sudden hormone overload and missed what he said next. When she realized he'd said something and was waiting for her to answer, she racked her brain for a good, non-specific response. "Ghlg," she said.

"Way to think on your feet," he said sardonically, and she stuck her tongue out at him.

"Look, if we're going to work together on this—and it looks like we don't have much choice—I'm going to need a little mature professionalism from you."

She sniffed, chin in the air. "I can be as mature as you can."

"Right." He turned his attention to the folder in front of him. "Okay, we need to leave pretty soon, since the target is already at the location. I want to get going this afternoon." He looked up at her. "I assume that's not going to be a problem."

She shrugged. "I work for myself, don't have any pets. Although I've been thinking about getting a puppy. Maybe a basset hound. What do you think of basset hounds? They're so cute and cuddly. And they look lazy, but Julie Metz, my best friend in junior high had one, and it was a maniac! It ate her tap recital costume and her mom was seriously tweaked. But they are really cute and since I work at home, I think it'd be okay…" She trailed off when she caught him staring.

"What? You don't like basset hounds?"

"I didn't notice you being this scatterbrained last night."

"Excuse me?" She narrowed her eyes at him. "I am *not* scatterbrained. I was merely commenting on my desire to buy a puppy."

"Yeah, okay." He opened the file folder and mentally reminded himself that he was stuck with this assignment—and her. And no matter how fantastic she was in bed, that was not a good thing. "The situation we're going into here, it's not that volatile. There's some inherent danger—since it's undercover and there's always a chance we could be made—but you won't be in direct contact with the suspects, and that's the only reason I'm even considering taking an amateur along."

"Why?"

"Why what?"

"Why won't I be in direct contact with the suspects?"

"Because you're an amateur and I won't let you."

She shrugged. "Okay."

He seemed a little startled by her easy acceptance of being called an amateur but he moved on. "First thing we need to go over is the cover. I'm not that thrilled with the scenario they've come up with, so I've made a few minor changes. I think it'll be easier for both of us to maintain if we go in as—"

"Hey." She waited until he looked up. "I'm hungry, I didn't get breakfast. Gordon caught me right as I walked in the door this morning, and then…you know—" she made a vague gesture with her hands " —all this."

"So?"

"So, how about we hash this out over breakfast?"

"Breakfast."

"Yeah, breakfast. You know, the meal you eat in the morning." He was still staring at her blankly. "Wow, you weren't this serious last night. You're really all business aren't you?"

He tapped his finger on the file. "It's serious stuff, Lacey."

"I know. And I promise, I'm taking it seriously. But I really am hungry, so how about you let me buy you breakfast? And I promise, we'll go over it all."

He was silent for so long, she was beginning to think she'd made a mistake. Then, abruptly, he closed the folder and got to his feet. "Okay."

She smiled, breathing a silent sigh of relief. "Great. I know the best place."

Chapter Twelve

Twenty minutes later they were sitting at a window table for two at the West Egg Café on Monroe. Lacey had taken the seat facing the door, leaving him with his back to the room, and he couldn't get comfortable.

"What's wrong?"

He turned from scanning the room to find her watching him curiously, that gamine face frowning. "What?"

"You're all twitchy, like you're looking for assassins around every corner."

He sent her a sardonic smile. "The things we do to stay alive."

"Well, nobody's going to storm the West Egg so just order breakfast." She smiled at the approaching waitress. "Hi there. I'd like chocolate chip pancakes, bacon and two eggs. Scrambled. Oh, and some wheat toast with honey and a large orange juice."

"Christ, are you a teamster?" he asked, goggled at the amount of food she'd just ordered.

"Hey, I worked up an appetite last night."

He shook his head. "I'll have the same," he told the waitress, "but make my pancakes blueberry and the orange juice a coffee." He handed her the menu, waiting until she'd walked off to face Lacey again.

God, she was cute. He simply couldn't think of another word that fit as well. Since she was preoccupied with arranging her napkin in her lap, he took a moment to study her freely.

The Devil and Ms. Johnson

Her hair, washed clean of the styling product that had it sticking up in curly spikes the night before, was sunshine bright and baby-fine. Wispy bangs flirted with delicately arched brows in a lightly darker shade of blonde. It was cut short, just brushing the back of her neck, and emphasized the pixie quality of her features. She had a small nose with a dusting of freckles dancing across the tip, a rounded chin and a pink little bow of a mouth.

It was the face of a bimbo. Cute, but empty. Until, he mused, you got a look at her eyes. Velvety brown in color, they were sharply intelligent and focused—at least when they weren't clouded by champagne—and he had a feeling that a lot of people missed what was in those eyes, making the mistake of seriously underestimating Lacey Johnson. It wasn't a mistake he'd be making again.

"So." He waited until she looked up, focused that laser gaze on his face. "How'd you get hooked up with the feebs?"

She grinned. "Do you ever call them that to their faces? They HATE that nickname." She took a sip of her ice water. "It's a funny story, actually. I met Gordon when he was giving a speech at career day."

"Career day?"

"Yeah, you know. When local professionals visit local high schools and describe their chosen professions in an attempt to illustrate to young people the opportunities available to them upon graduation."

He chuckled. "You sound like a brochure."

She shrugged. "That's what the letter they sent said. A friend of mine is a reading specialist. I did some work for her on a website when she decided to do private tutoring on the side, and she thought having a web designer for career day would be interesting. So I signed up." She gave the waitress a big grin as she dropped off the drinks and took a steady drink of her orange juice.

99

"It was pretty interesting," she continued, "and kinda creepy, to boot."

"Creepy?" He reached for the sugar. "How so?"

"High school." Lacey gave a shudder that wasn't entirely feigned and took a fortifying sip of OJ.

"Aw, come on." He grinned at her as he stirred his coffee. "I bet you were great in high school. Let me guess—captain of the cheerleading squad, student council, prom committee and valedictorian."

She snorted, nearly snuffing orange juice. "Valedictorian, yeah. But you're way off on the rest of it. I was a major nerd. Geek city. The only time the cheerleaders even talked to me was when they needed a grade changed."

"Ah, yes, the hacker. How much did you charge them?"

Lacey smirked. "Oh, never cash. That was too easy, since Mummsie and Daddums would've forked it over for their little darlings with no questions asked. No, I prided myself on being more subtle than that."

Devon waited a few beats then said, "Oh, don't leave me hanging."

She chuckled. "Well, I made the prom queen renounce her throne as patriarchal, sexist and degrading to women."

He started to laugh. "You're kidding?"

She sighed at the memory. "Nope. She had to do it right after being crowned too, or I wouldn't fix her trig grade. Wrote her speech myself, and it was a magnificent commentary on the glass ceiling, the trials of working mothers and the tragic fall of the ERA. It was a moment, with tears and all."

"She cried?"

"Tears of rage and hate, but it still looked fabulous. Hey," she protested, "I didn't make her do it. It was simply my price, and if she'd studied for the damn tests instead of banging Bobby McLane under the bleachers, she wouldn't have had to pay."

She grinned, quick and bright. "Man, she *hated* me for that."

"I bet." He eyed her, considering. "The Equal Rights Amendment?"

"Solidarity, sister. Although I think Ainsley had a few salient points."

"Who's Ainsley?"

"Ainsley Hayes. Associate White House counsel. Republican. She thinks the ERA is redundant."

"You know an associate White House counsel?"

She stared at him. "Jesus. No, from *The West Wing*."

"Oh." His face cleared. "The TV show. It's okay. A little unrealistic."

"I love that show. And what do you mean, unrealistic?"

"I live and work in Washington. Believe me, the real politicians aren't that smart, aren't that good-looking and certainly aren't that interested in serving the public."

"Please," she held up a hand. "You'll crush my dreams. My goal in life is to be interesting enough for Stockard Channing to play me in the movie of my life."

"Well, the prom queen was a good start. Maybe this little assignment will push you a little farther along in that goal."

She grinned. "Yeah, that one's going in my memoirs." She took another slug of orange juice. "So what is this assignment anyway?"

Devon waited for the waitress to plunk down their overloaded plates and walk away before he answered. "The simple version is that we need to stop a well-known arms dealer from selling a very sophisticated set of counterfeit plates."

Lacey was concentrating on getting just the right amount of powdered sugar on her pancakes and didn't look up. "American currency?"

"Yes. Also British and the Euro."

"Wow. That'd throw the world economy into a tizzy in the wrong hands, wouldn't it?" She took a bite and closed her eyes in ecstasy. "Oh, that's good."

"Yeah. A tizzy."

"Umf," she mumbled, swallowing her mouthful of pancake. She pointed to his plate. "You're not eating. Is your food okay?"

"I'm sure it's fine. I'm just not used to women actually eating." He picked up his fork.

Lacey shrugged. "Their loss. These pancakes are amazing."

Devon took a bite. "Yeah, they're pretty good."

They ate in silence for a few moments then Lacey spoke up. "So how're we supposed to stop this guy—what's his name?"

"You don't need to know that."

She rolled her eyes. "Okay. I'll just call him Ignatius. So how're we supposed to stop Ignacious from selling the plates?"

"You can't call him Ignatius."

"I have to call him something. I can't call him the big, bad counterfeiting man, that's a little too obvious."

"Okay, fine. Call him Ignatius."

She smiled. "Thank you. So how're we supposed to keep Ignatius from selling the plates to his buyers? Do we know who they are, by the way?"

He shook his head. "Just that it's a couple."

"Okay, we'll just call them Tiffany and Sheldon. So we're supposed to—"

"Wait, wait, wait." He held up a hand. "Tiffany and Sheldon?"

"Captain of the cheerleading squad and the quarterback. Most obnoxious couple in the world. They have three kids and a house in the suburbs now. He sells life insurance and she cheats on him with the guy who mows their grass. Anyway," she went on while Devon choked on his pancakes, "how are we supposed to stop them from getting the plates?"

Devon took a sip of his coffee. "He's meeting them at a resort. It's a popular vacation spot, there will be plenty of people around. We'll find him, figure out who they are and go from there."

"So you know what this guy looks like, then?"

He nodded. "We've tangled before."

Lacey frowned. "Then doesn't that make going undercover kind of impossible? I mean, if the guy recognizes you, we're toast."

He shook his head. "Won't be a problem. I was always behind the scenes, he doesn't know my face."

"What about your voice?"

"No, he's never spoken to me."

"Okay, then. So what's the plan?"

Devon polished off the last of his pancakes and set his fork down. "Well, the Bureau has us going in as a couple on a romantic vacation. And if I were going in with a seasoned field agent, I wouldn't have a problem with it. But since you've never done field work before…"

Lacey polished off her toast. "You don't think I can handle it?"

He shrugged. "I don't know if you can or not. It can be pretty stressful, pretending to be a couple under circumstances like that. I'd prefer not to take chances."

"Okay." She finished the last of her orange juice and sat back with a satisfied sigh. "So this is the part you decided to change?"

He tossed his napkin onto his empty plate. "I think it'll be better if we go in as business associates."

"Business associates. At a vacation resort?" She shook her head. "I don't know."

He sighed. "I agree it's not ideal. But going in as lovers is a lot of pressure."

"Why?" she asked. "We're already lovers."

He blinked, startled by the matter-of-fact way she threw that out into the conversation. "True...but we don't know each other."

She nodded. "Yes, but business associates at a vacation resort is completely illogical. Look—" she leaned forward " — where does it say we have to be long-term lovers? It makes better sense to pretend we've only been dating a little while and we're taking a little weekend trip to get to know one another better."

"That's a good point."

"I know. And we can cover the small stuff on the way." She looked at her watch. "It's ten-thirty. Where exactly are we going for this little adventure? Gordon said something about an island. We can do the whole first-date-getting-to-know-you spiel on the plane."

He shook his head. "No, no plane."

She frowned. "No plane? How do you get to an island with no plane? We can't be taking a boat."

He grinned suddenly, a sly, amused twist of his lips. "Mackinac Bridge."

"Oh, man!" She tossed her napkin on the table. "We're going to Mackinac Island?"

He rolled his eyes. "Say it a little louder, I don't think the chef heard you."

"This bites," she grumbled, folding her arms. "I thought I was going to get to go to a tropical island. Instead I get nine hours in a car, a trip over a bridge that can't possibly be safe, to a ferry that's just a death trap on water, to an island that doesn't allow internal combustion engines."

He chuckled. "We don't have to cross the bridge, we'll take the ferry from the lower peninsula, and I drive fast so it'll probably only be eight hours in a car. And besides, it's quaint."

"Quaint." She snorted. "It's an anachronism. But," she said, feeling marginally cheered, "they do make killer fudge."

"The silver lining," he drawled.

Lacey sighed. "Okay, when do we need to leave?"

Devon signaled for the check. "Can you pack and be ready to go in an hour?"

"No."

He blinked, startled again. He had the uncomfortable feeling that he was going to be doing that a lot around her. "Huh?"

"No, I cannot pack and be ready to go in an hour."

"Why not?"

"Why not?" She started ticking the reasons off on her fingers. "One—you haven't told me what to pack for. Casual, dressy, sporty? I need to know these things. Two—what's the weather like? Is it cooler because it's on the water? Three—an hour is just not enough time. I might have to stop by the dry cleaner, I may need new shoes. Four—"

"Enough!" Devon held up a hand. "I get it. How much time is it going to take you to pull a weekend bag together?"

She shrugged. "Couple hours, at least."

"Twelve-thirty?"

"Hmmm…" She considered. "Better make it one-thirty. Just in case."

"Just in case what?"

"Some kind of emergency."

"A packing emergency?"

She regarded him solemnly. "It doesn't pay to take chances."

"Uh-huh." He reached in his pocket for his wallet.

"Hey. I asked you to breakfast. I should pay."

He flashed a grin and dropped a very generous tip. "Nope. Uncle Sam pays."

She got up from the table to follow him out of the restaurant, eyebrows raised at the wad of cash he'd just left a very lucky waitress. "Okay, you don't need to impress me. You've had me, remember?"

"Oh, I remember." She shivered, taken aback at the sudden dark heat in his voice. He'd been so normal and business-like during breakfast and at the field office, she'd almost let herself forget that he'd banged her like a drum the night before.

He turned to hold the door for her and caught her staring at him. "What?"

"Nothing." She shrugged when he just raised an eyebrow at her as they stepped into the street. "Okay, something. You seem to switch gears awfully quickly."

"What do you mean?"

"I mean, one minute you're Super Spy, all business, and the next it's 'Oh, I remember'," she said, lowering her voice to a decent mimic of his rumbling growl. She saw his lips twitch before he suppressed the motion. She shrugged again, feeling foolish. "Just a little disconcerting, that's all."

He chuckled. "Sorry. It's just habit." When she looked up at him quizzically, he explained. "I've been at this job for a while now. And you learn pretty quickly to stay focused on business or people die."

She winced. "Well, that's a pretty thought."

"Hey." He put a hand on her elbow, pulling her to stop in front of him. His eyes were serious. "It's not a pretty business. The situation we're going into on Mackinac, it shouldn't be dangerous. But you never know, so I need to know if you can handle yourself."

She frowned. "Handle myself? Like, go all Sydney Bristow and kick bad guy ass?" She shook her head. "Hello? I'm a web designer, not a Bond girl. I mean, I'm in good shape, so I can run away from the bad guys like a champ. But that's about it, so if you need Wonder Woman for this deal…"

He shook his head, a wry smile twisting his lips. "No, that's not what I mean. It's likely we won't ever confront this guy, so you won't need the magic rope and wrist bands."

"Gold magic rope," she corrected.

He stared at her. "Right. Anyway, I mean I need to know if you're going to fall apart if things get sticky. Get hysterical, flutter your hands…be a girl."

She scowled. "I *am* a girl. Doesn't make me a cream puff, you chauvinistic pile of yak."

He blinked. "Pile of *yak*?"

"Yeah." She folded her arms. "Just because I'm female you assume I'm going to turn into a simpering moron? Get in your way, queer the deal, fuck things up? You're a jackass." She nearly spat the words at him then turned on her heel to walk away.

He caught her elbow before she'd even taken two steps, spinning her around to face him. If she wasn't already so steamed herself, she might've been taken aback by the thundercloud expression on his face. "What?" she snapped.

He took a deep breath—she could practically hear his teeth grinding—and said, "That's not what I meant."

"Really." She was unconvinced.

He tried again. "I just meant… Look, things could get tricky. If we get into a tight spot, I'm not going to have time to explain things to you and give you a list of options. We'll have to move and move fast, and I need to know if you can follow orders or if you're going to get your panties in a wad over it."

"Nice talk." She yanked her arm out of his grip. "So what you need to know is, can I run from the bad guys?"

"Umm…"

"Because I think I just finished saying that. And for the record, I'm well aware that your experience in this area far outweighs mine and I'm perfectly willing to follow your lead. I'm not stupid and I don't relish the idea of getting hurt—pain doesn't really do it for me."

He winced at the venom in her voice. "I didn't mean—"

"Not done yet, Super Spy." She jabbed him in the chest with her finger. "I'm not afraid to ask questions and I won't argue with your authority, but don't treat me like a bimbo. I've got a brain and I can use it. Got it?"

He cleared his throat. "Yeah, I got it. And I'm sorry." He grabbed the finger she was using to drill a hole through his sternum. "Really sorry. I know you've got a brain, I didn't mean to imply otherwise."

"Humph."

"Honestly. But I needed to make sure. Who's in charge isn't negotiable and both our lives could depend on it."

She shrugged, mollified. "I know. And you don't know me that well so I guess you could be forgiven for making assumptions."

"Well, the FBI vouched for you."

"Yeah, well…they're not exactly a confidence-inspiring bunch over there."

He nodded. "Gordon…and the Acting Asshole in Charge."

"Right. So, you're forgiven for your skepticism."

"And I don't think you're a bimbo. Really."

She smirked. "I know. After all, a bimbo couldn't have juked you out of a hundred bucks last night."

He grinned. "You're right. I should've let you pay for breakfast."

She chortled. "Ha! Too late, sucker."

He chuckled. "Yeah, this is going to be a smooth assignment."

"Oh, don't be such a pessimist," she admonished, and started walking again. "Can I ask you something?"

He fell in step beside her, shortening his stride to match hers. "Sure."

"You don't seem all that excited about doing this."

He waited a beat then looked over at her. "That was more of a statement than a question."

She rolled her eyes. "Funny man. *Why* don't you seem all that excited about doing this?"

"Because I was supposed to be retiring and going into the security business with Ian, and I've basically been blackmailed into doing this last thing for Uncle Sam before they let me go."

"My tax dollars at work," she said drolly, startling him into laughter as they reached her car.

They climbed in and Lacey pulled into the heavy Saturday morning traffic. She negotiated the construction and the throngs of people trying to make their way to the lake, suddenly painfully aware of the man sitting next to her.

Now that they weren't talking about business or arguing about who's dick was bigger, she found herself thinking once again about...well, about his dick. She slid a sideways glance toward his lap, which turned out to not be a good idea. The front of his pants was decidedly tented, which seemed to trigger a flood of moisture into the crotch of her own jeans.

"Um, can I ask another question?"

He looked at her, his expression inscrutable. "Sure."

She nodded toward his lap. "Do you always run around like that or is there something in your current environment that's causing it?"

He smiled. Not the grin he'd been favoring her with all through the morning, but a slow, sexy stretch of the mouth that made her own start to water. "It's not the current environment—it's you."

She swallowed. "Well, I thought so, but I didn't want to say in case it made me sound conceited."

"It's not conceit when it's true."

She cleared her throat. "Right. So. Right."

"You're flustered," he exclaimed, delighted. He twisted in his seat so he could look at her fully.

"Maybe just a little," she admitted, hating the flush she could feel climbing up her neck.

"A little, hell. You're flustered a lot. And you're blushing?" She scowled at his grin. "I don't get it," he said. "You were bold as hell last night, no stammering or blushing or hesitation at all. So why the shy maiden act today?"

She rolled her eyes. "Shy maiden. You wish."

"Well, you're blushing and you won't look at me—"

"I'm not looking at you because I'm *driving*. I have to watch the *road*."

"—and your lips are puckered so tight you look like you're sucking on a lemon, so something's up. What is it? You don't want to sleep with me again?"

"No!" The denial burst out with a little more force than she intended, and her blush deepened as he chuckled again. "No, that's not it. I just…"

"You just what?" he asked when she stayed silent.

"I'm having a little trouble keeping pace with you, is all. It's all business on the street then it's boners in the car. It's a little hard to keep up!"

"Sorry," he said, sounding like he was choking on a laugh.

"And if we're going to be spending the next I-don't-know-how-long pretending to be lovers, then I guess you'd better go over the rules with me." She pulled up to a stop in front of her building and shut the car off.

"That's fair," he allowed. He waited for her to look at him then grinned. "But you're cute when you blush."

"You ass," she laughed.

"That's better," he said. "Okay, ground rules. First of all, unless you tell me you want something different, we won't be 'pretending' to be lovers—we will be lovers." He looked at her expectantly.

She smiled. "No, I don't want something different."

"Good," he practically growled, and hooked one hand around the back of her neck to haul her in for a hard kiss. "Second," he said while she tried to remember her own name, "we've already gone over this but it bears repeating. I'm in charge."

She nodded. "Right, right. You're in charge, you have the biggest dick, all hail the Devil-Man."

He laughed, rolling his eyes as she went on. "But can you let me know when it's play time and when it's work time? Remember, I'm an amateur at this. If you tell me it's time to work and be serious, that's cool, but it might take me a minute to switch gears."

"Fair enough."

"Cool." She looked at her watch then back down to his lap where his erection didn't appear to have faded at all. "Um…do you still want to leave in a couple of hours?"

"Yeah, we need to hit Mackinac City by tonight. We'll probably have to take the ferry over to the island in the morning as it is. Why?"

"Because I either have time to seduce you again or pack. You pick—work time or play time?"

He looked at his own watch. "Fuck. Work."

She grimaced and opened her car door. "I was afraid you were going to say that."

"Is it really going to take you that long to pack?" he asked as he climbed out and walked with her to the front door.

"Yes." She fit her key to the lock. "And you still haven't told me what to pack for." She paused by her front door and looked up at him expectantly.

He sighed. "You're really going to spend the next three hours packing. Okay, pack casual. Throw in a couple of dressy things in case we have to hit the town or have a fancy dinner, and bring a couple of sweaters and at least one jacket."

She nodded. "Okay, can do." She opened her front door, watching him over her shoulder. He was just standing there, looking like someone just drowned his puppy. "What's wrong?"

He stared at her, incredulous. "I have a boner the size of a cruise missile and you're packing."

"Sweetie." She reached up and cupped his check in her hand. "It's big, but it's not that big. And besides—" she patted his face and grinned " —you're the one who said work."

"Don't remind me," he grumbled, and turned to head up the stairs, her laughter ringing in his ears.

Chapter Thirteen

✿

Exactly three hours later he knocked on her door. "Lacey, you ready?"

"Come on in," she hollered, "the door's open."

He opened the door and stepped in, looking at his surroundings with interest. A person's living space said a lot about them. For example, Jane's barrage of color and quirky taste in art told him she was eccentric, her one-thousand-count Egyptian cotton bed sheets spoke to her sensuality and the bowling cherubs on her ceiling...well, he wasn't sure what that said about her, except that she wasn't boring.

Now, Lacey's living space... He looked around the room. There were piles of books, with titles ranging from *In Defense of Pornography*—maybe he'd borrow that, it looked interesting—to *Hamlet* to *Choke*. There were half a dozen romance novels scattered around as well, which told him she had varied tastes and interests. There was a pair of battered track shoes tossed by the front door—she was a runner or worked out regularly. He spotted a Chicago Cubs jersey slung over the back of a chair and a Blackhawks coffee mug on an end table, so she liked sports. A supermarket tabloid was sharing a sofa cushion with a cereal bowl, and a laundry basket full of—clean? dirty?—clothes sat on the coffee table.

He turned when Lacey emerged from the hallway, carrying a leather shoulder bag the size of Rhode Island and pulling a wheeled carryon bag behind her. "I think I got everything," she said, lifting the carryon over an unidentifiable lump of fabric in the middle of the floor. "I just need to get my jacket." She looked up at him and stopped. "What?"

"My God," he said, and looked around the apartment once again. "You're a slob."

"Hey," she frowned. "That's rude."

"But true." He pointed. "What's that?"

She looked over her shoulder. "My bathrobe and the towel I used this morning."

"Why is it on the floor?"

She looked at him. "Because they need to go in the wash and if I hang them up I'll forget and use them again, and like I said, they need to be washed."

"Why don't you put them in the dirty clothes hamper?"

"I don't have one. I used to, but I'd keep forgetting that I had laundry to do. I just throw everything in a laundry basket now." She opened the hall closet and pulled out a lightweight leather jacket. He got a glimpse of jumbled disarray on the closet floor before she pulled the door shut.

"So why didn't you put them in the laundry basket?" He pointed at the basket sitting on the coffee table.

"Those are clean clothes."

"Then why are they still in the basket, instead of folded and put away?"

She walked up to him, narrowing her eyes and peering at him closely. "What?" he said.

"I'm just wondering how my mother got inside your head and took control of your brain."

"Okay, it's none of my business," he allowed. He was silent for a moment then, "But look at this place!" He spread his arms out. "How can you live like this?"

"Quite happily, actually."

He shook his head. "I don't get it."

She rolled her eyes. "Well, unless you're planning to move in, you don't really have to."

When he just stood there, staring, she cleared her throat loudly. "Aren't we in a bit of a rush, Hazel?"

"Yeah." He shook his head one more time then turned to her. "Is this it, these two bags?"

"Yep." She handed him the shoulder bag and he grunted a little, unprepared for the weight of it.

"Jesus, what's in this thing?" he muttered as he adjusted it on his shoulder.

"Shoes."

"A whole bag of shoes?" He followed her out the door, waiting while she locked up. "And only one bag of clothes to go with all the shoes?"

"Hey, you can completely transform an outfit with just a shoe change," she said as he held the door for her. "And how come you're in such a crabby mood?"

"I'm sexually frustrated," he said starkly as he walked to the rented SUV parked at the curb. He tossed the shoulder bag in the backseat then turned to take the carryon case from her. "I can't believe it took you three hours to pack two lousy bags."

"Well, it's a science. You can't rush it." She climbed into the passenger seat and belted herself in.

"I thought you couldn't rush art," he said as he climbed in next to her.

"That too," she said, and popped the seat into the reclining position. She settled herself comfortably against the headrest and stretched her legs out in front of her. "Wake me when we get to Michigan, would you?" she yawned and closed her eyes.

She could practically feel him staring at her as he stared the car. "This assignment already sucks," he commented, and she grinned as he put the car in gear and drove.

* * * * *

Four hours later he shook her awake. "Wake up, sleeping beauty. We're in Michigan."

Lacey yawned and popped one eye open. "How long have we been driving?"

"I've been driving for just over four hours. You've been sleeping."

She pulled the lever to bring her seat upright, blinking sleep out of her eyes. "Wow, I was really out of it. I slept though Gary?"

"Yeah, I couldn't believe it. Man, that place has a stench."

She laughed around another jaw-cracking yawn. "No kidding." She looked around. "We've stopped."

"I need to check in with the Washington office and I need a landline." He nodded at the truck-stop diner they were parked next to.

"Oh good." She unbuckled her seatbelt. "You find a pay phone and I'll find the restroom."

She left him at a bank of payphones just inside the restaurant and went to find a bathroom. She got confused for a minute when she went into the truck-stop shower room by mistake, but a truck driver named Lem with a nose ring and a tattoo of a snake wrapped around his neck pointed her in the right direction. She made quick use of the facilities, splashed some water on her face to clear the rest of the sleep fog out of her mind and wandered out to find Devon.

He was still hunched over a payphone, one eye on the door. She rolled her eyes at his back and started to wander aimlessly. The truck stop was divided into two parts, half Fifties-style diner, complete with roller-skating waitresses and cracked vinyl booths. The other half was a retail store chock-full of all the things a truck driver could ever conceivably need, and several things she was certain no person would ever need for any purpose. The two halves were bisected by a long lunch counter with short-order cooks working behind it under a sign that said, "Ask Us About Our Homemade Ice Cream".

Delighted with the hodgepodge of useless gadgets and tacky T-shirts, she lost track of time. She was eyeing a T-shirt with a recipe for Roadkill Surprise on it as a present for Jane when a heavy hand came down on her shoulder.

"What're you doing?"

Lacey barely controlled the automatic squeak of alarmed surprise. "Having a heart attack," she said, turning to look at Devon. "Don't sneak up on a person like that."

He folded his arms across his chest. "Sorry. Are you ready to go?"

She frowned. "Okay, as apologies go? That sucked. And, no, I have to buy my T-shirt."

He narrowed his eyes on the garment. "You're buying a hot pink shirt with instructions for cooking roadkill."

"It's a present for Jane." She headed up to the checkout counter. "And I want some ice cream." She smiled at the clerk. "What do you recommend?"

The clerk, whose nametag read Beverly Ann, snapped her gum. "Well, for my money the butter pecan is the way to go. But that's only if you're going to get it in a waffle cone. We make those here too, you know."

"What about if I want a milkshake?" Lacey asked.

"Hmm." Beverly Ann blew a thoughtful bubble. "Then I'd go with chocolate."

"Yep, the classics never go out of style." Lacey dug in her pocket and pulled out a twenty. "I'll take a large milkshake, chocolate." She looked at Devon. "You want anything?"

He looked up at the hand-lettered sign over Beverly Ann's head. "I'll take a small strawberry malted."

Beverly rang up their shakes and bagged the T-shirt. When she handed over the shakes, Lacey chuckled. Her large shake was so large she could barely hold it with one hand and Devon's small looked like a child's toy in his big hand.

"Sorry," she murmured when he looked at her funny. She followed him out to the SUV and climbed in, keeping her shake balanced between her knees as she buckled herself in.

He looked over at her as he pulled out onto the highway. "You going back to sleep?"

She shook her head. "Nope, I'm wide-awake now. I usually don't nap like that in the middle of the day, but the last few weeks have just been crazed. Being maid of honor is a lot more work than I was led to believe."

"Really?" he said. "All the best man has to do is plan the bachelor party."

"Well, I got to do that too—the bachelorette party, I mean. But I also had to do the shower." She shuddered. "I was just going to make it a bachelorette party-shower combination, but Jane's mother about had a heart attack. So two parties. Plus all the planning I had to sit in on."

"This is the planning where your mind would wander and you'd look at my picture?"

She sighed. "Yeah, I should thank you for that. That picture is the only reason I didn't have Mrs. Denning kidnapped."

"Oh, I think you thanked me last night."

She suppressed a shudder at the dark heat in his tone and tried to look stern. "Are you flirting with me on an interstate highway?"

He grinned. "Yep."

"Oh." She tried drinking her milkshake while she contemplated how to answer that, but it was still too frozen to get much through the straw.

"How's your shake?" he asked.

"Fine," she said, startled. "Still pretty frozen." She had expected him to continue the conversation along the flirting vein, instead of normal conversation.

He saw her watching him warily and grinned. "What, did you think I was going to talk dirty to you the rest of the way to Mackinac?"

"Well, yeah," she said. "I kinda did. You mean you're not going to?"

"Hell no."

Lacey frowned. "Why not?"

"Because I've already got half a hard-on from just smelling your skin for the last four hours, and since we don't have time to find a motel to stop for a few hours, I'm not about to drive myself even crazier."

"Oh...well. That makes sense." Lacey smiled.

"You like that idea, don't you?"

"What, that you can barely keep your hands off me? Of course I like it, I'm not stupid. But if we're not going to talk dirty, how're we going to pass the time? We've got what, another four hours of driving?"

"At least that," he said.

"Okay then, we should be able to find something to talk about that doesn't involve sex." Lacey thought for a second. "Can you tell me about your last assignment?"

He shot her a "get real" glance out of the corner of his eye.

"Okay, that's no good. How about you tell me about your family?"

"Don't have one."

"Everybody has one," she said. "Even if they're all dead, they're still family."

"Well, then mine's all dead. I was an only child, my mother raised me on her own after my father died in Vietnam and she passed away when I was in college."

"I'm sorry," Lacey said softly, oddly disturbed by the matter-of-fact way he spoke of his mother.

He smiled at her. "It's okay, Lacey. It was a long time ago. I still miss her, but it's fine."

She shrugged. "I'm still sorry."

"Thanks."

She nodded. "Okay, I'm out of conversational gambits, unless you want to tell me about this guy we're going to look for."

Devon shrugged, unable to think of a good reason not to tell her at this point. "His name is Deveraux."

"What's his first name?" Lacey tried the milkshake again and got a little through the straw this time.

"Simon."

"Simon Deveraux." Lacey grimaced. "Sounds like a French accountant. I think I like Ignacious better. What's his major malfunction, anyway?"

"Oh, he's your average, run-of-the-mill, psychotic killer arms dealer with delusions of grandeur and a God complex."

"Nice. And now he's decided to try his hand at counterfeiting?"

"So it would seem."

"And how exactly are we supposed to stop him?"

"We're not. Not unless we absolutely have to. Our information tells us that he's already got a buyer lined up. So we're just going to observe, try to identify the buyer and let Treasury know when they can move in." There was a slight sneer in his voice when he said "Treasury".

"I assume by Treasury you mean the Treasury Department."

"Right. Secret Service, to be exact. Counterfeiting is their jurisdiction."

"Then how come you're involved in this? You don't work for Treasury, right?"

"Right."

Lacey frowned. "So how come the FBI is involved?"

"The FBI is coordinating, that's all. And I don't exactly work for them either."

"I'm confused. Who do you work for?"

"Technically, I work for an agency you've never heard of that doesn't officially exist."

"So, what, they loaned you out for this?" He nodded. "Why you?"

He grimaced. "That's kind of a long story."

"Uh…" She made a point of looking out the window at the landscape speeding by. "You going anywhere?"

He sighed. "Well, Treasury knows I've had dealings with Deveraux before. Since they don't really have any intelligence on him, they consulted with the FBI to try to find out what to expect and decided rather than train one of their agents in a short period of time, they'd do better to borrow someone with the experience. In this case, that would be me."

"Uh-huh. And you're pissed off at this because…?"

"Because I was blackmailed into it. They won't let me retire until I take care of this problem for them, and the Treasury Department hates me so I'm pretty sure they're having a good time with it."

"Really?" Lacey said. "The entire Treasury Department hates you?"

She watched, fascinated, as a flush darkened his cheekbones. He muttered something under his breath.

"I'm sorry, what was that?"

"I said, the director of the Treasury Department hates me."

"Oh, you're going to have to do better than that," Lacey said, enjoying herself immensely. "You must've done something. What was it? Or," she said slyly, "who was it?"

She howled with laughter when his blush deepened. "I don't believe it! You slept with somebody you shouldn't have, didn't you?" She frowned suddenly. "It wasn't somebody's wife was it?"

"No!" He looked aghast that she'd even ask the question.

"That's all right then." She started giggling again. "So who was it? Somebody's daughter? Sister?"

He stayed silent for a moment then muttered, "Niece."

Lacey couldn't stop giggling. "Whose niece?"

Devon sighed. "The director's."

"And, what, he didn't want her dating a spy or something?"

"That, and I think he was a little put out at finding us on the living room floor of his beach house."

"Oopsie," Lacey said, still giggling. "Bet that put a hitch in the festivities."

He looked over at her. "You enjoying yourself?"

"Oh, totally!" she said gleefully.

He shook his head. "New topic, please."

"Spoilsport."

"I thought you wanted to know about Deveraux."

She sighed. "Well, if you're not going to spill the gory details, then I suppose that's the next best thing." She slurped at her milkshake. "So, about Deveraux?" she prompted.

"He's a little guy, five foot eight inches. Blond hair that he bleaches so it's almost white and very pale blue eyes."

Lacey rolled her eyes. "Devon, there's a photo in the file folder that'll tell me all that. Tell me about his personality."

Devon shrugged. "He's smart, he's charming and he's bat-shit crazy. He saw the end of the cold war as the opportunity of a lifetime. All those weapons that the superpowers had been stockpiling? Once there was no use for them anymore, several less-than-civic-minded government employees—on both sides of the Iron Curtain—started shopping for buyers. Deveraux was happy to play broker."

Lacey frowned. "I don't remember seeing that on the news. I mean, I was in college and more interested in soap operas than the evening news. But still, I'd like to think I'd have heard if nations were selling off nuclear weapons to the highest bidder."

"It wasn't publicized, Lacey. And most of those deals were intercepted before they could actually be made. At least on the big stuff like missiles. His bread and butter is the small arms deal—assault rifles, large caliber semi-automatics. He does pretty well with that, especially in high-tension areas, and also uses his own inventory when the price is right.

"Over the last couple of years, we've managed to punch enough holes in his network to make him nervous. Last year we almost managed to nail him in a sweep but he slipped through. I guess he figured it was time to get out of the game before he got pinched."

"So he thought counterfeiting was the way to go." Lacey nodded. "I can see that."

"Don't be fooled. The game might be different, but it's just as dangerous, if not more so. Money makes the world go 'round, after all."

"I thought that was love."

"Not in politics, darling."

"Okay." Lacey put her feet up on the dashboard and reclined the seat a few notches. "So we're just supposed to keep an eye on him and let the good guys know when they can move in."

"That's about the size of it, yeah."

"Sounds like a pretty cushy last assignment to me. Couple of days in a resort on the government dime. How come you're so pissed off about it?"

"I don't like having my strings pulled, that's all."

"Apparently," she said. "Why did they want you again?"

He shrugged. "I've had the most experience in dealing with Deveraux. It makes sense to pull me in, even if they hate the idea as much as I do."

"Yeah, but it seems like a pretty run-of-the-mill assignment. They just need someone to watch the guy, right? So why pull in a seasoned field agent for that, even if he does have the most experience?"

"There's always a chance something could go wrong, even on the most routine and mundane of missions," he explained. "Deveraux has a lot of dangerous friends. If any of them are involved in this new venture of his, they don't want a rookie at the wheel."

"Do they think he has any buddies with him?"

He shook his head. "There's nothing in the intel about a partner or accomplice, but I'd be willing to bet he's got Felicity with him."

"Oooh, there's a woman. Who is she?"

"His woman, his lackey, his gal Friday. She's always with him, so I imagine she still is."

"They're lovers?"

"So far as anyone knows. They're very close, he barely makes a move without her."

"Then don't you think it's a little weird that they wouldn't even have mentioned her in the intel report?"

He frowned. "It is. Unless she's not with him anymore. He went underground last year after we almost nabbed him. I'd always assumed she'd gone under with him."

"So, what, we just wait and see?"

"No, I'm going to make a phone call when we stop for dinner. I don't like surprises."

Lacey kept silent while Devon continued to frown over the holes in the intelligence report supplied to them by the FBI.

They were a little troubling to her too. She was new at this espionage game but, to her logical mind, it seemed reasonable that if the bad guy had a girlfriend, that would be helpful information to have. Especially if that girlfriend was a bad guy too.

"So." Lacey cleared her throat. "We just observe then?"

Devon was still frowning. "Yes."

"What're we going to do with ourselves otherwise?"

"I figured we'd be fucking our brains out. That sound good to you?"

The dark heat was back in his voice and suddenly it was all she could do not to climb in his lap and bite him.

"I don't know," she said, striving for cool nonchalance. "I was kind of hoping for a spa treatment or two. Maybe a seaweed wrap or a pedicure." She sucked desperately at her straw, thinking the frozen shake might cool her off. The only thing it did was give her an ice cream headache.

He took his eyes off the road to stare at her. "Lady, if you think I'm not going to have you flat on your back at the first available opportunity, you're out of your mind. You've been teasing me all day."

Lacey did her best to quash the rising heat with indignation. "I have not! Name one sexual thing I've done since I got out of bed this morning."

"You smiled, you laughed and you smell too damn good."

"It's hardly my fault if you're susceptible to such things," she said, folding her arms across her chest so he wouldn't see her nipples poking through her T-shirt.

"And you took three hours to pack."

"Again, not my fault. These things take as long as they take."

He laughed, a low burst of sound that held a wealth of sensual promise. "I hope you remember that later when I've got you under me with your knees pinned to your shoulders."

Lacey swallowed a moan at the image that conjured up. "That's so un-politically correct."

"Yep," he said.

She drew a deep breath. "When are we stopping for dinner?"

He grinned. "We'll stop when we get to Mackinac City."

"Right." At least four more hours. She raked shaking fingers through her hair and took a steadying breath. "How 'bout some music?" she asked, and reached for the radio.

"Good idea," he said as she hit the power button and the air was filled with the sharp twang of a steel guitar. He picked up his own frozen malt and resigned himself to a long drive.

Chapter Fourteen

ஐ

Four very frustrating hours later they pulled into the parking lot of a motel in Mackinac City. Devon threw the vehicle into park and looked over at Lacey. She was watching him, her face flushed and her breath coming quickly, and he had to make a serious effort to remember that he had business to take care of.

"I have to make a phone call," he said.

"I remember."

"I don't think we should head to the island tonight."

She shook her head slowly. "No, me neither. We should take some time, regroup."

"Right," he said. "So I'll go in, get us a room. Then make my phone call."

"Sure," she said, her voice sounding unnaturally loud in the quiet of the car.

"And just so we're clear, after I make my phone call, I'm going to fuck your brains out."

She let out her breath in a whoosh. "Talk fast," she whispered, and he groaned. He leaned over and took her mouth in a hard, brief kiss. When he pulled back, his breathing was as rough as hers. He reached blindly for the door handle and climbed out of the SUV.

He checked them into the motel in record time and before she knew it, she was standing at the threshold of room 24 while he did a security sweep. She wasn't sure what he was sweeping for—nobody knew they were there, for Christ's sake—but she was grateful for the time to gather her scattered senses.

127

God, the last four hours had been interminable. Once they'd talked about the case about as much as they could, they'd chatted about nonsense—what was playing on the radio, the sports report, whether or not baseball could still be called the national pastime. And all the while they were arguing foreign policy and hockey, there had been an undercurrent of sexual tension so thick it couldn't be cut with a chain saw. She'd spent more time in drenched panties in the eighteen hours she'd known him than the whole of her twenties, and she was pretty sure that if he even looked hard enough at her clit, it would explode.

"You can come in now," he said, and she looked up to find him standing a few feet away, watching her. He had that dark, dangerous, I'm-holding-back-but-watch-out look on his face that gave her shivers.

His eagle eye didn't miss a trick. "Are you cold?"

She shook her head and watched his eyes narrow with intent. "Turned on?"

His voice was a near rumble now and she felt it like a rough stroke over her skin. Slowly, she nodded her head and closed the door at her back.

He stayed where he was, several feet away with his hands clenched at his sides. "I have to make my phone call now." His tone of voice said he'd rather be making her.

"I know," she said. She swallowed and pointed to the bathroom. "I'll just…freshen up while you're doing that."

"Don't lock the door," he said, his voice tight with heat and anticipation.

"I won't," she promised, and walked to the bathroom before she forgot about business and attacked him where he stood.

She closed the bathroom door behind her and slumped against it, one hand pressed to her chest to hold her racing heart in. "Jesus," she breathed. "He hasn't even touched me and I'm so close to coming I can taste it."

She straightened and went to the sink, running the cold tap until the water was freezing then splashing it on her face until she felt seminormal. Then she just stood there and tried to breathe normally.

In the next room, Devon dialed the phone with shaking hands. God, if he didn't get his hands on her soon, he was going to lose it completely. He heard running water in the bathroom and pictured her in the shower, lather running down her body as she worked the soap with her hands, rubbing the fragrant suds over her silky skin.

He got lightheaded and had to sit down, and by the time he shook the image loose his call was picked up.

"Yo."

"Jack, it's Devon."

"Devon! What's up, pal? How's retirement treating you?" His old friend's voice turned from taciturn to friendly when he realized who he was talking to.

Devon grimaced. "Not so good. I got roped into one last gig."

"Ouch. Need a hand?"

"No, but I could use some information. Feel like going digging?"

"For you? No problem." He heard rustling sounds then, "Go."

"Get me what you can on Deveraux."

There was silence on the other end then a low whistle. "You going back there, man?"

"No choice." Devon glanced over his shoulder at the bathroom door. The water had stopped, and his head conjured up images of Lacey toweling off. His cock grew impossibly harder at the thought and he pulled himself back to the conversation with difficulty.

"Okay. But I thought he got out of the game."

"He just found a different one to play. He's into funny money these days and I need to know who he's brought along with him."

"Felicity?"

"Her specifically and any other players he might've picked up along the way."

"Your gut telling you something's funny, Hoss?"

"It's telling me something, I'm just not sure what yet. Can you do a quick run?"

"Sure. I take it you're looking for current activity?"

"Anything within the last twelve to eighteen months. I need to know who he's running with these days. You can send it to my email." He rattled off the address, keeping an eye on the bathroom. He'd rather not have Lacey walk in on this conversation. For one, she was a civilian and the less she knew the safer she'd be. And two, if she came out before he'd taken care of business, it wasn't going to get taken care of. He'd be inside her before she took two steps.

"You got it." Jack paused, then said, "Take it easy, okay? If you decide you need someone on your six, you know where to find me."

"Thanks, man. I appreciate it."

"Anytime."

Jack clicked off and Devon hung up the phone. If there was anything missing from the FBI file, then Jack would ferret it out. He rubbed his hands over his face, suddenly incredibly tired. He was looking forward to a nice, quiet civilian life where he didn't have to constantly wonder what—or who— was lurking around the corner.

His head snapped around when he heard the bathroom door open and everything ceased to exist except for the woman who stood in the doorway.

She was fully dressed and her hair was dry. "I thought you were taking a shower."

She shook her head, twisting her hands together. "I thought about it, but figured that'd just be a waste."

"How?" he asked, slowly standing up.

She shrugged, a ghost of a smile on her unpainted mouth. "I'm about to get all sweaty and sticky." Her eyes twinkled at him, all flirtatious female power, and the control he'd been holding on to all day frayed thin.

He started toward her, his stride measured and deliberate. He watched her eyes widen as he drew close, saw the reflexive step backward she started to take before catching herself. He stopped in front of her, so close his chest almost brushed the stiffened peaks of her breasts that were clearly visible through her T-shirt.

"Last chance to say no," he said, his voice so low and rough she could barely make out the words.

Her eyes grew heavy-lidded with arousal and the tip of her tongue sneaked out to wet her lips. He tracked the movement, aching to trace the path with his own tongue, to sink deep into her mouth. But he waited for her to answer, knowing that once he started he wouldn't be able to stop.

She reached out, placing her hand high on his chest. "I don't want to say no," she said. She fisted her hand in his shirt and tugged, bringing his head closer to hers. "I want you to fuck me," she declared in a growl of her own, and crushed her mouth to his.

Devon's control snapped clean and with a low growl, he wrapped his hands around her rib cage. He took over the kiss, sliding his tongue into her mouth. She moaned and curled her tongue around his, sucking at it, and he tore his mouth free.

"God," he muttered, panting. He lifted her up. "Put your legs around me," he ordered, and she blindly obeyed. He shifted his hands, wrapping one arm around her lower back and fisted the other hand in her hair. He tugged her head, angling it the way he wanted, and dove back into her mouth.

She whimpered under the onslaught, and suddenly he couldn't wait any longer. He turned, walking by memory to the low dresser against the wall. It held a lamp, an ice bucket and travel brochures advertising all the fabulous attractions of Mackinac. One sweep of his arm sent the lot of it clattering to the floor. Lacey jumped at the noise, tearing her mouth from his to look around. He tightened his hold on her hair, keeping her from turning her head. She looked at him with eyes dazed with lust, her lips damp and swollen from his kiss.

"I want inside you," he muttered, and set her down on the edge of the dresser. He gripped her hips with both hands, bringing her fully against him.

"Yes," she hissed, and let go of his shirt to tear at her own clothes. She whipped the T-shirt over her head then reached behind her to unsnap her bra. The position thrust her chest forward, and while she wrestled her way out of the garment, he took immediate advantage, planting one hand in the middle of her back to hold the arch of her spine and sucked one turgid nipple deep into his mouth.

Lacey let out a hoarse scream, her head falling back and hitting the dresser with a thunk. She laced her fingers in his hair, holding his mouth to her flesh as she ground her pelvis into his. He reached down and shifted her hips, bringing the rigid arch of his cock into direct contact with her aching clit.

"Oh, God," she sobbed. Devon could feel the heat of her through the thick seam of her jeans and ground into her. Her heart pounded a frantic rhythm under his lips. He raised his head, leaving her nipple red and wet from his mouth, and looked at her face. Her lips were parted, her eyes wide and blind as her hips surged desperately against his. He watched the flush spread across her chest as her pants turned to whimpering moans.

"Are you going to come for me, baby?" he whispered, and scraped his teeth along the ridge of her collarbone. She moaned louder, her hips pumping harder. "Are you?"

"If you move just a little bit higher…"she moaned, grabbing his wrists where they gripped her hips and tried to grind against him where it would do her the most good.

He grinned, delighted with her, and ruthlessly held her hips in place. "Is that a fact?" he drawled.

"God!" she wailed, digging her nails into his hands. "I'm almost there, please!"

"Jesus," he muttered, his eyes all but crossing in lust. He let go of her hips to tear at the fastening of her jeans, suddenly desperate to feel the wet heat of her cunt without barriers. He jerked at her zipper, dragging her pants and panties to the top of her thighs and giving himself just enough room to wedge a hand between them.

His head swam as the scent of her desire hit him full blast, dark and wet and earthy, and he couldn't wait any longer. He tucked his hand in the notch of her thighs, held tightly together by the confining fabric of her jeans. The lips of her pussy were plump and flushed, her engorged little clit already poking out from between them. He felt the slickness of her cream coating his fingers as he pried her lips apart and delved between them.

She was so wet and ready he slid two fingers easily inside her, groaning as her inner walls immediately clamped down on them. "Oh, you like that, don't you, baby?" He pulled back, tugging them almost all of the way out of her before slamming them home again.

She keened, the sound high and wild as her hips bucked. "Oh yes, oh, right there! Oh please, just a little…harder!"

"Like this?" He pumped his fingers in her hard, hooking them slightly to rasp and drag against her sensitive inner tissues. At the same time he ground the heel of his hand against her clit and with a scream, she exploded.

The sight of Lacey convulsing in orgasm, her face flushed with pleasure combined with the feel of her cunt pulsing around his fingers was more than Devon could take. He tore at the fastening of his own pants with one hand, pulling his fingers from her only when he needed both hands to dig out a condom and hastily put it on.

He didn't bother stripping her jeans the rest of the way down, but simply turned her on her hip, slinging both of her feet over his left shoulder. The position left her backside turned up, the soft, damp flesh of her bare cunt exposed and vulnerable, and he wasted no time.

Her eyes flew open when she felt him lodge the broad head of his cock to her sensitive opening. Her pussy was still fluttering with aftershocks, little pulls and pulses that had him gritting his teeth with the effort to hold back. He wanted nothing more than to plow into her, to bury himself so deep it would be impossible to tell where he ended and she began, but he wanted her with him.

"Look at me," he said, his voice low and rough with the effort of restraint. He could feel her pussy growing wetter still, her body preparing the way for him, and he nearly lost it right then.

"Lacey!" He nearly shouted it in desperation, and finally she turned dazed eyes on him. He paused for a moment, savoring the sight of Lacey as she balanced on the fine edge of passion.

Her hair was in complete disarray, the blonde strands tousled and sticking to her skin with perspiration. Her brown eyes were heavy-lidded, the pupils dilated with desire. Her breath came in pants, and he knew he'd have to have the sweet heat of her mouth wrapped around his dick again soon.

Her chest was flushed, her nipples drawn hard and tight, the red peaks still glistening from the touch of his mouth. Her rib cage rose and fell with rapid, panting breaths, the slight curve of her belly quivering with them.

A sudden groan tore from her lips, bringing his gaze back to her face. She was staring at him, her hands cupping her breasts. As he watched, she pulled her own nipples, tugging and twisting the hard little nubs and wringing whimpering cries from her throat. He could feel her pussy clutching, pulling him inside, and he growled. "Tell me what you want, Lacey."

Her only answer was another whimpering moan and a blind thrust of her hips that took him in another inch before he gripped her thighs to halt her movements. He was shaking now, sweating with the effort it took not to plunge blindly into the grasping depths of her pussy.

"Tell me!" he barked, and her head came up off the dresser.

Her eyes were wild, her soft, supple mouth curled into a near grimace. The thought hit him that this was not a supplicant woman, begging her lover for pleasure. No, this was a woman, despite her obvious physical disadvantage, who was willing to fight to get what she wanted. And what she wanted right now was his cock in her.

"Fuck me," she half hissed, half moaned, and pulled harder on her nipples. The action wrung a shudder from her and she bucked her hips again. "Fuck me hard, now!"

Devon gripped her thighs tight, muttered, "Hang on, baby," and drove his cock into her with one brutal thrust.

Lacey screamed, her back arching, but he didn't stop. He didn't even slow down. Instead, set a hard, driving pace that took him to the heart of her with every stroke. Devon groaned, feeling his balls draw up tight, his climax drawing embarrassingly near. The grip of her cunt was so tight it felt as though she held him in a heated velvet vise. The position of her legs, held tightly closed by the restriction of her jeans, made the fit even tighter, and he felt as though each thrust was the first one.

He was determined to make her come again before he lost himself completely in the hot clasp of her flesh. He shifted his grip on her legs, pulling so her hips were off the edge of the dresser and he could bend over her more fully. The position pushed her legs back to her chest and canted her hips higher, and he felt himself slide even deeper into her.

He barely heard her scream, her sobbing pleas for more. He was completely focused, driving both of them toward orgasm. Sweat ran in rivulets down his face to drip onto the quivering mounds of her breasts. Those pale mounds with their hard, red tips beckoned to him and, with a growl, he leaned over and captured one engorged peak.

The motion drove him even deeper into her clinging sheath, and with a shrill scream she came apart. Her cunt clutched him fiercely, milking his hard flesh as her body jerked and arched up into him. He released her nipple with a hoarse shout, driving into her once, twice more before he followed her into orgasm.

He came endlessly, his body locked to hers as he pumped himself dry. The rhythmic pull of her body milking him made him feel as though the top of his head would fly off and spin across the room. When it was over, he slumped over her, his body locked to hers. The spasms that shook her body and tightened her pussy kept him hard and, despite the pleasantly fatigued feeling that a good, strong orgasm always left him with, he suddenly couldn't wait for round two.

Catching his breath, he levered himself up on his elbows and looked down at her. She was sprawled in limp abandon across the top of the dresser, her eyes closed. Her breath was coming in shuddering sobs, and he realized suddenly that he had her knees pinned practically to her chin, which might make breathing more difficult for her.

He pushed himself up, groaning as the movement inadvertently seated him even farther inside her. She whimpered, her pussy shivering around him convulsively, and he gritted his teeth against the sensation. He pulled out, doing his best to ignore her groan and the shimmy of her hips as a fresh round of aftershocks shook her. He straightened her legs slowly, easing her more fully onto the dresser so that her legs were supported. He stroked the quivering muscles of her thighs in an attempt to ease any cramping she might have and she sighed.

"Okay?" he murmured.

"Mmmmm," she said, not bothering to open her eyes, and he felt a primitive pride in the satisfaction in her tone.

"Don't move," he said, leaning over to plant a soft kiss on her lax mouth. "I'll be right back."

"I'll be here," she sighed, and he chuckled as he walked to the bathroom to clean up.

He dealt quickly with the condom, grinning at his reflection in the mirror over the sink as he shucked his clothes the rest of the way off and washed up. Great sex always made him feel revved, almost like he had super-human strength, and the way he felt right now he figured he could probably bench press a tank.

He was hard-pressed to remember the last time he'd had such a hot time in bed with a woman. Like so much of his life lately, sex had become routine, almost boring. The women who inhabited his world were always the same—dangerous, hard-living, hard-loving, and gone when the sun came up. It was a good arrangement most of the time, considering he didn't have time or room for romantic entanglements. Having to tell a woman he was leaving for a "top secret mission" never seemed to play well. Even if they did believe him, not many were willing to put up with that kind of relationship—never knowing where he was, when or if he would contact them. It was too much to expect of someone, and he'd learned long ago to distance himself emotionally from his sexual encounters, as well as picking partners who knew the score.

All of which had made for a pretty routine sex life over the years. Lacey was the first woman who he'd been with in years out of more than just a need for release. He liked her. God knew he liked fucking her, but it was more than that. Her sense of humor and sharp intelligence were entertaining, and he couldn't remember the last time he'd had a casual conversation with a woman.

Spending the day confined in the SUV with her, he'd been surprised to find that he enjoyed her company. He couldn't remember the last time he'd been relaxed enough with another person—besides Ian—to enjoy a simple conversation. And even though he'd been half hard all day, he'd genuinely had fun just talking to her.

All of which was slightly confusing for him. It had been so long since he'd had any kind of real relationship with a woman, he felt a little out of his element with her. Even though they were thrown together on this assignment, he knew he couldn't treat her like any other agent who knew the game. Like it or not, he was responsible for her on this mission, and he had no intention of putting her in harm's way.

He frowned as he dried his hands. He didn't think they'd run into any trouble with Deveraux, but the holes in the FBI's profile did give him some concern. He didn't think it would amount to much since he had Jack working on filling in those holes, and he was grateful for that. He didn't like leaving his flank vulnerable. Plus, if this assignment turned out to be as cushy as he thought it was going to be, he was going to have plenty of time to try and figure out what made Ms. Lacey Johnson tick.

He left the bathroom, his eyes narrowing as he crossed the room to her. She didn't seem to have moved from where he left her. Her arms were still hanging limp by her sides, her legs lying lax on the dresser, thighs still trapped in the confining denim of her jeans. In the dim light of the bedside lamp, he caught the sheen of sweat on her skin, and the slick layer of juice that still clung to her bare pussy. He felt his cock, which had remained half hard, swell to full hardness once again.

"Round two," he declared, and after a brief pause to snag the full box of condoms from his duffle and place them on the nightstand, started toward her.

* * * * *

Lacey lay boneless across the dresser, her limbs heavy and her mind a fog. She knew she should move, but her limbs had that puddle-of-wax feeling that great sex always seemed to provide, and she couldn't seem to muster up any interest in moving.

She'd been well and truly plowed, she thought, and couldn't manage to get overly upset about it. On the contrary, as soon as she could make her brain work again, she planned to thank him profusely. She felt her lips curl in a faint smile. The day had been torturous, long and boring with nothing to do but listen to bad radio and fantasize about all the things she'd like to do naked with Devon. She hadn't pictured this scenario, and even though her back was bruised from laying on the hard dresser and her thighs were cramping from being twisted up in her pants for so long, she wasn't going to complain.

She sighed, too limp to even shift enough to get out of the confining pants, and wondered if she could fall asleep without falling off the dresser. She was seriously considering it when she heard him come back from the bathroom. He growled something she couldn't quite make out, and then suddenly his hands were on her.

She moaned softly when she felt his hands slide down her still trembling thighs, let out a hiss of discomfort when he began tugging her pants down her legs. He murmured, "Easy," as he drew them down and off. His hands returned to her thighs, massaging firmly.

"Better?"

"Mmmm." She opened her eyes lazily to find him poised over her and, despite herself, caught her breath at the decadent picture of sensual satisfaction he presented.

His eyes were heavy, almost lazy with repletion, even though a hint of interest still lurked in their amber depths. His face was relaxed, the normal stern, hard planes of it curiously eased, as though he'd let go of some of the worries and pressures that weighed him down. And his mouth—oh, his mouth. Its normal sensual firmness was softened somehow, giving him a very satisfied, almost smug look.

"You look pleased with yourself," she managed, and fought back a shiver when he favored her with a slow smile.

He saw the shiver and his smile deepened. "You didn't think I was done, did you?"

Her eyes widened and a squeal burst from her lips when she felt him grasp the backs of her thighs and hoist her into the air. She grabbed reflexively at his shoulders and fought to keep the room in focus as he swung toward the bed. "Devon!"

"What?" he said, and set his lips to the curve of her shoulder, using tongue and teeth on the sensitive skin.

She felt her eyes roll back in her head as renewed heat flooded her pussy. She could've sworn two minutes before that she had no sexual impulses left, and with just a nibble of her shoulder he had her primed and ready to go.

"Oh, my God." She let her head fall back and laced her fingers into his hair, hanging on for dear life. "How do you do this to me?"

The room revolved again as he shifted her in his arms and when it stilled, she found herself straddling his hips as he reclined on the bed. She looked down to find him watching her. "What?" she gasped.

He raised one eyebrow, that sensual smile still in place. "I don't think you're done either."

She swallowed, unsure of the answer herself. He saw her hesitate and, in a preemptive strike, slid one long finger through the slick folds of her sex and straight into her.

She gasped, her body arching hard as she struggled against the riot of sensation that one long finger bought to screaming life. "I could be done," she gasped.

He chuckled. "Really?" he asked, and hooked the finger forward to scrape along the sensitive front wall of her sheath.

She felt her body tighten, gripping that magical finger with clutching muscles. She heard him hiss out a curse and she felt the edges of her vision dim once again as she started sliding toward orgasm.

Lacey whimpered in distress when he suddenly slipped his finger from her, her hips blinding surging, seeking his touch. She struggled to focus her hazy vision and to balance herself as he twisted to reach the nightstand. She saw him snag a condom from the box there, watched while he tore open the foil and rolled it on his cock with jerky, frantic movements.

When it was in place, he lifted her by her hips, holding her poised over him, and slowly began to lower her down.

"Wait," she gasped, and braced her hands on his stomach. He stopped immediately, holding her barely impaled, just the head of his cock breaching her tender opening.

She hung there for a moment, her entire attention focused on the tight, stretched feeling in her pussy as it struggled to accommodate him. It was a delicious combination of searing pleasure and slight discomfort, and she bit her lip against the dual assault.

"You okay, baby?" he said, and she looked down at his face. He was watching her with a predator's face, hard and unyielding, but there was a shadow of concern in his eyes, and she knew if she told him she was too sore, he'd let her up.

It made her all the more eager to have him.

"Yes," she breathed. "But I want to do it." She moved one hand, balancing herself on the other, and grasped his wrist. She dragged his hand up to cover her breast, holding it firm to her swollen flesh.

He took the hint, and with a low sound of approval moved his other hand so that he covered both breasts, massaging and kneading. She braced herself once more, hands firm on the taut muscles of his abdomen. Slowly, so as to draw out the sensation as much as possible, she began to lower herself onto the rigid length of him.

His long, groaning sigh mixed with her keening moan as she slid down, taking him fully in one excruciating, slick stroke. Her head reeled with the unbelievable feeling of fullness. She was tight, swollen from before, and felt as though he'd fill her to bursting.

She rose up, delighting in the delicious friction as he dragged along sensitive nerve endings. She lifted herself nearly completely off him before reversing course and sliding back down again. She found it so pleasurable she did it again. And again, and again, until they were both moaning on every stroke.

Her skin became slick with sweat, the effort of keeping the pace rhythmic and steady taking its toll. Part of her wanted to race to the finish, grab the brass ring of an orgasm that she knew was waiting for her without further delay but, oh, the delicious feel of him inside her, the fullness and friction and scent and sound of him as she rode him were too wonderful to give up.

So she held back, and when he shifted his grip to her waist and she felt him start to lift her, to take control, she would have none of it. "No," she hissed, her nails scraping his abdomen as she continued to ride slow and steady. "I want to do it."

He groaned, his hands flexing on her waist, gripping hard enough so she knew she'd have fresh marks tomorrow. "God, you're killing me here," he said, but he let her continue to set the pace.

"Don't worry," she gasped. "I'm almost finished." She could feel the storm gathering inside her, the coil of tension winding tighter and tighter with every downward stroke.

"Thank God," he said. He watched her with glittering eyes that missed nothing. She knew he could see the flush that signaled her impending orgasm, the quiver of her belly as the contractions began.

She whimpered, her vision blurring as her orgasm hit, no less powerful for having come so slowly. Suddenly desperate to feel his mouth on hers, she leaned forward.

He met her halfway, his hands leaving their death grip on her waist to tangle in her hair as he buried his tongue in her mouth as deeply as his cock was buried in her body. The pulsing contractions of her slick sheath were too much, milking him relentlessly and, with a hoarse shout that was muffled in her mouth, he came.

Lacey slumped onto his chest, her mouth sliding from his as her head suddenly became too heavy to hold up. She tucked her nose into the side of his neck, loving the musky scent of his skin, and tried to get her breath back.

His chest was heaving with the effort to draw breath, and she suddenly realized she was probably making that difficult for him. She slid to the side, curling up against him as he removed the condom. He dropped it into the trash can next to the bed and turned back to her.

"Come here," he rumbled, and gathered her up in his arms. He pulled her back up onto his chest, and she settled with a happy sigh.

"I'm too heavy for you," she said sleepily, her eyelids already drooping shut.

She felt rather than heard his snort. "Please. You barely weigh anything."

She yawned. "Still, this probably isn't comfortable for you. I can move."

"It's fine," he assured her, one hand stroking lazily up and down her back in a soothing stroke that was already putting her to sleep.

"If I don't move now, I'm going to fall asleep on you," she warned, and felt his arms tighten around her.

"Feel free," he rumbled, and with a sigh, she did.

Chapter Fifteen

ം

Lacey woke the next morning still lying on top of Devon. Her head rested on his shoulder, her legs tangled with his. One brawny arm was wrapped around her back to hold her in place, the other was flung out on the bed. His chest rose and fell with his breathing — he was dead to the world.

She stretched cautiously, not wanting to wake him. She felt fabulous. Rested, satisfied. She winced as her skin stuck to his then pulled free with a slight sucking sound. And sticky. Very, very sticky.

She grimaced in distaste, very aware of the fact that she'd fallen asleep before cleaning up last night. The combination of sweat and sex that had been so much fun last night had dried in a sticky layer on her skin, and suddenly a shower was the first thing on her agenda.

She moved quietly, sliding out from under his restraining arm in an attempt to let him sleep in, but he must've felt her move. His eyes snapped open, pinning her in place.

"Hi," she whispered.

"Hi," he yawned, rubbing one hand over his stubbled jaw. "Where're you going?"

"I need a shower," she said, and made a face. "I'm sticking to myself."

"I'll join you," he said, and sat up.

Lacey watched as he swung his legs over the side of the bed and stood up, stretching. It was fascinating to watch, all those muscles bunching and shifting. It was almost enough to make her think of having another go at him. Then she stood too, wincing as the muscles of her inner thighs screamed in protest. Almost.

"Okay," she agreed as she minced her way around the bed to the bathroom. "But you just keep that thing to yourself." She gestured to his morning erection, which waved in front of him like an eager flagpole.

Devon grinned, following her. "Aww, is somebody a little sore this morning?"

"Yes," she said, shooting him a wry glance over her shoulder as she turned on the shower. She adjusted the temperature then stepped under the spray. "Not that I'm complaining, but still. No playing 'hide the salami' this morning."

He stepped in behind her and closed the curtain. "How about 'suck the sausage'?"

She laughed and splashed water in his face. "No, not that either."

"Well, a guy can hope." He grabbed the little complimentary bottle of shampoo and squeezed some out onto her hair.

"Thanks," she said dryly, and began to work it into a lather. She moved to the side so he could dampen his hair, grinning when he cursed the scalding heat of the water.

"Christ, is it hot enough?" he groused, lathering his hair briskly.

She nudged him back out of the way. "I have sore muscles, remember? The heat is good for them." She sighed as she stood under the spray again, rinsing the suds from her hair.

She reached for the mini bottle of conditioner. "Of course, if I had Raul, I could work the kinks out much faster."

"Ah yes, the infamous Raul." Devon took a bracing breath as he rinsed his hair as quickly as he could then stepped back out of the spray. He stripped the paper off a new bar of soap and worked it between his hands. "Baby, you won't be needing Raul."

She rolled her eyes at him as she worked the conditioner into her hair. "I meant it'd be useful to have a handheld massager to work on the sore muscles of my legs."

"Oh." He handed her the bar of soap and nudged her out of the way again to rinse off. "Well, that might be handy. But you don't need him for anything else, not while I'm around."

The boasting, arrogant tone of voice might've irritated her if he hadn't already proved that point several times. But she couldn't resist a little, tiny dig and tucked her tongue firmly in cheek. "Well, I can probably do without him for a while. Yesterday's session with him should hold me for a while, at any rate."

She grinned as she ducked under the spray again and waited for the explosion. She didn't have to wait long.

"What do you mean, yesterday's session?"

His voice had gotten considerably lower, growly even, and she opened one eye to see him glaring at her.

She shrugged in unconcern and lathered up the soap. "I mean yesterday. As in the day before today."

"Yesterday when?"

"Yesterday morning, after I went back to my own apartment."

He glowered. "Why?"

"Because I wanted to, that's why." She grinned at him, enjoying herself immensely. "I told you I was going to."

"I didn't believe you."

She choked back a giggle at his fierce scowl. "Is something wrong?"

"Yes, something is wrong," he ground out. He was practically glowering at her. "I spent yesterday in a sexually frustrated hell and you'd scratched your own itch!"

Lacey bit back a chuckle. "You could've done the same, you know."

"I was rushing to get to that meeting," he reminded her, unappeased.

She shrugged and idly soaped her arms. "Well, you could've done it while I was packing. After all, I took three whole hours."

He folded his arms across his chest and harrumphed. "I didn't think of it."

"Well, that's hardly my fault," she pointed out reasonably, and finished rinsing off.

He shut off the water and followed her out of the shower. "I'm going to pay you back for that."

"How very small of you," she said, the words muffled under the towel she was using to dry her hair.

He wrapped his own towel around his hips and stormed past her. "I ought to jack off in front of you, just to make you suffer."

She chuckled and walked into the bedroom. "Are you seriously sulking over this?"

He sat on the bed, a mulish expression on his face. "It's rude," he muttered.

"Oh, forgive me. How very rude of me to see to my own needs, in my own home, without regard for the manly ego of my one-night stand."

"We're not a one-night stand," he protested.

"Not now we're not, but we both went into this thinking it was a one-off, and don't try to tell me different," she said when he opened his mouth to interrupt. "Besides, you're not mad I got off without you, you're just mad I got off when you didn't."

He had the grace to look sheepish. "Okay, that's true. But I'm still going to pay you back for it. Leaving me to suffer all day when you'd already gotten yours," he muttered.

"Awww, poor darling," she said, and patted his cheek while he glowered at her. "If it'll make it up to you, the next time I decide to take matters into my own hands, you can watch."

He perked up like a small boy with a new toy. "Really?"

Lacey shook her head. "Men," she said, and giving up, went to find her suitcase.

* * * * *

They found a diner near the hotel that specialized, as all diners do, in fabulously greasy, unhealthy food. They were both ravenous, having completely forgotten to eat dinner the night before. While Lacey polished off a second helping of banana pancakes, Devon made a phone call.

"Jack," he said when the phone stopped ringing. "You have any answers for me?"

"More questions than answers at this point." Devon could hear the frustration in his friend's voice. "I'm running into a few snags. It's going to take me a bit longer to get what you need."

Devon tamped down his impatience with effort. "Do the best you can," he said. "I'll give you a call tonight."

"Hopefully I'll have it by then. Later, buddy."

"Yeah, later." Devon hung up the payphone, frowning. If Jack was having trouble getting information, Deveraux had covered his tracks well, and probably with some help.

He pondered the significance of that on the way back to the table. Lacey looked up at his approach.

"What's wrong?" she asked, and only then did he realize he was frowning.

"Nothing," he assured her, picking up the check from the table. He glanced at the total and dug out some bills, tossing them on top of the check. "You ready to go?"

She looked at him curiously. "Sure." She stood up, slinging her purse over her shoulder. He put one hand on the small of her back as they left the restaurant, guiding her steps in a way that felt both protective and intimate. She silently admonished herself. This was clearly "work time", so she needed to get her mind out of her pants.

"So we're heading to the island, right?" she asked as they climbed into the rental.

"That's the plan," he said, still scanning the parking lot for, she assumed, any sign of a threat. Though what kind of threat they'd encounter in what she considered to be the wilds of Michigan was beyond her.

"Have you ever been there?" he asked as he pulled out of the parking lot. "Mackinac Island, I mean."

"Sure."

He looked at her. "Really?"

"Couple of times as a kid." She shrugged. "My family was big on camping trips. We hit campgrounds all over the Midwest in the summers."

"Yeah?" He grinned at her. "You mean like in tents and shit? Roasting hot dogs over a campfire? Making whatayacallems?"

"Whatayacallems?"

"Yeah, you know," he said, gesturing vaguely. "The things with the marshmallows and chocolate and cracker things."

"S'mores?" she asked, incredulous that he didn't know their proper name. "Yeah, we had those. No sense having a campfire if you don't make s'mores."

"I bet it was fun," he said, sounding wistfully sentimental.

She chuckled. "Sure, if you think getting eaten alive by mosquitoes, squabbling with various siblings and cousins, and sleeping on the hard ground a good time."

He braked for a traffic light and looked over at her. "You didn't have fun?"

Lacey smiled. "No, we did. It's just at the time it all seemed like such a pain, you know? Packing up the car, setting up camp, arguing over who got to do what, who *had* to do what. It sure couldn't have been easy for my parents. All those kids running around, screaming and picking fights, and just...generally being kids."

She looked over at him. "But now, when I think about it? Those summers were great. When we all manage to get together for a wedding or new baby or just a reunion, it's the one thing everybody loves to talk about."

"It sounds nice," he said, and the quiet tone of his voice reminded her that his childhood probably hadn't been so carefree.

"Did you and your mom ever go on vacations when you were a kid?" she asked quietly.

The light turned green and he accelerated through the intersection before answering her. "We always did little things together. Baseball games, pizza in the city."

Lacey had enough friends on the East Coast to know that when they said "the city", they meant New York City so she took a guess. "You lived in New York?"

"New Jersey," he said, making a left turn. "We'd go into the city a few times a month, find something fun to do. My mom, she could make anything an adventure."

"That's a great skill for a mom to have," she said.

"Especially a mom with a growing son who was into everything," he agreed, and turned right onto Lake Street. "She was great that way, you know? A lot of kids I knew had moms that just wanted their kids to shut up, be quiet, settle down." He shook his head. "She always found a way to encourage me."

"She sounds great," Lacey agreed.

"Yeah, she was." He pulled the SUV to a stop. Lake Street ended at Huron and he pointed across the street to the right. "There's the ferry dock."

She looked around. "What're we doing with the car?"

"They've got secured parking for overnight guests to the island." He flipped on his blinker and pulled across the street into the dock lot to a waiting valet. "We'll leave the car there. It's a rental, so if we have to ditch it, anyone looking for it won't be able to trace it back to us."

She looked alarmed. "Why would we have to ditch it?"

He took the parking ticket from the valet and got out. She followed suit and walked around the back of the car to stand next to him while he pulled their bags from the backseat. "Why would we have to ditch the car?" she hissed.

He glared at her, cutting his eyes to the hovering valet. She got the message—shut up until we can talk privately—and swallowed her words. She waited impatiently while he tipped the valet then fell into step beside him as the SUV roared off and he made his way to the ticket booth.

He bought the tickets—paying cash, she noted—and gestured her over to a cement bench along the water. She sat down, waited for him to do the same, then lit into him.

"What did you mean, if we have to ditch the car? I thought we were just supposed to watch this guy."

"Say it a little louder, Lace. I'm not sure the family of six over there heard you."

She rolled her eyes. "Sorry," she muttered, casting a wary glance over her shoulder to make sure no one was listening in. "But you make it sound like you're expecting trouble—a *lot* of trouble—and that's kind of contradictory to what you've been telling me to expect so far."

Devon leaned back against the bench, the picture of casual nonchalance in his faded jeans and navy blue T-shirt.

He smiled at her and stretched one arm out along the bench, toying with the ends of her hair as they danced in the breeze.

"I'm not expecting any trouble," he lied, deciding then and there not to tell her about the funny feeling he had about their lack of accurate information on Deveraux's associates.

She looked at him, clearly disbelieving. "Then why the whole, 'if we have to ditch the car, no one can trace it to us' talk? That's not the talk of an unworried person."

He kept the smile on his face but his eyes narrowed. "It's just a habit, honey. I'm used to making sure I can get out fast if I have to. I've been doing this a long time, you know."

He saw her shoulders relax a little and frown line between her eyebrows smoothed out. "Oh. You're sure?"

She looked so earnest, he felt a little twinge about lying to her. Just a little one though. "Yes, I'm sure."

"Okay then." Lacey leaned back, turning so her head was nestled on his shoulder. "When does this ferry leave?"

He looked at his watch. "About five minutes, actually. We should probably get onboard."

They tussled briefly over whether or not Lacey could carry her own bags, which nearly ended with both of them in the lake. Lacey capitulated with a, "Fine. Be a Grand Canyon mule," and they fell in line with the vacation crowd waiting to file onto the ferry.

They boarded the ferry in relatively short order, the crowd moving quickly. The wind was whipping off the water and most of the early morning travelers meandered toward the enclosed lower deck for the ride to the island. Lacey was planning to join them but Devon nudged her toward the stairs leading to the open upper deck.

Assuming he wanted privacy to talk about the plan for when they reached Mackinac, she trudged up the steps, one hand on the rail for balance. She hit the top step and breathed deep the fresh morning air, her face turned to the sun.

"Wow," she sighed. "The city doesn't smell like this. Hey!"

She turned to scowl at him, rubbing her butt where he'd jabbed it with his duffle bag. "Do you mind? I'm having a moment here."

He rolled his eyes. "I'm stuck on a stairway that's way too narrow for a pack mule." He nudged her with the duffle again. "Can you have your moment all the way on the deck?"

"You have no poetry in your soul," she sniffed, and strode onto the deck.

"There once was a man from Nantucket," he began, and she laughed.

He dumped the bags on one of the benches lining the rail and grinned at her. "See? Poetry."

"I stand corrected," she chuckled, and turned to face the open water.

The lake was choppy, stubby little waves capped with white rolling over each other to bang against the hull of the boat. Seagulls dipped and swooped, catching breakfast as the waves tossed it up. Lacey braced her legs apart, her sea legs coming back to her with ease even though it'd been a dozen years or more since she'd been on a boat.

She shivered in the stiff breeze, her summer-weight T-shirt not providing much of a barrier against the brisk wind. She felt Devon's arms come around her from behind and she snuggled into the warmth of his broad chest with a sigh.

"What's on your mind, baby?" he murmured into her ear.

She stayed silent for a moment then, "Is it wrong that I'm totally jazzed about this?"

"About the assignment?"

"Yeah." She twisted in his arms, laying her hands on his chest and leaning back to look him in the face. "I mean, I get that it's a big deal and a matter of national security and blah, blah, blah, but I'm still so *jazzed* about it. Is that horrible?"

He chuckled. "First, if you'll say 'national security blah, blah, blah' to my boss when this is all over, I'll buy you a new car. Second—no. It's not wrong. It's the adrenaline."

She frowned. "I'm not a danger junkie."

He shook his head. "That's not what I mean. It's a chemical reaction, basic human response to fear or danger. Even though this situation isn't all that dangerous, it's new and unusual and exciting. The trick is to know when the adrenaline will help and when it's time to really be scared."

"And how am I supposed to know that?"

He dropped a kiss on her forehead. "In your case? I'll tell you."

She grinned. "Since I have no earthly idea what I'm doing, that'll work."

They grinned at each other. Lacey's brows rose as she felt the boat shift beneath her feet. "I think we're shoving off."

Devon looked over his shoulder, saw the Star Line employees untying the lines, pushing the boat off the dock. The rumble of the hydro-jet engine nearly drowned out the screeching of the gulls. "Looks like," he agreed.

Lacey turned in his arms so she faced the water again, placing her hands over his where they rested on her abdomen. The boat began to pick up speed, kicking up spray as they began to plow through the waves.

Lacey laughed, sheer joy in the eruption of sound. She felt so alive, so ready for whatever was waiting for them on the island, she couldn't seem to help it.

She heard Devon chuckle in her ear. "You really are jazzed."

"I know!" She laughed again, loving the way it felt, and lifted her arms to the sky. "I just feel like I could do anything. I've got all of this energy with nowhere to go."

Devon's arms tightened around her. "Energy, huh?" She felt the warm wash of his breath on her neck and shivered.

155

"How long is this ferry ride?" he murmured, his voice low in her ear.

Lacey grinned. "Not long enough," she said, nudging his pelvis with her backside. His cock had gone from semihard to fully erect in the space of seconds—she'd swear she could feel his pulse through his jeans.

He shook her gently. "How long?"

She raised her arms to encircle his neck from behind. "Fifteen to twenty minutes at the most." He groaned, his head dropping to her shoulder. "See?" she said. "Not enough time."

"Lady," he said, spinning her around and pinning her to the rail. "You obviously don't know who you're dealing with."

Lacey stifled a giggle at that and raised one eyebrow. "What was your name again?"

"Ha." He took her mouth in a hard kiss, a tangle of tongues and teeth that made her feel like she'd lost her sea legs all of a sudden.

"I think I remember you now," she panted when he lifted his head.

He grinned at her. "Fifteen minutes is plenty of time for what I have in mind."

She rolled her eyes. "Maybe for you, quick draw, but you couldn't even get me halfway to the promised land in fifteen minutes."

He drew back, one eyebrow disappearing into his hairline. "That," he said in slow, measured tones, "sounds like a challenge."

She shrugged, secretly thrilled but trying desperately not to show it. "I'm just saying."

Now both eyes went narrow and his face settled into stern lines. He let go of her to cross his arms over his chest. "Wanna make it a bet?"

It was Lacey's turn to regard him with narrowed eyes. "What is this, some lame attempt to win back your C-note from the other night?"

He shook his head. "No, I wasn't thinking of betting money. I was thinking more along the lines of a service agreement."

She crossed her arms, mimicking his pose. "Service agreement?" she asked delicately.

"Yep."

"Explain."

He smiled, a feral, predatory smirk that told her he knew he had her. "Simple. Loser has to spend one night doing whatever the winner wants."

The idea of that had her panties going damp. Well, damper. She swallowed hard. "And what's the bet?" she asked, relieved to find her voice sounding somewhat normal, if a little strained.

His flashing grin told her he hadn't missed a trick. "I bet that I can get you to come before this ferry docks. I get to do anything that won't get us arrested and all you have to do is hold out."

She nodded slowly, giving her tongue time to unstick from the roof of her mouth. "And what does 'anything' entail?"

He spread his hands. "Whatever the winner wants, of course."

She frowned. "Sounds a little too dangerous," she said, envisioning herself naked in the hotel dining room, giving him a lap dance. "No bet."

She could tell she'd surprised him, but he recovered quickly. "Too rich for your blood?"

Lacey smiled thinly. "I'd be a fool to agree to something as broad as 'anything'. And so would you."

He nodded. "Fair enough. How about we amend 'anything' to exclude public, painful or humiliating acts."

"And the loser gets to determine if something falls into one of those categories."

"As long as the loser is honest about it and not just trying to welsh."

She thought about it for a second. "Okay. You got yourself a bet." She held out a hand and he shook it to seal the deal.

"So," she said, leaning back against the rail with a smirk. "Seduce me."

Chapter Sixteen

It was all Lacey could do to keep the grin on her face and her body relaxed. God, he was so potent, just being in the same space with him made her want to jump his bones. She had no idea how she was going to hold out for the next fifteen minutes, since just *talking* about him making her come had her primed and ready to go. She mentally cursed her gambler's heart. It had never gotten her into trouble with money — she was too smart and too careful for that, and besides, gambling wasn't about the money for her. It was about the thrill, the challenge of beating the odds. And from the gleam in his eye, it looked like she was about to get the thrill of her life.

Devon stepped forward, crowding her against the rail. His head ducked down, his lips hovering over hers, just a breath away. She started to close the distance between them, was in fact already rising to her tiptoes to take his mouth when she remembered she was supposed to be resisting. She rocked back to her heels and tried to control the blush.

She heard him chuckle and knew she'd been unsuccessful. He ducked his head down to look into her face and the mirthful triumph in his eyes made her want to poke them out.

"Easy there, trigger," he chuckled. "Don't make it too easy for me."

She tossed her hair back. "Reflex. I briefly forgot myself. Don't count on it happening again."

He winked and had her gritting her teeth against a snarl. "I won't. Now, let's get you situated." He grabbed her by the waist and spun her around so she was once again facing the churning water. He pushed her forward slightly, taking her

159

hands and placing them on the rail in front of her. He put his foot between hers, his knee between her slightly splayed legs.

"There, that's nice." He gave her ass a stinging pat. "Comfy?"

She shot him a fuming look over her shoulder. "And not remotely turned on," she assured him.

He gave a short bark of laughter. "Bullshit." He leaned over to growl in her ear. "I can practically smell the cream pouring out of you. You're so hot for me you can barely stand it. But you're going to have to stand it a little bit longer."

He straightened and moved behind her, so that if she wanted to keep him in her line of sight she had to crane her neck all the way around or move from her position. Since she'd agreed he could do anything he wanted to accomplish his goal, she had to stay where he'd put her or void the bet.

She opted to turn her head back to the front, unwilling to get a crick in her neck just to keep tabs on him. She'd find out what he had planned soon enough, and she didn't think he'd give it away unless he wanted to. Even if he did, it probably wouldn't do her much good.

She tried to distract herself by needling him. "And why will I have to stand it a little longer? Can't get it up, huh?"

He chuckled, unfazed at the poke at his male ego. "Trust me, sweetheart, that's not an issue."

She felt him stroke his fingers over her hair, trail them down the length of her spine in a lingering caress, and couldn't quite suppress a shudder. She felt more than heard his quiet, triumphant laugh, and his fingers danced over the curves of her ass, down the backs of her thighs. He kept his touch light, stroking and gliding them over her thighs, her abdomen, the sensitive undersides of her breasts. Her jeans and cotton T-shirt weren't effective as a barrier, instead, the clothing seemed to conduct the heat of his touch, leaving tingling trails of sensation wherever they went.

"Did I tell you I love your skin?" he whispered in her ear, and she jolted. She was concentrating so hard on keeping her breathing even and her reactions suppressed, she hadn't noticed that he'd all but draped himself over her back.

"I do," he continued, his voice like dark velvet. His breath washed over her neck as his hands stroked up her arms, over her shoulders. "It's like warm silk, soft and supple and sweet-smelling." He tucked his nose to her neck and inhaled, drawing her in and emitting a groan that made her pussy clench.

"And you've got all this wonderful muscle underneath," he continued, his hands sliding down her sides and over her flanks. He squeezed her thighs with gentle hands. "Feel the muscles there, how solid and strong they are. Strength is so sexy."

Lacey let her eyes drift shut, losing herself for a moment in the pleasure of his touch. Her skin tingled, and she could already feel a flush spreading over her body. She could feel herself getting wet—she was probably soaking through her panties at this rate. She barely swallowed a whimper and took a grip on her sanity.

Devon flicked out his tongue, barely scraping over the sensitive shell of her ear as his hands slid up the front of her thighs. "But you know what my favorite part of your body is?"

He seemed to be waiting for an answer so she managed a gargle he apparently took for, "No, what is your favorite part of my body?"

"It's right here," he murmured, his teeth scraping across her earlobe as he settled both hands across her lower abdomen. Her T-shirt had ridden up slightly with her bent-over position, and the feel of his rough, callused hands on her skin was almost more than she could bear.

"My belly?" she managed, her body all but vibrating under his hands. Jesus, he'd hardly even touched her and she felt like her head might blow off.

"Mmmm," he said, and stroked one hand across her abdomen, hip to hip, in a lingering caress that had her biting her tongue to hold back the moan.

"The skin here is so soft," he said, dipping one finger briefly in the hollow of her belly button as he continued to stroke. "And there's this gentle curve, this subtle and sweet curve to you here. It's so female and so sexy, I could spend hours nibbling right along this line." He traced the waistband of her low-rise jeans with his finger. "And I want to lick right here." He swirled his pinky finger around her belly button.

Lacey took a deep breath and tried to hold on to her senses. Her entire body felt as though it were lit up from the inside. The constant stroking and caressing, the sound of his voice so close to her ear and the penetrating heat of his body along her back were all combining to push her closer to the edge of orgasm.

She couldn't believe it. He hadn't touched her breasts, hadn't gone near her pussy, which was now pulsing insistently, begging for attention. He hadn't touched her with a heavy hand, something she usually needed during sex. Instead, he'd kept his touch light and slow, and the unexpectedness of it was driving her crazy.

"Your time's almost up," she managed. She could see the island in the distance and they were beginning to see more sailboats as they drew closer.

"Well, then I guess I'd better get busy," he murmured, and using the hand he still had braced on her belly, drew her up against him as he straightened.

She let go of the rail, letting her hands fall limply to her sides as he held her plastered to his body, her back to his front. His thighs felt rock-hard against hers, the tension there belying the easy way he held her. And that wasn't the only thing that was hard.

She almost lost her balance when he turned her in his arms again—she had to grip the corded muscles in his forearms to keep from toppling over. When she looked up into his face, she nearly lost it then and there.

His eyes were lit, blazing with lust, the pupils narrowed to tiny points. His cheekbones were flushed, his lips parted slightly with his breathing. He was looking at her like he was a big, bad wolf and she was Little Red Riding Hood, and he could gobble her up in one quick bite. Of course, it'd be better if he took his time, used a lot of little bites, devouring her bit by bit until she couldn't take it anymore...

Her thoughts splintered when he suddenly slid hard hands under her ass. Her eyes flew to his face as he lifted her, digging her fingers into his arms to keep her balance.

"Since I only have a few more minutes," he growled, "I'd better make the most of it."

"What—?"

That was all she managed to get out of her mouth before his slammed down, and then she couldn't think at all.

In contrast to all the gentle, gliding touches, the kiss was a marauder's kiss. He dove straight in, sliding his tongue across her teeth and into her mouth. He took her mouth like he couldn't take her body right then—with focus and passion and single-minded intent.

She whimpered, her arms reaching up to curl around his neck as she tried to climb him. Her tongue curled against his, instinctively suckling, and she felt his fingers dig into the tender flesh of her ass in response.

She tried to boost herself up, to twine her legs around his waist and get some friction for her aching clit, but he held her ruthlessly down. She cried out into his mouth, fighting his hold, not understanding why he wouldn't give her what she needed.

He tore his mouth from hers, panting for breath, before latching his mouth on the tender flesh under her jaw. He laved her with his tongue, licking his way to her ear, and said, "Too many boats. They'd know."

ry

Lacey blinked, not understanding, and let out a mewling whimper. "Devon," she groaned, clutching at him with desperate hands.

"Do you want to come, baby? Is that what you need?" He bit down on her earlobe with tender ferocity, and she keened at the sharp sensation.

"Yes," she said, half mad with the need for relief, still trying to lever herself high enough to get the friction she needed.

Devon growled in her ear. "How bad, baby? How badly do you need it?"

"Oh, God," she half wailed, unable to make her brain work enough to understand what he was saying. All she heard was the tone, the heat and the want and the strength of it.

"Tell me," he said, and slid one hard thigh between hers. She clamped her legs closed, keeping him there, and began to rock against his leg.

He urged her on, using the hard grip of his hands on her ass to guide her movements, to force her to move faster and harder, grinding her clit against the seam of her own jeans as he held her tight to him.

"Oh, God, oh shit, oh, God," she panted, her head going back as the waves of her orgasm came rushing in. "Oh yes!" she wailed, and then she couldn't say anything, didn't have the breath for it. The spasms hit hard and fast, throwing her cunt into convulsions that jerked her body against his and had her hands clenching and unclenching in his shirt.

He was unrelenting, keeping one hand on her ass, driving her harder still against him when she couldn't maintain the cadence. He tangled the fingers of his other hand in her hair, turning her face toward his and taking her mouth, smothering her gasping cries.

When she finally quieted, her hips still and her body slumped in his arms, he smoothed her hair back from her face. "Doing okay?" he murmured.

"Oh yeah," she breathed. She picked up her head and looked at him, bemused. "You did it."

She sounded incredulous and he chuckled. "What, you didn't think I could?"

"No, not really."

"Well, now you know not to challenge me in certain areas." He put a note of pompous pride into his voice. "Remember that tonight when you're playing my slave."

She rolled her eyes and managed a weak chuckle. "I don't remember anything about slave."

"Semantics," he said, and eased them both to sit on the bench. "Service agreement, slave contract. You say potato..."

Lacey narrowed her eyes. "Excluding painful, humiliating or public acts."

"I know," he said, a smirk on his face. "Trust me, I already know what you'll be doing. In the privacy of our suite, and it won't hurt a bit. Well, it might sting the pride a bit, but I think you'll get over it."

She worked up a scowl. "You're such a gracious winner."

"I know."

He said it with such blatant satisfaction in his tone, she couldn't help but laugh. She snuggled into his shoulder, her eyes closed.

"You're not going to sleep, are you?" he asked.

She shook her head, rubbing against him like a cat. "No, I'm just—" she broke off with a huge yawn.

"Hey." He poked her in the shoulder.

"What? I'm not sleeping." She muttered, opening one eye to stare at him balefully.

"Good, because we're docking." He nodded over her shoulder and she looked to see Mackinac Island off the port bow.

"That means I have to move, huh?"

"Yep."

She sighed. "Okay, but you're going to have to help me up."

He laughed. "Come on," he said, and hauled her to her feet.

It took them twice as long as Devon had expected to get to their hotel, mainly because Lacey couldn't seem to stop ogling everything like a tourist. She thought the bicycle rental shop was "too cute for words", she petted every horse they passed and bought an obscene amount of fudge from no less than four different fudge shops.

"Jesus, the fudge weighs more than your luggage," he complained.

"Why do you think I packed so light?" she asked around a mouthful of chocolate mint. "I'm taking a shitload of this stuff home with me."

He rolled his eyes. "Can we get to the hotel now?" he asked. "You remember why we're here, right? National security, secret mission? Any of this ringing a bell?"

Lacey was watching a family of four dive into their purchase of a fudge sample pack. The two little boys, barely toddlers, were giggling and shrieking with delight as they fed their faces, getting fudge everywhere.

She giggled, turned to look at him. "What'd you say?"

He glowered at her, exasperated, and she rolled her eyes. "Okay, okay. We'll go to the hotel. God, you're so crabby."

"Gee, I wonder why," he grumbled, lugging her bags as well as his as they began walking.

"You're such a baby," she admonished. "It's your own fault, you know. You're the one who made the bet, and you won. You should be happy."

"You know, I'd smack you around a little for that, except there's no blood left in my head and I'm afraid it'd make me dizzy."

Lacey laughed. "I'll make it up to you," she promised, and blew him a kiss.

"Damn straight you will." He pointed to a horse-drawn carriage parked along the side of the street. "There's our buggy. I asked them to wait."

She grinned at the old-fashioned, horse-drawn carriage. "Awesome. By the way, where are we staying?"

"Grand Hotel," he said, hefting the bags into the carriage. He realized she'd stopped walking when he turned around to help her into the buggy and she wasn't there.

"What're you doing?" he asked, walking back to where she stood stock-still in the middle of the road. "Are you okay?"

"The Grand Hotel?" she asked, sounding hoarse. "Did you say we're staying at the Grand Hotel?"

"Yeah." He was confused. "Why are you just standing there?"

"We're really staying at the Grand Hotel?"

"Yes." He was hanging onto his patience by the thinnest of threads. "If that's not okay, we can try to find another hotel. But I gotta tell you, we're in high tourist season here and we might not have a lot of luck with that. But if you want, I can make a phone call and—"

"Are you *crazy*?" she practically hollered, and launched herself into his arms. "Oh, my God, we're staying in the *Grand Hotel!*"

He winced as her screech made his ears ring. "I take it that's a good thing?" he asked.

"Honey, you have no idea," she said, grinning from ear to ear. "Come on, let's go!"

He shook his head as she dashed ahead of him to the waiting buggy and clambered in. He followed, nudging their waiting luggage aside to make room for his feet.

The driver clucked to the horse and they were on their way. Lacey was so excited she could barely contain it, all but bouncing on the seat. Devon shook his head. "What's the big woo about this Grand Hotel?"

"It's fabulous, that's what! The pool is named after Esther Williams, the front porch is the longest in the world and no two rooms are alike. Oh, and they make this desert that they only serve here, called a Grand Pecan Ball." She rolled her eyes and made yummy noises. "Out of this world, or so I hear. I can't wait to taste one."

She looked over at him in time to see him roll his eyes at her. "If you don't know anything about this hotel, why'd you pick it?"

He shrugged. "It's famous, unique and exclusive. It's the one Devereaux is most likely to be at. He likes his luxuries."

"Oh." Hearing that they'd probably be sharing their hotel space with a former arms dealer turned counterfeiter dampened Lacey's enthusiasm just a bit.

"Why is the pool named after Esther Williams?" he asked.

Lacey put aside visions of running into Deveraux in the dining room. "Because one of her movies was filmed there, using the pool. I forget which one."

"*This Time for Keeps.*"

"Huh?"

"It was called *This Time for Keeps,*" Devon said. "She plays Nora Cambaretti, an acquacade showgirl who falls in love with Dick Johnson—"

"*Dick Johnson?*" Lacey said, incredulous.

"—who just got out of the army and decides he wants a career in popular music. There's this really spectacular water ballet at the end."

He turned to find Lacey staring at him open-mouthed. "What?"

She started laughing. "How do you know all of that?"

He shrugged. "I like musicals. Hey," he protested as she began laughing harder. "It's a *good* movie!"

"I'm sure it is," she said, trying to choke back her laughter. "What other musicals do you like?"

"I'm not telling. You'll just laugh at me."

Lacey had to hide a grin at the grumpy tone of voice and schooled her face into sincere lines. "No I won't. I think it's great that you like musicals. I like them too."

He eyed her with suspicion. "What's your favorite?"

Lacey racked her brain to think of a musical. After a tense few seconds, she came up with, "*Guys and Dolls.*"

He relaxed, nodding. "Yeah, that's a good one. Although I think the stage version is better overall than the film, you just can't beat Brando and Sinatra."

"Right, absolutely." She nodded soberly.

He turned on the seat to face her. "What other musicals do you like?"

"Ah..." Lacey thought frantically. "Well, I liked the *Wizard of Oz*. And um...*Seven Brides for Seven Brothers.*"

He nodded. "Classics. Did you ever see *South Pacific*?"

"Is that the one with the song that goes, "I'm gonna wash that man right outta my hair"?" He nodded. "That's one of my mom's favorites."

"It's probably my favorite," he said. "Well, that and *A Chorus Line.*"

Lacey was saved from making any comment — which was good, because she had no earthly idea what to say — by their arrival at the hotel.

The carriage crested the hill the hotel sat on and they were treated to the breathtaking view of the hotel's front porch. Lined with thousands of geraniums that stood out in glowing red against the stark white of the building, it was a sight to behold.

"Wow," she said, her voice quiet with reverence.

"Yeah, some digs, huh?"

She dug an elbow into his ribs. "Hush. I'm having a moment."

He winced, rubbing his side. "Sharp elbows," he muttered.

She shot him a quelling look as the carriage came to a stop in front of a uniformed bellhop at the center of the porch. He came forward with a smile and offered her a hand.

"Oh." She realized after a minute that he was waiting to help her down and placed her hand in his gloved one. "Thank you," she said. She smiled then frowned slightly as he blushed and stammered out a "you're welcome" and hurried back to his bellhop stand.

Devon stepped out of the carriage behind her with the luggage and spoke in her ear. "Don't smile at the poor man like that."

"Like what?" she whispered.

"Like he's the answer to all your girlish dreams of Prince Charming."

"Well, he did help me out of a horse-drawn carriage, which is more than I can say for you," she sniffed.

He frowned. "I was in the carriage with you. How am I supposed to help you down if I'm still in it?"

"You should've gotten out first," she said, and started up the steps. "A gentleman would've."

Devon sent the bellhop a scowl that had him scrambling back and rethinking his offer to help with the bags, and followed Lacey up the steps of the portico. Checking in and getting to the room took nearly as long as getting to the hotel since Lacey couldn't seem to keep herself from oohing and ahhing all over everything.

By the time he finally got them up the stairs and to the suite, he thought she'd give herself a stroke from all the excitement. He stood outside the door and counted backward from one hundred, trying to tune out the conversation she was having with the bellhop.

"So, the porch is 666 feet long?"

"Yes, ma'am," the bellhop said as he fought with the old-fashioned key and lock. "And there are over twenty-five hundred geraniums planted in the flower boxes."

"Really?"

He nodded. "And a hundred rocking chairs."

"That's fascinating," she said, and opened her mouth to ask what Devon was sure was her eight-hundredth question about the hotel when the bellhop finally got the door open and she was rendered momentarily speechless by the suite.

So was he, but for entirely different reasons.

"Oh, it's the Wicker Suite!" Lacey squealed, and did a little dance around the room.

Devon dropped his head against the doorframe in despair. "The Wicker Suite."

The room was lovely, he'd give it that. Bright and airy with a big window. And all the furniture was white wicker. Wicker rocking chair, wicker bench under the picture window. He wasn't going to be able to sit down the whole time they were here.

The bellhop was extolling the virtues of the suite. "The bedroom's just through here," he said, opening a door to more white wicker. "The bath is just on the other side."

"Oh, it's just great, Bernard," Lacey gushed. She glanced over at Devon who was standing with his forehead still pressed to the doorframe, his eyes closed. "Um…I think we're okay now. You can put the bags down there." She pointed to the wicker settee.

Bernard did as bid but held up a hand when she dug in her purse for a tip. "Not necessary, ma'am. Hotel policy."

"Oh. Well, thanks very much, Bernard. You've been very helpful."

"It's been my pleasure." He tipped his hat, aimed a wary glance at Devon and scooted out the door.

Lacey rolled her eyes. "Oh, for the love of Pete," she said. She tugged him into the room and shut the door. "Do you have to be so dramatic?"

"Dramatic?" He stared at her, incredulous, still holding onto his small bag. "The whole suite is furnished with wicker!"

"Yeah, so? I think it's charming."

"I suppose I'd think it was charming too, if there wasn't a good chance I'd break it."

She scoffed at that. "Oh, please. It's not that delicate—it's made for people to sit on."

"Uh-huh. Just the same, I'm hoping the bed isn't made of wicker or I'm sleeping on the floor."

She thought he was being ridiculous but went to check anyway. "You're in the clear," she said from the bedroom doorway. "It's a queen-sized brass."

He breathed an exaggerated sigh of relief. "Thank God."

Lacey turned, braced in the doorway, and plastered a "hey there, big boy" look on her face. "Wanna try it out?" she asked coyly, batting her lashes.

She saw interest light his eyes and thought for a brief moment he was going to take her up on it. Then he shook his head and hefted his duffle bag. "As much as I'd like to, I think it's probably time to get to work."

Chapter Seventeen

ร∂

Lacey watched as he set his duffle on a wicker side table and unzipped it. He began taking things out—a thick file folder, a palm-sized flashlight that he flicked on and off a few times as if testing the batteries. A wand-like device that Lacey recognized as a handheld metal detector, a small silver box with an antenna and a series of lights on it and a box of rubber gloves.

She blinked at the gloves. "Kinky," she said mildly, and he looked up with a grin.

"Sorry, doll, just part of the spy gear. But we can improvise, if you like."

Her lips twitched, amused at the leering waggle of his brows. "I think we're doing just fine with the scripted program. No improvising necessary."

"Well, it was worth a shot."

Lacey folded her arms and leaned against the doorway. "Just out of curiosity, what can you do with a rubber glove that you can't do without one?"

Devon sent her a look that had her stifling an involuntary shiver. "Oh, darlin'," he drawled, voice gone low and thick with heated promise. "You have no idea the things I could show you."

If there was a woman alive who was immune to the potent sexuality in that look, she'd eat her hat. If she were wearing one, that is. "Uh…that's okay," she assured him, and tried to tamp down her raging libido.

He winked and went back to emptying his bag. Laptop computer, a small black case approximately the size of a pack of cigarettes, a mess of wires and cords, and a pistol.

Lacey didn't know much about guns. Okay, she didn't know anything about guns, beyond what she saw on television and the movies, and the bb gun her brothers had used to shoot at various inanimate objects, until Mama had caught them shooting holes in her best sheets as they hung on the line. So the sight of that gun took her aback a little.

"Have you had that with you the whole time?"

He looked to where she was pointing. "The gun? Sure."

"Did you think that might be important for me to know?"

He frowned, confused at the tension in her voice. "No. Why would it be?"

"Oh, I don't know," she said, sarcasm dripping from every word. "Maybe because I'm part of this whole secret mission thing and if guns are going to be a part of it maybe I should know about that?"

He stopped digging around in his bag and crossed the room to stand in front of her. "I'm sorry, I just assumed you knew I'd be carrying." He ran his hands down her arms to grip her fingers in his. "Didn't you wonder why I wouldn't let the bellhop carry my bag?"

"Yeah, I just figured it was more of your control freak thing."

He chuckled. "I guess it was, although it's more accurate to say that I didn't want it in someone else's hands." He squeezed her fingers gently. "Do guns make you nervous?"

She shrugged, feeling suddenly foolish. "Not exactly. But I don't know how to use one, I've never even held one. So they make me nervous that way."

"I'm sorry, I didn't think of it," he said. "I can teach you how to use it, if you want."

She grimaced, shooting the weapon in question a look. Even just lying on the stark white wicker of the end table—or maybe because of it—it looked ominous and threatening.

"No thanks," she said. "I'm not really crazy about the idea of having the power to take a human life."

Devon sighed and she looked up to find him watching her with a kind of quiet resolve that didn't bode well for her desire to remain fire arm ignorant. "You're going to show me anyway, aren't you?"

"We're in a weird situation here, honey," he said, drawing her toward the side table. "I'm not anticipating any major problems and I'm certainly going to go out of my way to make sure we don't run into Deveraux directly, but there's always the possibility that we could end up in a jam. And I'd really like to know that if you have to, you can pick up a gun."

"You're not going to make me shoot it, are you?" she asked.

Devon was stroking his hand up and down her arm in a soothing, reassuring motion. "No, because I doubt we could do that anywhere on this island and still keep this whole 'couple on vacation' vibe going. But you are going to hold it."

Lacey watched while he picked up the gun, hands tucked behind her back so she wouldn't accidentally get in his way. He held it out for her to see. "This is a nine millimeter," he said. "It holds fifteen bullets. Fourteen in the clip, which is here," he tapped the butt of the gun then did something that made it slide out into his waiting hand. He held it out to her and she dutifully peered in.

He seemed to be waiting for some kind of reaction, so she said, "They're stacked in there very neatly."

He stared at her, and she said, "What?"

"Never mind," he said, and turned his attention back to the gun. He laid the clip on the table. "The fifteenth bullet is held in the chamber," he explained, then pulled back on the top of the gun. There was a scraping sound and a bullet popped out. It landed on the table next to the clip.

"Is it supposed to just," she gestured with her hands, "pop out like that?"

"Yes."

"Oh. Okay." She rubbed her hands on the seat of her jeans nervously. "Now what?"

"Stop doing that," he said. "You're reminding me of that Gordon guy."

"Oh, jeez," she muttered, and shoved her hands in her front pockets.

"No, don't put them in your pockets," he said. "You're going to hold the gun now."

She winced before she could help it. "Why do I have to do this again?" she asked, not taking her eyes off the weapon.

"So you'll be able to use it if you ever have to."

"Right." She took a deep breath. "Okay, what do I do?"

"First, never point a gun at something or someone you don't intend to shoot." He held it out to her, pointed at the floor. "Whether it's loaded or not. In fact, always assume that it is loaded and always assume the safety is off."

She nodded. "That makes sense. How do I hold it?"

"Just like this." He reached for one of her hands then paused. "Are you right- or left-handed?"

"Right."

"Okay, give me your right hand." He put the gun in her hand, fitting her palm to the butt and wrapping her fingers around it. He nudged her index finger over the trigger guard.

"Now, when you're holding it like this, pointed at the floor, you want to keep your finger off the trigger." He demonstrated, positioning her finger. "Don't put your finger on the trigger unless you're preparing to shoot."

"Okay."

"Now, the safety is here." He moved her thumb over the little switch. "Right now it's on, and you just need to push it over to take it off." He had her do it two or three times.

"How does it feel?"

"Weird," she said. "Foreign and heavy. Not just heavy because of the weight of it, but heavy because of the *weight* of it, you know?" She turned her head and found him watching her. "You know?"

"I do," he said quietly. "It's a powerful thing, knowing you have the power to take someone's life."

Lacey swallowed hard. "Yeah."

"Okay," he said. "Is it feeling more comfortable?"

"Not really," she said, "but then, I don't really think it's ever going to."

"You'd be surprised," he muttered.

Lacey was beginning to feel silly, standing there pointing a gun at the floor. "Okay, are you going to show me how to shoot the thing?"

He laughed. "Can't wait to put it down, can you?"

"It's creepy," she said. "I'd like it safely back in the hands of someone who knows what the hell they're doing."

"Okay, we'll get on with it then." He moved so he was standing behind her, her back braced against his chest. "I really wish I could get you out on the range with this, because a nine mil has a bit of a kick, and you're not used to guns. But this'll have to do."

"Since we're not going for marksmanship here, we're going to skip all the fancy stuff about sighting down the barrel and aiming for the head."

"You don't think I could hit someone in the head if I aimed for it?" she asked, mildly insulted.

"That's not what I said," he began.

"Because I could," she muttered. "I could so shoot someone in the head if I wanted to."

"I never said you couldn't," he soothed. "But since we're don't have a lot of time, we'll stick with the beginner lesson — shooting to stop."

"Shooting to stop?"

"Right," he said. "Chances are, if you have to shoot, all you'll need to do is stop your assailant, not necessarily kill him. So aiming for a headshot isn't important and since you obviously don't like guns, it's probably best not to try."

Lacey grumbled but conceded the point. "So, where should I aim?"

"The broadest part of the body — the torso."

"Torso. Got it." Lacey chewed her lower lip then peeked at him over her shoulder. "How?"

"Here, let's do it this way." Devon turned them so they faced the mirror hanging on the wall beside the bathroom door.

Lacey started to giggle as she saw their reflections in the glass. Her, small and blonde and looking uncomfortable as hell. Him, tall and darker blond and looking serious as hell. She caught the rise of his eyebrow and schooled her features into more serious lines. "Sorry."

He sighed. "Just concentrate for me, okay? Now, since you're a shorter than average person —"

"I'm *delicate*," she argued.

"And short, and because of that you're probably going to have aim a little high in order to hit what you need to. So you'll want to bring your arms up," he slid his hands under her elbows, raising them to shoulder level, "to at least here, depending on how tall the target is."

"Okay. Should I lock my elbows?"

He shook his head. "Keep them slightly loose, it'll help absorb the impact of the shot."

"Check."

"You can use your left hand to support your right, if it feels uncomfortable or the gun is feeling heavy." He waited while she did as instructed, then said, "You'll point the gun at the target, pull the hammer back with your thumb—"

"What's the hammer?"

"This," he said, and put her thumb over the hammer and pulled it back with her. "If you're in a hurry, you don't have to. It's a double-action, semi-automatic weapon, so if you just pull a little harder on the trigger, the hammer will pop back on its own."

Lacey nodded. "Okay."

"So once you've got the hammer back, and you're pointing the gun at what you're supposed to be shooting, move your finger over the trigger and squeeze."

When she did nothing, he prompted again, "Squeeze."

She started, her eyes meeting his in the mirror. "Oh, sorry." She screwed her eyes shut and squeezed her finger on the trigger, flinching at the loud click in the quiet room.

She felt more than heard his heavy sigh. "Lacey, you need to keep your eyes open when you shoot."

"Right." She opened her eyes, took a deep breath and squeezed again.

"Again."

Click.

"Again."

Click.

"Again."

"How many times are you going to make me do this?" *Click.*

"Just a couple more. I want it to feel comfortable. Again."

"I told you, I'm never going to be comfortable with this." *Click.*

"Well, then I want it to feel not new. One more time."

Click.

"Okay. How'd it feel?"

"Awful," she said, and tried to hand it back to him.

"Hold on," he said. "I want you to learn how to load it."

"Why?" she said. "You said they're already loaded, why do I have to load an already loaded gun?"

"Relax," he soothed. "I just want you to know how to put the clip in and take it out, just in case."

He made her do it several times before he was satisfied. "Okay, that's good enough." He reached out, gently eased the gun out of her grip, muzzle down. "You doing okay?"

"Yeah." She swallowed and raked her hands through her hair. "It just feels so weird. I hope I never have to use it."

Devon flicked the safety back on and put the gun on the table next to his gear. He turned to face her. "Me too, baby." He brushed a kiss on her mouth. "But you are sexy as hell holding that thing."

Startled into laughter, Lacey buried her nose in his chest as he wrapped tight arms around her. "You're such a pervert."

"Bet your ass," he said, and smacked one broad palm down on her butt.

It made her laugh even harder. She picked up her head and grinned. "Does this mean work time is over?"

"Unfortunately, no. I need to go over my equipment, make a few phone calls."

She sighed. "Bummer. Do you need me for any of that?"

Devon shook his head. "I want to go over a few things with you later but, no."

"Well then," she said, "I think I want to go exploring."

He frowned. "I don't want you wandering around by yourself."

She blinked. "Why?"

"Because…"

"Because…why? I won't leave the hotel, I'll only go as far as the front porch. And I'll only be gone an hour." She glanced at her watch. "Then we can go have lunch and work on projecting our 'happy couple' vibe."

"Ah, but how would it look for one half of the happy couple to go wandering off before they've been on their romantic getaway for a full hour? People might talk."

"Well, I'll just explain to them that my honey pie had to tie up a few loose ends at work before we could start our love fest." She batted her lashes at him.

He grimaced. "Could you not call me honey pie?"

She laughed and patted his chest. "How about cuddle bear? That masculine enough for you?"

"No, not really." He watched her pick up a room key and head for the door. "Seriously, don't leave the hotel. I know we're just here to observe, but I don't like the idea of you floating around the island on your own."

Lacey stopped at the door and smiled at him. "Not to worry, love wolf. I'm just going to sit on the porch."

She blew him a kiss and stepped into the hall, choking back laughter when she heard him repeat, in a slightly baffled tone, "Love wolf?"

* * * * *

After a brief wander through the hotel, Lacey found herself a vacant rocking chair on the porch and settled in to enjoy the view. The weather was perfect—warm, with just a hint of cool breeze coming off the water, and none of the humidity that was one of the hallmarks of Chicago in the summer.

She rocked gently for a while, watching the boats bob in the harbor, breathing in the scent of the geraniums that lined the porch. Head laid back against the rocker, she closed her eyes and breathed deep, letting her mind wander aimlessly.

Inevitably, it wandered back to the guy currently cataloging his spy toys in the suite upstairs. She shifted in the chair, a resigned sigh escaping her lips as she felt her body start to respond to just the thought of him. God, she was getting so easy, she thought, feeling the familiar tightening in her pelvis. It was all she could do to walk out of the room and let him work. She'd been gone five minutes and was already wondering how much time she had to give him before she could go back up and jump his bones.

She checked her watch. "Probably needs more time," she muttered, and tried desperately to think of something besides Devon and sweaty monkey sex.

"Talking to yourself?"

Lacey looked around at the amused question and grinned at the willowy brunette who'd settled herself in the rocking chair to Lacey's left.

"It's when I start answering myself that I start to worry," she said. "Sorry, I didn't realize anyone was there."

The brunette waved a hand. "It's fine," she said, her voice faintly accented. "I was just enjoying the view."

Lacey turned to look out over the water again. "It's a stunner," she agreed.

"So what were you talking to yourself about, if you don't mind my asking?"

Lacey gave a little laugh and settled back in the rocker. "Oh, I was just wondering how much time I have to give my boyfriend to settle a little business before I go up and jump his bones."

The brunette laughed. "You're here with your boyfriend?"

Lacey nodded. She decided it couldn't hurt to talk about it, as long as she stuck to the cover story they'd agreed on. "We haven't been dating that long, only a few weeks. It's our first weekend away together."

"And he's working?"

Lacey shrugged. "He had a couple of things he didn't manage to get worked out before we left yesterday so he's making a few calls."

"Well, you're more understanding than I," the woman said, giving her head a little toss and sending a cascade of mink-brown hair over her shoulder. "I believe I'd be ready to chew glass if my man was working on something besides me on a weekend getaway."

Lacey snorted out a laugh. "Oh, I'm sure he'll make up for it. I'm Lacey, by the way."

"Corrine."

"Nice to meet you," Lacey said. "So what brings you to Mackinac?"

"Oh, I just needed to get away," Corrine said. Her pretty face twisted into a frown, her striking blue eyes clouding. "It's been a rough year or two."

"I'm sorry," Lacey said, not wanting to pry. For a second there, Corrine's serene face had looked decidedly hostile and Lacey figured whatever the problem was, it was a big one.

Some of her curiosity must have showed on her face because the other woman went on. "My boss died about a year and a half ago," she explained, her voice tinged with sadness.

Lacey winced. "Oh, I am sorry," she said, and going with her instincts, laid a hand on the other woman's arm. "Were you very close?"

Corrine started slightly at Lacey's touch but then seemed to relax. "Yes, we were. We'd worked together for nearly ten years. I was devastated when he was killed."

Lacey blinked. "He was killed?"

Corrine nodded. "He was a brilliant man, an innovator. One of his rivals in business arranged for his death."

"Wow. Did the police catch him?"

Corinne shook her head, sending waves of hair flying. "No, the police were never able to prove what happened wasn't an accident. I believe they didn't want to." Her accent became thicker as she continued to talk. "It was more convenient for them to simply file their reports and move on. They didn't care about Paul."

Lacey frowned. "That's awful."

"Yes, it was." Corrine took a deep breath. "So you see, it has taken me a long time to move past this tragedy."

"With good reason," Lacey said. "Did this happen in Europe?"

At Corrine's curious look, Lacey explained. "You have a slight accent and I don't remember hearing about this," she explained. "I pay fairly close attention to the news, so I assume it happened overseas."

The other woman nodded. "Yes, we were in Europe at the time, working on a new project of Paul's. It would have been revolutionary, had he been allowed to continue his work. But alas, his genius was extinguished by those jealous of his gifts."

Lacey had to struggle to hold back a smile at the drama in the woman's voice. She didn't want to appear insensitive since it was obvious her boss's death had had a very strong effect on her.

"What kind of business was he in?" she asked, curiosity prodding her to ask.

Corrine waved a hand. "Oh, he was interested in all sorts of things. He was a very talented man. He very much enjoyed envisioning something then using his mind to turn it into something real."

Lacey opened her mouth to ask what he was working on when he died when a movement on the porch caught her eye. When she glanced up, she saw the unmistakable outline of Devon standing at the foot of the steps to the main entrance.

"Guess he's done working," she said, and nodded in his direction when Corrine gave her a quizzical look.

Corrine turned to look and one delicate brow arched. "This is your boyfriend?"

"That's him," Lacey said, watching as he walked a few steps in the opposite direction from where they were sitting.

Corrine turned to smile at her. "You must be very understanding, indeed. If I had such a man at my disposal, I would certainly not let him work."

Lacey laughed, the sound carrying and bringing Devon's head around. He spotted her at the end of the porch and began walking in her direction.

Lacey whistled out a breath as she watched him walk, all loose-hipped and purposeful. "I really hope he's done working," she said, and Corrine laughed as she stood.

She held out a hand. "It was very nice to have met you, Lacey. I'll leave you to your romantic weekend." She cast a quick look over her shoulder at Devon then turned back with a wink. "He looks as though he has plans for the rest of your day."

"A girl can hope," Lacey said, shaking her hand. "Nice to meet you too. Maybe we'll see you around a little later."

"I'm certain we'll run into each other again," Corrine said, and with a smile, walked away to the end of the porch.

Devon came to a stop in front of Lacey just as Corrine was walking down the porch steps. "Who's your friend?" he asked.

Lacey glanced over her shoulder to see the brunette disappear down the garden path. "Just another tourist," she said. She smiled up at him from her seat in the rocker. "She thought it was very understanding of me to allow you to work on our first romantic getaway."

Devon frowned. "What'd you tell her?"

She rolled her eyes. "Only that we'd been dating a few weeks and this was our first trip away together, and that you had a few loose ends to tie up before we could really be on vacation."

When he kept frowning, staring at the spot where Corrine had disappeared down the path, she poked him in the stomach. "Hey," she said when he looked down, "don't worry. I stuck to the story."

He rubbed his stomach where she'd poked him. "It's just better to keep it simple."

"I know and I did. Anyway, she's just a tourist, and now if anyone asks around about us, the story's already planted."

He glanced toward the garden path one more time then seemed to shrug it off. He sat down in the empty rocker next to her and took her hand.

"Did you get your phone calls made?" she asked, trying to keep from leaping into his lap as he began playing with her fingers.

He nodded. "Talked to my contact in the Bureau. He's having a hard time coming up with any info on Deveraux's known associates."

"That worries you?"

"Yeah. It's just not like him to not have his crowd of admirers around him. Especially Felicity."

The absent way he was stroking her fingers was driving her crazy. After a quick glance up and down the porch to make sure there weren't any little kids around to traumatize, she levered herself out of her chair. She saw his eyes flare with surprise as she settled herself into his lap, straddling his legs and sliding her knees alongside his hips.

She smiled and took his other hand in hers so that their fingers were linked. "Tell me about Felicity," she said.

He laughed. "I'm supposed to talk business while you're sitting in my lap?"

"You're a professional," she said. "You can do it."

He raised an eyebrow. "Sounds like a challenge, cupcake."

She laughed so hard she nearly unseated herself. "No more challenges! I'm still not recovered from the last one."

"And you still owe me a night of sexual servitude." He waggled his eyebrows at her.

She snorted. "Yeah, yeah, yeah. Are you going to tell me about Felicity or what?"

"Sure." He set the rocker moving in an easy, gentle motion. "Where should I start?"

"At the beginning, doy."

"Doy?" He shook his head. "I swear, sometimes it's like you're thirteen years old."

"Lucky for you I'm not, or you'd be getting arrested right now." She grinned when he flinched at the thought, the rocker stopping its gentle motion.

"Ugh, don't even go there," he said.

"Felicity?" she reminded him, and he began rocking again.

"Felicity Merriweather," he began. "She's English, educated at Oxford and Harvard. Her IQ is somewhere around two hundred. She graduated from Harvard when she was seventeen."

"Wow. How'd she get hooked up with Deveraux?"

Devon leaned back farther in the chair, bracing his feet to stop the rocking and using his grip on her hands to pull her with him. Since it also kept her from bracing herself on her hands, she had no choice but to lean farther into him to keep her balance. She inhaled sharply as the ultrasensitive tips of her breasts came into contact with his chest. She saw him smile slightly, his gaze heavy-lidded and, when he continued, his voice was just the slightest bit rougher.

"Her mother was English, Merriweather is her name. But her father was German. From East Germany, back when there was such a thing, and he was fairly active politically."

"Communist?" Lacey asked, intrigued by the concept. By the time she'd reached high school, communism had been pretty much eradicated from the globe, saving China and North Korea, and she herself could barely remember the details of the Cold War.

He shook his head. "No, he was very much against communism. In fact, he was mostly active in the underground movements that espoused the violent overthrow of the East German government."

Lacey tried, but she couldn't really find fault with that logic. "I guess if I was living behind the Iron Curtain for most of my life, I'd have felt the same."

"No argument there," Devon agreed. "Unfortunately, he found that he really liked the violent part of his work. He figured out that there was a market for his particular brand of skills after the wall came down and started marketing himself rather aggressively."

"I'm guessing he was less than discriminating on the jobs he took," Lacey said.

"He managed to get freelance work with some of the most well-funded and destructive terrorist organizations in the world. Within five years, he was on the most-wanted lists of Great Britain and the US."

She shrugged. "Guess it depends on the kind of attention you're looking for."

He let go of her hands, letting her brace them on his shoulders as he slid his own palms along the outside of her thighs to curl around her hips. "Let's just say that very quickly, he was getting all the attention he could handle."

Lacey wiggled a bit, settling more comfortably on his lap and trying to ignore the gentle flex of his fingers on her hips.

Who knew hips were sensitive and erogenous? To distract herself, she concentrated on the discussion.

"So what happened?"

"Well, after a number of high-profile incidents in Europe, he was killed in a car accident in central London in 1991."

"Really. An accident." She made no attempt to hide her skepticism, and he didn't bother trying to persuade her.

He shrugged. "That's the official story. Struck by a taxi while crossing the street. Unofficially, he was taken out. By whom, I'm not sure and it doesn't really matter. Felicity was fifteen at the time and already away at Harvard, and she didn't take it well."

"I'm sure."

"Well, as soon as she got back from the States, she started making inquiries into his death. She tried to find the taxi driver and, of course, couldn't."

"Of course."

"She tried to get the House of Lords to launch an official inquiry. She tried to get anyone who would listen to launch an official anything. Unfortunately, she had a bit of tunnel vision when it came to dear old dad and she was convinced he'd been some sort of double agent, secretly working for the good guys.

"It took a while but she finally stopped asking for inquires, but she never really let up on her zealous defense of him. Even when her mother—who, by the way, had tried to forbid Carl to contact his daughter—showed her proof of his involvement with terrorism. All that really accomplished was her total estrangement from her mother."

"Daddy's girl to the end," Lacey said.

"The very end," Devon agreed. "While she seemed to come to believe that her father was indeed involved in terrorism, murder for hire, etcetera, she decided if it was good enough for Daddy, it was good enough for her. She put out feelers, trying to find people who knew him and worked with him, and she hooked up with a guy named Claude Batiste."

Lacey frowned. "Okay, he's a new one."

Devon shook his head. "He's one of Devereaux's flunkies. Or was. By all accounts he was killed during that last showdown eighteen months ago. He was the first contact she had with Devereaux's crew—"

"Hang on a sec," Lacey said, holding up a hand. "Why don't you ever use his first name?"

"Whose first name?"

"Devereaux's," Lacey said. "You never say his first name, it's always just Devereaux. His first name is Simon, right?"

Devon frowned, like he couldn't see how it mattered. "Right."

"Okay. Go on," she prodded him when he continued to frown at her.

He shook himself slightly. "Anyway, Batiste was her first contact—" He got only that far before she interrupted again.

"Here we go again with the last names," she said. "They're not hockey players or football players or privates in the Army. So why do you not use their first names?"

He seemed to be talking through his teeth when he answered her. "Because it helps keep people straight. You might have two people named John, so using their last name makes it easier to distinguish which one you're talking about."

"Oh." That made sense. "You don't do that with the women though. I mean, you don't call Felicity by her last name…it's never 'Merriweather'. Why is that? Why are you banging your head against the chair?"

He stopped pounding his head against the wood and looked at her, clearly exasperated. "I don't know why we do it that way, we just do. That's how they train us to do it, so that's how we do it. I've been doing it that way for almost twenty years, so if it's all right with you, I'll keep on doing it that way."

Lacey shrugged. "Fine by me, it was just a question."

"Do you have any more questions or can I continue?"

She sniffed and tried not to get tweaked at his surly tone. He was under stress, she reminded herself. Just let him talk. "Please, go ahead."

"As I was saying, *Claude*—" he looked at her pointedly when he said the name "—was Felicity's first contact with *Simon's* group. Her test, to see if she was really committed, and after she passed it, she met up with the man himself."

"And followed in Daddy's footsteps."

"There were a few steps along the way, but yes."

"She and Simon were lovers?"

Devon's shoulders shifted in a shrug. "We never had any concrete evidence, but we always assumed."

Lacey frowned. "And your friend can't find any trace of her?"

He shook his head. "It's possible that after he was almost nabbed he got rid of the excess baggage, but it's hard for me to swallow. She was essentially his right-hand man, he hardly made a move without her there. But Jack can't get anything solid on her after they scrambled eighteen months ago."

"Is it possible she was killed?" she asked.

"I guess," he conceded. "I know she made it out of the fire fight—she was spotted in Budapest the following week. But that's the last intel we have on her and considering her profession, it's possible she could've been killed in some other way."

"Poor thing," Lacey said quietly, and he swung incredulous eyes to hers.

"Excuse me?"

"Well, I'm not saying she's completely innocent or anything—"

"She isn't innocent at all," he muttered.

"—but it's gotta be tough being daddy's girl when daddy's a killer."

Devon grinned at that, curving his hands firmly on her butt. "Were you a daddy's girl?"

She grinned right back at him. "Oh, absolutely. My mother couldn't do a thing with me, but Dad just had to look at me cross-eyed and I'd fall right in line." She laughed. "I heard her say to him once, in this baffled, annoyed tone of voice, 'she just adores you'. She just couldn't understand why I obeyed him so readily when I stubbornly refused to even listen to her."

"Wish you obeyed me like that," he grumbled good-naturedly.

"Well, you're not my father, are you?" she whispered. She slid her hands from his shoulders to his neck and leaned in for a nibbling kiss. "And thank goodness he's not here because then I probably wouldn't be able to do this." She settled her mouth on his, sliding her tongue along the seam of his lips and dipping briefly between them. She tugged his bottom lip into her mouth, suckling it gently before releasing it with a soft pop.

"Mmmmm," he murmured, gathering her closer, his amber eyes glittering with purpose. "In that case, I'm glad he's not here either." He shifted his grip on her butt, tilting her pelvis and bringing her into full contact with the hard ridge of his cock.

Lacey hissed in a breath at the contact, the desire that had been on slow simmer all morning shooting to fast boil in a single heartbeat. She let her eyes drift shut as he set the chair going again in a gentle rhythm that rocked her needy cunt firmly into him. Every time he rocked back, she slid up his length, her clit hitting the hard curve of him, and every time he rocked forward, she slid back, her clit dragging down the his length.

It was an almost constant friction and within moments, she was whimpering. She clenched her fingers in the collar of his shirt, burying her face in the hollow of his throat to muffle the noise. She opened her mouth on his neck, flicking her tongue out to taste him. Unable to stop herself, she closed her teeth on him in a little love bite, suckling lightly as she stroked him with her tongue and held him with her teeth, and with a strangled groan, he snapped.

Chapter Eighteen

🔊

She squealed, her head popping up out of his throat at he surged to his feet. "What're you doing?" she squeaked, wrapping her legs around his waist and hanging on for dear life as he started walking with long, purposeful strides toward the hotel entrance.

"I'm getting us off this porch before I fuck you on it," he said, his voice so deep and guttural she felt it reverberate through his chest.

"Don't you think you should put me down?" she panted, fighting the urge to groan out loud as every step jostled her aching clit firmly against his hard cock. "I mean this looks odd."

"I don't really care," he said as he reached the steps. He took them two at a time, and she would've sworn her eyes crossed at the delicious, pounding friction.

"You should...at least...carry me...differently..." she gasped, clinging to him with desperate fingers. He was moving so fast—he was like a ride at some X-rated theme park she had to hold tight to in order to stay on. "We could...tell people...that I got sick."

He was striding down the hallway now, going right past the elevator to the stairwell, and she figured he either didn't want to wait for the elevator or he just wanted to keep torturing her with more stairs. He never broke stride, hitting the stairs like a distance runner in training, and she just buried her face in his throat and hung on.

By the time they reached the suite, she was a quivering mass of need. Her clit felt like it was on fire—the constant friction of his cock against it through their clothes making her feel as though her head would explode. It wasn't enough to bring her to orgasm, but it was keeping her hovering on the ragged edge, and if she didn't come soon she was sure she'd lose what was left of her mind.

The solid thump of wood against her back had her opening her eyes to find herself pinned to the door of the Wicker Suite. "Oh, thank God," she cried. "Quick, open the door."

"My hands are full," he muttered, his mouth attacking the soft curve of her neck. She felt the nip of his teeth, the stroke of his tongue, and tried desperately to remain conscious. "Where's your key?"

"It's in my...my front pocket," she gasped, uncurling the fingers of one hand from his shirt collar long enough to try and find it. She managed to wedge her hand between their bodies, fought the constraints of her jeans, and closed her fingers around the old-fashioned key.

She jerked it up with shaking fingers, nearly jabbing him in the eye. "Here. You. I can't," she managed to say between pants.

He took the key, shoving it into the lock on the third try and turning it with such force she worried dimly that he might break it off in the lock. The door banged open, slamming against the opposite wall, and then they were inside and he was kicking the door closed, propelling her through the sitting room to the bed.

She fought with his T-shirt, yanking it out of his pants and shoving it up under his arms. She couldn't get it over his head, not while he still held her clutched to his chest, so she contented herself with trailing kisses over his breastbone and nibbling his nipples with her teeth.

Devon finally reached the bed, tumbling her to her back in the middle of it. The impact jarred her grip free and he took the opportunity to shed himself of his clothes, taking the time to fish a condom out of his pocket before turning his attention to her. He had her out of her shirt and bra in five seconds, her jeans, panties and shoes in ten, then he was flipping her over onto her stomach.

He dragged her hips high, bringing her to her knees. She barely had enough time to shake the hair out of her face and brace herself on her hands before he plunged into her without warning.

She screamed, the sound piercing the quiet air of the suite as he thrust deep into her, hitting bottom and holding himself there. She screamed again, feeling herself pulse around his hard length, her body struggling to adjust to the sudden invasion.

"Are you all right?" he managed between pants, and she turned to look at him over her shoulder. His face was flushed, his eyes glittering wildly as he held himself still, waiting for her response.

"Yes," she moaned. "Now fuck me."

His eyes flared, his lips peeled back in a near snarl as he began pounding into her.

Lacey clung to the bedspread, pressing her forehead into the backs of her hands as he fucked her. In this position, with her hips tilted high and her shoulders on the bed, she could feel every firm, fiery inch of him as he speared into her, hitting her G-spot with every thrust. She could feel the knot of tension coiling tighter and tighter in her belly, pushing her higher, faster and, within seconds, she came screaming.

It seemed to go on and on, his continuing thrusts keeping her spasms going until he let out a hoarse shout of his own. He held himself deep within her, the pulses and shivers of her orgasm milking him dry. They hung there, suspended, for long moments until finally he collapsed over her.

Lacey felt her knees slide out from under her, the sudden lack of support causing him to fall with her, seating his semihard cock even deeper into her. She moaned as the action set off a fresh round of spasms in her pussy.

"Jesus," he panted, his cock twitching inside her. "You're going to kill me."

She laughed weakly. "I think that's my line."

They lay there, both of them panting for breath. He nuzzled her hair away from her neck to place a soft kiss there. "Am I too heavy for you?"

"No," she sighed. "Not yet, anyway."

"Well, before I get to be..." He slid out of her, eliciting shivers at the drag of his cock along her sensitive flesh. She felt him roll to his side, heard him moving around as he dealt with the condom then he was tugging her into his body so they nestled like spoons on top of the coverlet.

Lacey sighed, snuggling deeper into the cocoon of his arms. "This is nice."

"Mmmm."

"Know what would make it even better?"

He pushed her hair aside to kiss her ear. "What, baby?"

"A club sandwich."

A moment of silence followed that declaration then the bed started to shake with his laughter.

"What?" She turned over to look at him as he rolled around chuckling. "I'm hungry!"

"Way to kill the romance!" he said, practically doubled over with laughter now.

"Hey, in a minute, my stomach is going to start growling. How romantic is that?" She poked him in the ribs, which only made him laugh harder.

She grinned. "Oh-ho, what have we here?" She poked him again, delighted when he twitched convulsively. "You're ticklish!"

"That's not—hey!" He grabbed at her hands, cursing when she evaded his grasp, cursing a blue streak when she danced her fingers down his side.

"Really ticklish!" she giggled, and started tickling in earnest.

Devon howled a protest and started defending himself aggressively, cursing whenever she managed to slip past his guard. They grappled, rolling around the mattress, the air ringing with laughter and grunts and panting breaths. He finally managed to pin her to the bed, her hands caught up by her ears, both of them out of breath.

She tugged at her hands. "Let me go."

"You promise not to tickle?"

She swallowed the giggle that threatened to break free and tried to look sincere and somber. "I promise."

He frowned, obviously suspicious, so she blinked innocently. "Okay," he said slowly, still not trusting her, and released her hands.

He was all tense and expectant, obviously just waiting for her to go for that sweet spot between his ribs again. So she tucked her hands behind her head and smiled.

"What're we going to do for lunch?" she asked, barely managing to keep from laughing out loud at the relieved expression on his face.

He dropped a quick kiss on her lips before levering himself up to sit on the side of the bed. He picked up his cell phone from the bedside table and checked the clock display. "Christ, it's two-thirty already."

"No wonder I'm hungry." She rolled to her side, suppressing a yawn. "Listen, since we've got dinner here in the main dining room tonight—"

"We do?"

"Duh! It's in the brochure. Anyway," she continued, "since we're doing dinner here tonight, let's find someplace else for lunch."

"Okay." He twisted, leaning over to nuzzle her neck. "We should probably get a shower first."

"Mmmm," she tilted her neck to give him room to nuzzle. "Before we do, I just want to do one thing."

He raised his head slightly, brow raised. "Really?" he rumbled. He stroked his palm down her body, smiling slightly as she shivered. "What's that?"

She raised her head, bringing her mouth within a hair's breadth of his. "This," she whispered, and, raising her foot, dug her toes into his ribs.

He jerked, cursing even as she shrieked with laughter. "Oh, you're gonna get it now," he warned, and pounced on her.

* * * * *

It took them another hour to make it to lunch as the tickle battle continued in the shower they shared. He'd gotten her to agree to a cease-fire by holding her under the freezing cold spray of the shower until she finally relented.

They found the Bagel and Deli shop, where they made pigs of themselves over sandwiches then found dessert in the form of ice cream cones at Waffle World.

By the time they got back to the hotel, Lacey was yawning almost constantly. Devon laughed at her as he put the key in the lock.

"What's wrong with you?" he asked, grabbing her elbow when she nearly stumbled into the wall.

"I'm just tired," she said around another yawn. "It's not like I've gotten a lot of sleep in the last few days."

He shut the door behind him and steered her into the bedroom. "Why don't you get a nap?" he suggested. "We don't have anywhere we have to be and I could use a couple of hours to go over a few things, see if Jack's gotten anything solid on Felicity by now."

"Are you sure?" she asked, already kicking off her shoes and flopping facedown on the bed.

He chuckled, shaking his head. "Yeah, I'm sure. Here, scoot up." He tugged her toward the top of the mattress. "How's that?"

"Is good," she murmured. "C'n I have a blanket?" she asked drowsily.

"Sure, baby." He unfolded the quilt at the end of the bed and draped it over her. "Comfortable?"

When she didn't answer, he peered down into her face. "Lacey?" A slight snore was his only answer.

He shook his head. "Somehow, even the snoring doesn't turn me off," he told her sleeping form wryly. He shut the bedroom door behind him softly and settled gingerly in one of the wicker chairs in the sitting area.

When it seemed as though it would hold his weight, he grabbed his briefcase and went to work.

He had a detailed dossier on Deveraux, but it was Felicity's he decided to start with. Something about her was bothering him, hovering just on the outer edges of his consciousness, and he hoped that going over the details of her life might jar it loose.

Even though he knew most of it already, he went back to basics and read through the background on her, the information in the file echoing what he'd told Lacey about her earlier in the day. Her father's death, her subsequent search for something to validate his life in the eyes of the world. And when she couldn't find it, her eventual crossover to his way of life.

There were the notes from the psych experts—several of them from a number of agencies that had profiled her over the years. The conclusion most of them arrived at was that she'd compensated for the lack of love and affection from her father by believing he was doing important work, saving the world from monsters. When it came to light that he was one of the monsters, she refused to believe ill of the man, and simply switched allegiances.

Her association with Deveraux just followed the same pattern. A dominant male, in a position of authority, he gave her the attention she'd always craved from her father and never got. Toss in the fact Deveraux was in essentially the same business as her father had been and he'd been all but irresistible to Felicity.

Devon frowned as he flipped through the photos in the file. There were multiple shots of her and Deveraux in a variety of poses and locations. She was a very pretty girl, with a tumble of red hair and blue eyes that he knew could sparkle with warmth or turn frosty and cold. She fooled a lot of people with that cheerful, pretty face—it's what made her such an asset to Deveraux and his crew.

Devon flipped the page, pausing as he came to a black and white photo of Felicity and Simon in Paris. It was a fuzzy shot, grainy and distant, of the two of them at the base of the Eiffel Tower. He'd taken the picture himself, and it was the only time he'd ever seen them act even remotely physically intimate with each other. They weren't touching, but were leaning into each other, looking each other in the eye the way couples do when they know one another.

He'd told Lacey the truth when he said that they'd never had any proof that the pair had been lovers. It was always assumed, as neither one of them ever seemed to become involved in other relationships, but he'd never really felt right with that assumption. They were close, yes, but it had always appeared to him as more of a sibling relationship than a romantic one. He'd offered that opinion more than once and had been brushed aside by both his superiors and fellow operatives. It was unreasonable, naive even, to think that they weren't "bumping uglies" as one rookie spy had once put it.

Most of the other members of the intelligence community thought the same. They lived in the same home in Spain, they worked in each other's pockets. It was a natural assumption that they'd be lovers, but Devon had never been able to fully swallow it. Everyone agreed that Felicity's hero worship of her father had been transferred to Simon Deveraux, and he just couldn't see her being intimate with a father figure. It was possible, he supposed, but he'd spent the last ten years of his career watching them and he just didn't see it.

He picked up the phone, punching in Jack's number. "Jack, it's me," he said when the call went through. "Tell me you found something."

"Dev. Man, I wish I could."

Devon swiped a hand over his eyes and swore. "Still nothing?"

"I've gone over every bit of data on Devereaux since Prague—what there is of it—and aside from that one sighting in Budapest, there's nothing about Felicity."

"Dammit, that just doesn't make sense," Devon grumbled.

"That's the least of your worries," Jack said. "What kind of info have they given you on Devereaux?"

"What're you talking about?"

"Just humor me. How much information have you got on his activities over the last year?"

Devon slid the folder out of his bag and flipped it open. "Everything. Wherabouts, activities…"

"Is there a lot of it or is it sketchy?"

"Well, there's not much on associates, which struck me as odd considering he hardly made a move without Felicity. But other than that, it's a full report."

Jack swore. "I was afraid of that."

"What the hell are you talking about?"

"Dev, I dipped into the files on this one—"

"You hacked the Bureau? Jesus, Jack, you better be able to cover your ass."

"My ass is covered, okay? Just listen. When I dug into the file and took a look at the data log, it showed that about ninety percent of the data for the last year was added in the last six weeks. Someone's padding the evidence."

Devon waited a moment then said, "I'm waiting for the punch line."

"It's not a joke. Someone seriously padded that file—sightings, intercepted communications, the whole works. Everything that has to do with this counterfeit enterprise. All added in a two-week span a month and a half ago."

Devon's mind was racing. "What possible reason would someone have to make all of this up?"

"I can only think of one real possibility and it's not a pretty one."

"You think someone did it deliberately to get me on the job."

"You got it."

Suddenly too agitated to sit, Devon got up to pace the length of the room. "Devereaux was always one of my active files, and practically my only job for nearly a year. I spent a full six months doing nothing but putting the sting in Prague together."

"Why didn't they keep you on it after Prague?"

Devon grimaced. "For one, they blamed me for not getting him in that sweep. For another, it wasn't a big secret I was looking to get out altogether. I was bringing a couple of junior agents up to speed, and then I was out. That was always the plan."

"But you were the one with the most experience with him, right?"

"Yeah."

"Then they probably looked at this as a guarantee to pull you back in. And even if it wasn't enough hook to get you back on your own, it was enough for someone else to force you back."

"Dammit!" He cursed, then darted a guilty look at the bedroom door. He lowered his voice. "I need to get a look at the undoctored files."

"Can you get to your computer? I can do an email draft."

He darted a look at the bedroom door again. He didn't want to let Lacey know what was going on, not until he knew himself what was happening. "Yeah, but I don't want to do it from here. There's an Internet café about a ten-minute walk away, I'll pick it up there. Give me the account info."

He dug out a pen and paper while Jack rattled off his AOL screen name and password. "Okay, set now and I'll call you back after I get a look at it."

"Doing it now," Jack assured him. "Watch your back, Dev."

"Count on it."

Devon clicked the phone shut. "Fuck."

For someone to go to all the trouble to fabricate a situation just to pull him into it was not a good thing. It meant that whoever was pulling the strings had money, contact in the intelligence community and a big grudge.

Which was worrisome enough for him but he had Lacey to worry about too. She was a computer geek not an agent, and she was ill-equipped for a situation like this. Hell, the only reason he'd agreed to bring her along on this trip was because it was supposed to be strictly observational. Identify Devereaux, alert the Chicago office, they'd tag Treasury, and they'd swoop in and do their thing.

Now he was looking at a much more serious situation, one that could land them both in a lot of hot water. He cursed softly, hating the feeling of helplessness flooding through him. He needed to get to the cyber café and take a look at Jack's email to see exactly how elaborate a setup he was dealing with. Then he could worry about how to best get Lacey off the island and out of harm's way while he dealt with what was.

He dug in his bag for the nine millimeter, loading it and tucking it into his jeans at the small of his back. He slid his phone in his front pocket and walked to the bedroom door. Easing it open, he saw that Lacey had rolled to her back. One hand lay low across her stomach, the other palm up by her face, the fingers gently curled. He felt a little clutch in his chest at the sight and suddenly he was furious with whoever had set him up. He was used to taking risks with his life—it was his job, and part of the territory that he'd always accepted as the price of doing business. But she was innocent, just a web designer with a talent for hacking, and she didn't have the background or the training to deal with something as serious as what he was afraid they were up against.

He checked his watch. He hated to wake her, but he didn't want her to wake up alone either, wondering where he was. He was saved from making a decision when she started to stir.

She yawned, stretching her arms toward the headboard, causing the blanket to slide down her body and her T-shirt to ride up, exposing a narrow band of silky belly. Her eyes fluttered open, blinking as they focused on him.

"Devon?" she murmured. "What're you doing?"

"Just watching you wake up," he said easily, keeping his voice even with effort. He was furious, but she wouldn't know that it wasn't with her and he didn't want to alarm her. "I didn't want to leave without waking you."

"Where're you going?" she asked around a yawn.

"Want to pay that cyber café a visit," he said, having decided to keep things as close to the truth as possible. She was a sharp cookie when she was awake, and he didn't want

205

to give her anything to worry about until it was necessary. "Jack had some information to send me and I don't want to use the laptop here."

She frowned, sitting up and rubbing the sleep out of her eyes. "It's just as dangerous to access it at the cyber café. Email is email, after all. If they can track it here, they can track it to the café."

He shrugged. "He's not actually sending an email. He'll write it, save a draft of the email, but never actually send it. Then I access the account and read the draft. Nothing actually gets sent, so nothing gets traced. And he set up this account just for this, so no one knows about it but the two of us."

"Okay." She smiled at him, sleepily sexy. "Give me a kiss before you go."

He grinned, bending down to cover her mouth with his. She gave a little hmmm of delight as he stroked his tongue into her mouth. She tasted warm and spicy, and he knew if he didn't get out of there right away, he wasn't going to.

"I have to go," he murmured, feathering kisses along her jawline.

Lacey sighed. "Okay. Bring me back some more fudge, will you? I'm getting low."

"You have three pounds," he corrected.

"I know," she said. "But that's really just an emergency stash. I don't want to touch it if I don't have to."

He laughed despite his worry. "Okay, I'll get you more fudge. Any particular flavor?"

"Try to find some maple with no nuts." She frowned. "Why do they screw it up by putting nuts in it, anyway?"

He shook his head, marveling at the way her mind worked. "I've no idea. What're you going to do while I'm gone?"

"I think I'll take a bath," she said. "There's some lavender bath salts so I may just dig out a fashion magazine and have a good soak."

"Really?" He grinned. "Don't use all the hot water—I'll join you when I get back."

"Yeah?" She grinned. "It doesn't threaten your masculinity to smell like lavender and sit in a bubble bath?"

"Of course not," he said. "Lavender oil has been used for centuries to relieve sore muscles, headaches, tension."

She blinked. "It has?"

"Yep." Devon tapped the end of her nose and grinned. "It's a strong herb. Very butch."

She laughed and pushed at him. "Get out of here, go do your spy thing."

"Okay, okay, I'm going." He pushed off the bed and headed for the door. "Maple with no nuts, right?"

"Right. Oh, and maybe some vanilla!"

He waved over his shoulder at her and disappeared out the door.

Lacey flopped back on the bed and tried to breathe evenly. It didn't do much to control the butterflies in her stomach. She was getting very attached to her secret agent man. She didn't like the idea that they'd be going their separate ways once they got back to Chicago. Just thinking about it gave her a little twinge of dread in her belly.

She winced. That was not a good sign, getting droopy over the thought of breaking things off with a guy she'd only technically known for less than three days and wasn't even technically dating. Sleeping with someone did not a relationship make—all she had to do to remind herself of that was think back on her entire junior and senior years of college.

Still, it didn't feel like fuck buddies. It felt like, well, like a relationship. She frowned a bit at that as she rose from the bed. She headed into the bathroom and put the stopper in the old-fashioned claw-footed tub. Grabbing the bath salts with bubbles she dumped in a generous handful and turned on the taps, adjusting the water to just this side of scalding. As she watched the tub slowly fill with bubbles, she forced herself to be honest with herself about her feelings for Devon.

She felt her chest go tight as she realized the simple truth was that she wanted to be with him. She liked who he was—his humor, his sense of reluctant responsibility to the government that had already taken more than its fair share of his life. God knows she liked his looks and she absolutely adored his sex drive.

"Well, that makes me sound shallow," she muttered. Then she shrugged—it was the truth. She liked that he was intune with his sensuality, that he wasn't afraid to be bawdy or silly or goofy or—God help her if he ever overheard her saying this—dominant. She wasn't a girl with a lot of tie-me-up-big-daddy fantasies, but when he looked at her with that light in his eyes—the one that made her feel like if she wasn't naked and on her back in five seconds, he'd put her there himself—the feminist in her all but disappeared and the sex kitten sat up and begged.

She shivered at the thought and turned off the water. She was just standing to peel out of her clothes when she heard her cell phone trill from the other room. Thinking Devon had forgotten something, she trotted out to answer it.

"What'd you forget?" she asked when she answered.

"Lacey?" The voice on the line was faint but unmistakable. She frowned.

"Gordon?"

"Yeah, it's me. It's me, Gordon."

"Gordon, what're you doing calling me?" Lacey wasn't too well-versed in this spy business, but she was pretty sure phone calls from the FBI while technically on an undercover mission were not standard procedure.

"Listen, I gotta talk to you, okay? I gotta talk to you." He sounded even more agitated than usual, which was like saying the Dallas Cowboy cheerleaders were perkier than usual.

"Why?" A sudden thought occurred to her. "Has something happened?"

"Yeah, something happened, that's it. Can you meet me right away?"

"Meet you? You mean you're *here*?" Now she was getting alarmed. Why would Gordon be here unless something was very, very wrong?

"Yeah, I'm here, I just got here, I came on the ferry. I didn't like the ferry, made me feel sick. Did you get sick on the ferry? Boy, I did. All that rocking, and bouncing—"

"Gordon!" Lacey fairly screamed his name. "What're you doing here on the island? What's wrong?"

"Uh, no, not on the phone. It's just—it's bad, okay? It's bad. So can you meet me?"

She was already pushing her feet into her sandals. "Where are you?"

"Um... Hold on." She could almost hear his head whipping around as he looked for something to tell him where he was. "It's a fudge shop."

Lacey swore as she fumbled for a pen on the writing desk. "Which one, Gordon? There are dozens of them on the island."

"Really? Why do you think they eat so much fudge up here? Maybe because in the winter it gets so cold—"

"Gordon!"

"Sorry. It's right by where I got off of the ferry. There's a blue awning with red stripes, but I can't see the name."

"Don't worry about it, I'll find you." She looked around for something to write on and settled on the back of a Fort Mackinac brochure. "I'll be there in ten minutes."

"Okay, but hurry, okay? You should really hurry."

"Right." She clicked the phone shut and scribbled a quick note to Devon, cursing him for not having given her his cell number. She had no idea how long it would take him to check the email account his friend had created but she didn't want to wait for him to get back to see what had Gordon in such a twist. The man wasn't a field agent—if something were important enough to get him out of his office and up here on a Sunday, then she didn't want to wait. The Internet café was about a block from the fudge shop Gordon was waiting at so, with luck, she'd be able to find him quickly if she needed to.

She was tucking the extra room key in her pocket and turning toward the door when she spotted Devon's bag on the table. She hesitated for a moment, gnawing on her lower lip, then peeked inside.

The gun that he'd had her practice with was gone—she assumed he had it with him. There were a few other guns there. He'd told her while they were at lunch that they pretty much all followed the same procedure—loaded the same, fired the same. He told her he'd had her practice on the heaviest one so she'd be able to handle the weight of it even though, if they had to get into anything iffy, he'd likely give her one of the smaller ones.

She eyed the selection. He'd said something about a nickel-plated one that he wanted her to try handling later, so she picked up the only shiny silver one in the bunch, grimacing as she held it in her hand. She remembered what he said about all the guns being loaded then decided she'd better check. She only fumbled once getting the clip out, saw it was indeed filled with little bullets that scared the bejeezus out of her just to look at them, and popped it back in. She checked the safety like Devon had showed her for good measure, and took a deep breath.

She wasn't sure why she was taking the gun, but the little hairs were standing up on the back of her neck in a way she'd learned not to ignore. Granted, the last time she'd felt them all on end like this was right before she caught Matt Fisher under the bleachers with Melanie Redding the day before he was supposed to take her to the prom, so it had been a while. But her mama hadn't raised any fools, and only a fool would ignore the little hairs on the back of one's neck.

She slid the gun carefully into the front pocket of her jeans—thank God, she'd screwed up and brought the comfy, baggy ones instead of the tight, sexy ones—and headed out the door, praying she was overreacting.

Chapter Nineteen

ॐ

Devon walked down the hall toward their suite trying to get a handle on his temper. He didn't want to let Lacey in on how dire the situation was until he had some answers, so he was reining it in until then. But when he found out who was responsible for this debacle, he was going to make certain of two things—that they never worked for the FBI or any other federal, state or local law enforcement office ever again, and that they would need crutches for at least a month.

He'd stumbled into a huge mess. *Correction*, he thought savagely, *I've been* led *into a huge mess.* The file the Chicago field office had, and even the file that the director had been given, had been heavily doctored, and it looked like about ninety-five percent of the information in it was pure bullshit. Jack had pulled everything he could find out of the data logs, and all of the information detailing Devereaux's supposed counterfeit activities, his supposed buyers for the fake plates and even his relocation to Canada was bunk.

The only data that Jack had been able to verify as having been entered legitimately were a few sketchy sightings in Europe that dated back just over a year, and the information on those was scarce. Felicity's appearance in Budapest after the botched operation in Prague was there, and he knew that was legitimate because he'd still been working the case. Aside from that, the entire file, all the intelligence and data gathered on Devereaux seemed to be nothing but smoke and mirrors.

Devon bit back a curse as he came to a stop in front of the suite door. He had to get it together before going in or Lacey was going to know something was wrong right away. She wasn't a stupid woman or a very patient one, and he knew she wouldn't let it drop until he told her what was going on.

He took a deep breath, but it didn't do much to calm his rage, or his worry. There was only one reason he or Jack could come up with for someone having gone to that much trouble to doctor the files. Whoever was behind this was gunning for him specifically, and the thought of it had little fingers of cold dread dancing up his spine.

Not for himself. He was pissed enough about the deception—and the knowledge that someone inside either the FBI or the Treasury department was responsible for it—that had he been on his own he would go after the bastards, guns blazing. The only thing that kept him from doing that very thing was the woman who was most likely lounging in a bubble bath just a few rooms away.

Lacey had nothing to do with whatever grudge someone had against him—it had to be a doozy for them to go to this much trouble to set a trap—and the idea that she'd been put in unnecessary danger had him seething with anger. He had to figure out a way to get her off the island, and fast. He frowned as he slid his key into the lock, trying to come up with a reason for her to leave without him. It had to be a good one, she wasn't going to buy some lame excuse like he didn't need her anymore. He could try it, but he imagined she'd punch him in the nose and tell him to go to hell, and they'd be right back where they started.

He turned the knob, unable to put off going in any longer. It was already late in the afternoon, so if he was going to get her off on the last ferry, he was going to have to figure something out, and fast. If he had to, he'd use his Bureau ID to enlist the help of local law enforcement. He mentally winced at the idea of having to force her off the island, or the slightly less scary notion of having to place her in protective custody. She would not be happy. In fact, she'd likely raise holy hell and try to tear his head off, but she'd at least be safe. He'd worry about how to get back on her good side later, when the danger was past.

He pushed aside thoughts of all the groveling he'd have to do—he had no doubt that it would be considerable—and walked in the door. The sitting room was empty, but the air felt slightly damp and he could smell lavender, so he set his key on the side table and called out. "Lacey, I'm back. You still in the tub?"

He didn't get an answer, but he heard the gentle lap of water coming from the direction of the bedroom, so he assumed she was still in the bath. He slid the gun out of the waistband of his jeans, laying it on the table alongside his duffle bag. He was turning away to join her in the bathroom when something about the duffle caught his eye. He looked at it, frowning. It was in disarray, the contents all jumbled together, and the hairs on the back of his neck stood up.

"Lacey," he called again, an urgent thread in his voice this time. He was reaching for his gun when the voice behind him stopped him cold.

"Oh, I believe she had to run out."

Devon felt the bottom drop out of his stomach. He knew that voice, had heard its coolly British tone on numerous surveillance tapes, and the fact that she was standing in his hotel room with Lacey nowhere to be seen was not a good thing.

He turned, his face carefully blank. "Hello, Felicity."

* * * * *

By the time Lacey got to the fudge shop, she'd managed to work herself into a lathering panic. All sorts of scenarios were flying through her mind, none of them pretty and the gun felt like it weighted a hundred pounds sitting in her pocket.

She found the store with the blue and red striped awning and ducked inside, dodging a couple of giggling teens with belly button rings and hair extensions, and headed for the counter. She spotted Gordon immediately. He was wearing what she was sure he thought of as normal summer vacation clothes—Bermuda shorts, athletic socks with sandals, and a Jimmy Buffet *Margaritaville* T-shirt. He had a handful of fudge and was sampling with gusto.

"Gordon."

He turned to her, his round little face lighting up with a smile that showed fudge-stained teeth. "Lacey! Have you had the fudge here? It's great, it's better than my mother's homemade. But I wouldn't tell her that, would never tell her that, because she'd just—"

"Gordon!"

He blinked at her. "What?"

She glared at him. "You called me down here, you tell me 'what'."

"Oh, right!" He hurriedly wiped his fingers clean, pushing the rest of his fudge in its paper bag. "Yeah, I'm supposed to get you, cause there's a problem. A problem with the—" he paused, looked around, and lowered his voice to a whisper that everybody could hear just fine "—the *mission*."

Lacey tamped down her impatience with an effort, grabbing him by the elbow and dragging him out of the shop. "What's going on, Gordon? Is Devereaux on to us?"

He nodded, his round head bobbing so fast she got a little dizzy watching it. "Yeah, he's onto you, onto you and the other guy, so we gotta leave. We gotta leave now."

"Okay, I'll go get Devon and we'll go." She swung around in the direction of the cyber café and had taken two steps when a hand clamped on her wrist.

"No, we gotta go now, Lacey." Gordon's face was red, his eyes frantic. He began pulling her with surprising strength toward the marina. "That Devon guy, he's already onboard, so we gotta go."

Lacey had to jog to keep up with Gordon, his grip on her wrist tight enough to make her wince. He led her past the wooden docks lined with boat slips, sailboats and sport boats bobbing on the water. "Onboard where?"

"There," he said, and pointed to a boat at the end of the last dock where the pump-out station was located. A sailboat was tied up there, a beautiful sloop with a teak deck.

"Devon's already here?" she asked. "You must've caught him right after he left the hotel."

"Yeah, right after, right outside the hotel. The um...the other agent saw him there, and brought him here."

She frowned. "Then why the hell didn't he just go back inside and get me?"

Gordon drew to a stop beside the boat. "Because he was almost spotted. He was almost spotted by the bad guy, that Deveraux. We had to get him out of there."

Lacey frowned. "Where was Devereaux? Why didn't they just nab him right there?"

"I don't know, they just told me to call you. We gotta go, Lacey, we really gotta go." He pointed at the boat. "We really gotta go."

"Okay, okay," she muttered. She stepped onto the boat, climbing nimbly over the lifeline that encircled the deck and stepped down on to one of the bench seats that lined the cockpit. The hatch was open so she stepped into the cockpit and peered into the companionway, but the interior was too dark for her to see much. "Devon," she called, loudly enough for him to hear her but not so loud that the sound would carry very far. No answer.

She looked over her shoulder at Gordon who was hanging onto the lifeline so hard she thought he might rip it off. She waited until he managed to get into the cockpit. "Where's Devon?"

"He's down there, he's already onboard."

"Then why isn't he answering when I call?" she asked, suddenly very nervous. The little hairs on the back of her neck were standing up again.

"He probably can't hear you, it's a big boat."

Lacey turned to face Gordon, keeping her feet firm on the deck and her knees soft to absorb the sway and bob of the boat. "It's a fifty- or sixty-footer, Gordon. Big, but not big enough for him to not hear me. What's going on?"

"I'm sorry, Lacey, I'm really sorry, but there's a problem, a big one, and I don't know what to do." He looked stricken, his hangdog face tense, and Lacey felt herself starting to panic big-time.

"Gordon, if you don't tell me what the hell is going on, I'm getting off this boat and I'm finding a cop." She waited five tense seconds then turned, intending climb out of the boat.

She got one foot up on the bench when she heard something rustle behind her. She turned her head slightly, saw the sun flash against something metal then pain flashed in her skull. She staggered, trying to shake the stars from her vision, then pain came again and everything went dark.

Chapter Twenty

❧

Devon walked down the dock, mentally castigating himself for getting caught unawares. Felicity walked at his side, staying slightly behind him, her hands comfortably tucked into her pockets, and he knew she had one hand on the gun tucked into the pocket of her loose chinos.

He could take her down, it wouldn't be hard. He outweighed her by at least a hundred pounds and could have the upper hand physically in a matter of seconds. But she had Lacey.

When he'd seen her in the hotel room, leaning casually against the doorjamb, a pistol held easily in her hand, his blood had run cold. He recognized her now as the woman Lacey had been speaking to on the porch that morning. She'd changed her hair, dulling the red fire of it with a nondescript brown, and the once razor-straight style had been softened into waves. But her face was the same, and there was no way she could disguise the evil in those icy blue eyes.

"What brings you here, Felicity?" he asked, crossing his arms casually across his chest. *"Got a hankering for some fudge?"*

She shrugged delicately, a faint smile that didn't reach her eyes curving her lips. "It seemed as good a place as any."

He kept his voice even. "For what?"

"For revenge, of course," she said, her voice chilling a few degrees.

"Revenge for what, Felicity? I've done nothing to you."

"Oh, but there is where you are wrong, Mr. Bannion. Or may I call you Devon?"

He smiled without humor. "Only my friends call me Devon."

She shrugged. "We'll stick with Mr. Bannion, in that case. And you have done something to me. In fact, you have done many things to me, but we will concentrate on the big issue."

"And what would that big issue be?"

Her eyes narrowed just a bit. "Simon," she said, biting the word off. "He is the big issue."

Devon raised an eyebrow in casual inquiry. "And where is Simon? I would have thought he would be here with you."

"I am certain he would be," she'd practically snarled at him, "if you had not killed him. Ah," she said, watching the surprise he couldn't conceal on his face, "I see you were unaware that your little trap in Prague was successful."

"We found no evidence that he'd been killed."

"Because he did not die in Prague. I was able to get him out, to Budapest, before your men could close in. But his injuries were grave."

"Bummer."

Devon kept his features passive as she snarled at him. "You should not be so glib, Mr. Bannion. We were unable to get him to a doctor. Since you and your agency were still hunting us, we couldn't risk it. So he suffered, for more than a week, before he finally succumbed to his injuries."

"This is all very interesting," he said. "But what does any of it have to do with me?"

"Do you think I don't know that it was you hunting Simon? It's because of you that he suffered the way did, and so now you will suffer as he did."

"How do you think you're going to manage that?" Devon asked. He kept his voice easy, slightly bored. "I have the height, weight and weapons advantage," he said, gesturing to the duffle bag behind him, "so I'm curious as to how you think you're going to make me suffer."

She smiled, eyes like ice chips, and he felt a cold knot of dread form in his gut. "Yes, you do have all of those things. But I have Lacey."

Devon kept his face passive, his voice unaffected. "I have no proof of that. And even if you did, what makes you think that would matter to me in the slightest?"

"I will soon have your proof for you, please don't worry about that. And it will matter, because I know you."

"Is that right?"

"Yes, that's right. You see, all the time you spent studying us, we were also studying you. You've an unfortunate personality trait which, I'm afraid to say, is going to be your downfall. You're a hero."

"Excuse me?" Devon managed to inject a note of subtle amusement into his tone, but it was an effort.

"A hero. You have that unfortunate affliction so very common among law enforcement. You won't be able to live with yourself if Lacey goes to her death because of you. You'd do anything in your power to stop that happening, especially since you've personal feelings for her."

Devon remained silent, all his attention focused on maintaining his façade of calm uncaring.

Felicity laughed softly. "No fervent denials? Yes, you have feelings for her and so I'm confident you won't be uncooperative."

"I still don't have any proof that you have her," he said, and as soon as the words left his mouth, his phone rang.

She looked at him, a cruel imitation of a smile twisting her lips. "Perhaps you should answer that."

He dug the ringing phone out of his pocket, keeping his eyes on her face. "Hello."

"Devon? Devon, what's going on?" Lacey's voice was faint and pain-filled, and his heart clutched at the sound.

"Lacey, are you all right?" he asked, unable and unwilling now to keep the tension out of his voice.

"Head hurts," she moaned. "You were supposed to be here…where are you?" she asked, then he heard a rustling noise just before a man's voice came on the line.

"Do what Felicity says," he said, the voice sounding vaguely familiar, "or she suffers."

The line went dead. Devon flipped the phone closed and put it back in his pocket. "Where are we going?" he asked.

She smiled that terrible smile again. "For a little boat ride."

Devon cursed again as he thought over the conversation. There wasn't anything he could've done differently, but he was kicking himself for not listening to his own instincts. Something had felt off from the start, but he'd let himself get distracted. He should've known better, should have remembered that even the most innocuous seeming assignment could turn to shit.

He came to a halt at the feel of a restraining hand on his elbow. They were at the pump out, a fifty-foot sloop bobbing gently on the water in front of them. Felicity prodded him none too gently in the back. "Climb aboard," she said, and he did so, making his way down the dim companionway with Felicity right behind him.

He found himself in a small galley, a berth directly to his right and a salon with bench seating straight ahead. He knew the closed door on the other side of the salon likely led to the forward cabin and the one facing it in the short hallway was probably the head. He didn't see Lacey anywhere.

He turned. "Where is she?"

"In the forward cabin." She prodded him in the back again. "Get going, hero."

He bit back a snarl and did as he was told, angling his shoulders to fit in the narrow passageway. He opened the cabin door and felt his stomach drop. Lacey lay on the bed that filled the small space, her hands and feet bound, a gag in her mouth. Her eyes were closed and she wasn't moving, her skin pale and waxy. Devon felt a surge of rage that he didn't bother to control.

"What the hell did you do to her?" he snarled. He leaned one knee on the bed, reaching out to touch her face. Her skin was warm to the touch, her breathing soft and even, and he couldn't prevent a sigh of relief.

"Oh, isn't that touching." Felicity smiled when he turned to glare at her.

"What did you do to her?" he repeated, holding on to his temper by a thread.

"It's just a little bump on the head, Mr. Bannion, nothing to worry about." She raised an eyebrow. "My associate was very cautious with her, I assure you."

"Your associate."

"Yes, I believe you know him?" She raised her voice slightly and called out. "Darling, where are you?"

The door to the small bathroom banged open, revealing Lacey's handler at the Chicago field office. "Gordon," he growled, the rage threatening to choke him.

"Hi, Mr. Bannion, hi. She's okay, I promise. I wouldn't hurt her, I really wouldn't. She woke up though, and she was really mad. Boy, I didn't know a girl could curse like that, I really didn't, and I was afraid she was going to try to get loose, she was struggling so hard, so I had to hit her again. But she's okay, she really is."

He stopped talking, panting slightly from his speech, and some of what Devon was feeling must have shown on his face because the little man's eyes widened and he took a convulsive step back. He slammed into the wall, stumbled over the raised threshold of the bathroom and crashed to the floor.

Felicity never took her eyes off Devon while she whipped the gun out of her pocket. Pointing it straight at his chest, she said over her shoulder, "Darling, are you all right?"

"Yeah, I'm fine, yeah."

"Good. Why don't you go untie us from the dock so we can get moving?"

"Okay, sure, okay." Gordon stumbled his way out of the bathroom, and with a last look at Devon over his shoulder, headed up the companionway.

"What the hell," Devon said, his voice tight with control, "makes you think I'm going to let you do this?"

She tilted her head to the side as if considering his words. "I don't really see as you have a whole lot of choice," she said, and pulled the hammer back on the gun.

Behind him on the bed, Lacey stirred, shifting and moaning slightly. He whipped his head around at the sound and almost immediately felt a sting on his hip.

"Dammit," he swore, spinning back around, but Felicity had already moved back out of reach, the syringe in her hand held aloft like a trophy.

She smiled. "Like I said, Mr. Bannion. I don't really see as you have a lot of choice."

Devon snarled and tried to take a step toward her, but suddenly the room tilted dangerously and he staggered. He shook his head violently and tried again, but this time he fell back onto the bed while the room spun sickeningly around him.

"What'd you give me?" he managed, blinking fiercely to try and clear his vision. He tried to raise his arms to push himself up, but his limbs felt suddenly like lead and they dropped limply back to his sides.

Felicity's face suddenly loomed in his vision, her features blurring as the drug wound its way through his system. "Just a little something to make certain you don't give me any more trouble," she said, her voice sounding tiny and faint over the ringing in his ears.

"If you...hurt her...kill you," he managed, fighting unconsciousness.

Dimly, he heard her chuckle. "I'm afraid, Mr. Bannion, that you're in no position to negotiate."

And the last thing he saw before the lights went out was the door closing behind her.

* * * * *

Lacey woke up to find herself lying on her side facing the hull. She came awake suddenly and completely, as if jerked alert by invisible puppet strings. She immediately knew two things—first, her head hurt like a son of a bitch, and second, the boat was no longer docked. The boat was tilting at an angle, or keeling, and she could tell by the slap of the waves against the hull that they were plowing through the water at a fairly steady pace.

She reached up to touch the sore spot at the back of her skull where that fucking little toad Gordon had sucker punched her with something—probably a winch handle—and noticed dumbly that her hands were tied together. Badly. There was enough rope wound around her wrists to make a hammock, and the knot was roughly the size of her fist. She twisted her head around, wincing at the jarring pain of the motion, and saw a similar wad of rope wound around her ankles.

She turned her attention back to her hands. "Thank God, Gordon was never a sailor. Or a Boy Scout," she muttered, and went to work on the bulky but inefficient knot with her teeth. It took her under five minutes to work the knots loose and shed the ropes and she immediately sat up, intending to work on the ropes at her feet. She dropped right back down again, curling into a fetal position as the dull throb in her skull escalated into a screaming roar.

"Fuck," she said, gritting her teeth against the pain. She rolled to her back before trying to sit up again, hoping that the lack of twist in the motion would help keep her head in one piece. She pushed herself to her elbows, and when her head seemed to stay in place, shifted her hands under her to push herself all the way up. And barely stifled a scream as her hand landed on warm flesh.

Her head whipped around before she could remind herself not to, and the resulting wave of nausea had her gritting her teeth in an effort to keep her lunch down. When she could breathe again without puking, she blinked her vision clear, hoping there wasn't a dead body or something equally disgusting lying next to her.

"Oh, shit," she whispered when she realized it was Devon sprawled out on the mattress. He wasn't tied, but he also wasn't moving. His skin had that waxy, pale look corpses on TV always had, and she was suddenly nauseous for a completely different reason than her concussed skull.

She scrambled awkwardly to her knees, ignoring her bound feet and the pain in her head. "Please, oh please, oh please, oh *please,* don't be dead," she chanted, laying two fingers against his neck. She felt the slow, steady beat of his pulse beneath her fingertips and nearly went boneless with relief, tears stinging her eyes. She blinked them back and tried to focus on his face.

"Devon," she whispered. "Devon, wake up."

He didn't stir, didn't even twitch, and she frowned. Thinking he might have been jumped from behind and hit on the head as well, she leaned over, reaching around behind his head to gingerly check for fresh wounds. There was nothing there, no bump, no blood, nothing to indicate he'd been knocked out. Which meant they'd probably slipped him something.

"What'd they give you, baby?" she murmured. She lifted his eyelid, wincing at the size of his pupil. "Whatever it was, they gave you a bunch of it," she muttered.

She had to start waking him up. She had no idea where they were, no idea who they were up against—except that traitorous little insect Gordon, but somehow she figured he'd be the least of their worries—and she was starting to panic.

225

She had no way of telling how long it had been since Gordon had called her, but she guessed it to be several hours. There was no sunlight coming in the small porthole and even in the close confines of the cabin, the air had a crisp bite that told her it was likely well after dark. Despite the heat of the summer, the nights were considerably cooler in the northern part of Michigan and especially so out on the lake. If they'd been sailing for several hours, they were probably halfway to Canada by now.

Lacey forced back the rising panic and tried to think what to do. The first thing was to get herself completely untied, so with a last, lingering look at Devon's still face, she twisted back around to a sitting position. She leaned forward to reach her feet, and something hard bit into her hip. She leaned back, putting a hand over her pocket, and her fingers encountered the hard outline of the gun she'd stuck in her pocket.

"Well, there's a lucky break," she breathed, even as the feel of the weapon made her want to cringe away. Gordon must not have searched her before dumping her in the cabin, thinking she was an amateur and unlikely to be carrying a weapon. And he would've been right, had she not gotten a sudden attack of the paranoids from his creepy little phone call.

She laid the gun next to her then went to work on the ropes around her ankles. It took her a lot longer this time, because she kept looking back at Devon, hoping he'd magically come around and take charge of the situation. She was not equipped to handle this shit, and she'd have given every Ferragamo pump and Prada slingback in her closet if he would just wake up.

By the time she got the ropes undone, she was nearing full panic stage again, so she hung her head between her updrawn knees for a few seconds. When the room stopped spinning and the nausea faded, she turned her attention back to Devon.

She frowned. Had he moved? She thought he might have shifted position, rolling slightly to his side, but that could be attributed to the motion of the boat. She leaned over, pulling his eyelid up. "Devon, are you awake?" she asked, louder this time, knowing that the sounds of the water would block any sound but a full-out scream from their captors, and he blinked his eyelid out of her grip.

"Why're you poking at my eyes?" he mumbled. He flailed one hand up, most likely to push her away, and smacked himself in the nose.

"D'ju hit me in the nose?"

"No, sweetie, you did that yourself." She grabbed both of his hands, holding them to his chest as she leaned over him. "Baby, can you see me?"

He blinked repeatedly. "Sure, course I can." Her sigh of relief was cut short when he continued. "Can see both of you just fine."

"Damn," she muttered. "Devon, listen. Listen to me." She held up two fingers. "How many fingers am I holding up?"

He squinted. "Four."

Lacey nearly whimpered in despair. "Shit, shit, shit," she chanted quietly.

"Hey." Devon struggled to sit up, looking around blearily. "Where are we? What happened? Where'd Felicity go?"

"Felicity?" Lacey frowned. Maybe they'd hit him over the head *and* drugged him. "What's she got to do with it?"

"She was waiting for me, in the room. Woman you were talking to on the porch."

Lacey had to take a minute to decipher that. "Felicity was the woman I was taking to on the porch? The brunette?" He nodded jerkily. "That lying bitch."

He nodded again. "Yep. 'S a good liar. She didn't lie 'bout you though."

"What do you mean, she didn't lie about me?"

"She said you were here and you are." He struggled to focus on her face. "Why're you here? How come you didn't wait for me to get back?"

"Gordon called after you left," she explained. "He said there was some kind of problem, that our cover had been blown and we needed to get out. He said you were meeting us here." She shrugged. "It wasn't until we got to the boat that I realized he was in on it. And by then he'd already conked me on the head with something."

He was watching her intently, his focus exaggerated as he tried to concentrate. "He hit you?"

"Yes, but I'm fine," she soothed as she saw his expression darken.

He wasn't appeased. "He hit you more than once, didn't he?" he asked. When she didn't answer, he said, "He said that after he called me and let you talk, he had to hit you again to get you to cooperate."

She shrugged again. "I never could keep my mouth shut."

Devon looked grim. "I'll kill him." He tried to stand up and wavered on his feet like a drunk. She rolled her eyes and snagged his arm, hauling him back to sit on the bed.

"You can kill him later. Right now we need a game plan."

"Right." He shook his head as if to clear it. "Do we know where we are?"

He was sounding more lucid, his eyes seemed to focus better on her face, and she felt herself relax, tension she didn't know she was holding onto easing out of her muscles. She shook her head. "No, but we're out on the lake and I'm thinking we're probably heading north."

He looked at her quizzically. "It's just a guess," she said. "If I were kidnapping people and running afoul of the FBI, I'd be taking the fastest route out of the country."

"Good point," he conceded. He rubbed absently at his temples. "Was there anyone else onboard that you saw besides Gordon?"

She shook her head. "Just him. How many people came on with you?"

"It's Felicity's show," he said. "I think it's just her and Gordon, and my guess is she'll get rid of him as soon as she doesn't need him anymore."

"What's the deal, anyway? Did she tell you why she's doing this?"

"She blames me for Devereaux's death."

Lacey blinked. "Huh? I thought he was running a counterfeit ring?"

Devon shook his head, wincing slightly with the motion. "Me too, but apparently that was an elaborate ruse to get me assigned to the case. He died after that last mission eighteen months ago."

"And nobody caught on to this?"

"Nope. Looks like Felicity went to extremes to plant evidence to the contrary. With a little help from your pal Gordon."

"Little bastard," she said, feeling the lumps at the back of her head and wincing.

Devon caught the movement and eased her hand away. "Let me see," he said. He probed the wound with gentle fingers. "Damn, baby," he muttered. "I'm sorry."

The tender concern in his voice was her undoing, and she lost her fragile grip on her control. "Oh shit," she whispered, burying her face in his shirt.

"Hey, what's wrong?" he asked, worry evident in his tone as he gathered her close.

She sniffed into his shirtfront. "Nothing, really. It's stupid. It's just... God, I was so scared when I saw you lying there! I thought you were dead, I really did, and I just didn't know what I was going to do."

He was stroking her hair, her back, whispering soothing sounds, but she couldn't stop talking. It was like the floodgates were opened and she couldn't stop the flow of words. "I don't know what I'm doing with all this espionage crap, I can't do this on my own, and I thought I was going to have to. What with you being dead, and we're in the middle of the damn lake and it's been fifteen years since I've been sailing, and even if I did manage to figure a way out of this mess, I don't even know if I could pilot the damn boat!"

She took a deep breath. "And I was mad, oh, I was so mad, because I don't want you to be dead, because I really think I'd miss you." She picked up her head, looking up at him with imploring eyes. "I know we've known each other for like, thirty-six hours or something ridiculous like that, but I have feelings for you and I don't think they're going to go away, so if you die I'm going to be really pissed off."

He stroked his thumbs over her cheeks, wiping away tears she hadn't even been aware of. "Get it all out?" he murmured.

She drew in a hitching breath. "Yeah, I think so."

"Good. Now listen to me." He waited until she raised her eyes to his. "We are going to find a way out of this. And we are going to be okay. And I'm glad to hear you have feelings for me because, God knows, I don't think I could let you go now."

"Really?" She sniffed. "I wasn't sure if this was, you know, usual mission mode for you."

"Mission mode?"

"Yeah. You know, like maybe you always hook up with your partner on every mission, make mad, passionate love to her then say something corny like, 'It's been real, baby', and ditch her." She felt herself go defensive at his incredulous look.

"Hey, how'm I supposed to know? I've only known you for thirty-six hours!"

"Well, my partner for a lot of these situations was Ian, so I'd hope you know me well enough to know that I wouldn't be doing to him the things I've been doing to you."

"Oh yeah!" she said, smiling. "Somehow, I can't quite picture that."

"God, I hope not," he muttered. "Let's get something straight, okay? I've never 'hooked up' with a partner or a member of my team. This is a first for me and, thank God, this is my last job, because it's shot my concentration all to hell. I should've spotted something wrong about this from the start. Hell, I *did* spot something wrong, but I kept getting distracted by your delectable body and all the things I wanted to do to it."

"You're not blaming me, are you?"

He rolled his eyes. "No. Jesus."

"Okay, just checking." She peered up at him. "So, what happens now?"

"Now we find a way out of this mess," he said. He dropped a hard kiss on her mouth. "We need to figure out where we are."

"Good luck with that," she said dryly. "There aren't exactly any road signs out here."

"My cell phone has a GPS locator in it."

"Oh. Well then, bitchin'." She watched as he pulled his phone out of his pocket and keyed in a sequence of numbers. "By the way, do you realize that this whole thing could probably have been avoided if I'd had your phone number?"

He grinned at her while he waited for his phone to relay their GPS coordinates. "Like I said, I kept getting distracted."

Lacey snorted. "You're very easily distracted."

"When the distractions come packaged like you, damn straight." He grunted in satisfaction at the numbers that appeared on the tiny screen. "You have anything to write with?"

She shook her head. "I didn't exactly grab my purse on the way out the door." She looked around the small cabin. "Maybe there's something here."

They searched for a few minutes, but the built-in cubbyholes and shelves had been picked clean. "They probably didn't want to leave anything we could use as a weapon," he muttered.

"Well, they missed this," she said, holding up a stubby pencil. "It was under the mattress."

"Great." He dug into his pockets and came up with a crumpled receipt. He quickly jotted down the numbers and gave her the paper. "Keep this in your pocket. I spotted a radio on the portside just off the galley. As soon as you can, radio the Coast Guard and give them the coordinates. Tell them the boat was hijacked, that you were kidnapped, whatever you can think of to get them here on the run."

She took the paper and tucked it into her front pocket. "Okay. What're you going to do?"

His face was grim. "I'm going to take care of Felicity and that little shit Gordon."

"Wait." She put up a hand, twisting around to look behind her. She swiped her hand through the tangled bedclothes until she hit metal. "Here." She held up the gun, muzzle down.

"Where did you get that?"

She shrugged. "Gordon spooked me with his little phone call, so I stuffed it in my pocket before I left to meet him. He must not have searched me before he dumped me in here."

He grinned at her and took the gun, tucking it in the waistband of his jeans. "I think I could fall in love with you, Miss Lacey," he drawled.

She narrowed her eyes at him. "What is that, some kind of adrenaline-induced confession? 'Cause I'm telling you right now, if you're going to say something like that, I don't care if a polar bear is sitting on your chest and your life is flashing before your eyes. If you say it, you better damn well mean it."

He grabbed her chin and brought her face close to his. His eyes were flashing gold fire at her. "I mean it," he said, and slanted his mouth over hers.

She moaned into his mouth, opening automatically for the invasion of his tongue. He stroked hard into her mouth, growling low in his throat as she curled her own tongue around his in unmistakable invitation.

He tore his mouth from hers, breathing hard. "Damn, I wish we had time to finish that," he whispered, and swiped his tongue across her swollen bottom lip.

"Me too," she whimpered. She licked her lips, savoring the taste of him that lingered there. "Tell you what. Soon as you get us out of this mess, I'll make good on that night of sexual servitude I owe you."

The heat in his eyes flared higher at that and he took her mouth again in a quick, hard kiss. "Baby, you got a deal."

He scooted off the platform that held the mattress, pulling her by the hand so she stood plastered to his back in the narrow space between the platform and the door. He gave her hand a reassuring squeeze. "You know what to do, right?"

"Find the radio and get the Coast Guard."

"Right. Ready?"

She nodded, trying to project bravery and capability, but she must've let some panic and ineptitude show on her face, because he carried her hand to his lips and kissed the knuckles. "It's okay, baby. I promise."

"I know," she said, smiling brilliantly to cover up the return of her nausea. "I'll be fine. We can go." He opened the door and started to pull her into the narrow passageway when she grabbed his arm. "Wait."

"Honey, we can't just sit here and wait for them to get us wherever we're headed," he protested, giving her hand a little tug. "We have to go."

"I know, I know, but feel," she said, holding up her hand and concentrating. "We're slowing down."

He paused, listening intently. "You're right."

The boat was slowing down considerably, the rushing sound of the hull plowing through the water fading to the gentle slap of waves against fiberglass as they all but came to a stop.

"Did we lose the wind?" he wondered out loud, keeping his voice much lower now that they'd lost the camouflaging noise of the water.

Lacey listened intently. "No, I don't think so," she whispered. "Hear that sound? That's the jib sheet flapping in the wind." She turned to look at him, a grin breaking over her face. "I don't think our hosts are very good sailors."

He started to say something then stopped when he heard raised voices coming from above deck.

"Do you even know what the hell you're doing up there?" Felicity's voice carried plainly from the stern of the boat, her tone strident and angry.

"No!" came the equally frustrated answer, from right above their heads. They both looked up at the forward hatch to see a foot planted in the middle of the Plexiglas cover. "I'm not a sailor-type person, I told you I don't do outdoor activities."

"Well you better damn well figure that thing out, and try to do it without strangling yourself. I don't want to dilly-dally around in the middle of this flaming lake all night."

"I'm doing the best I can, I told you I'm not good at this." There were more rustling noises over their heads then a loud thump. "Ow!"

Devon frowned. "Is he hopping up and down?" he whispered, and Lacey grinned as they listened to the unmistakable thump, thump, thump of Gordon hopping on one foot.

"I think he stubbed his foot on the windlass."

"The what?"

"It pulls the anchor up," she whispered. "Shhh, listen."

"I think my foot is broken, it's broken! I need a doctor!" Gordon's whining shriek of pain made Devon wince. Somehow, he didn't think Felicity was going to be sympathetic.

"You little rodent, I don't care if your foot rots and falls off, we are not taking any detours to any hospitals! I've got to get to Sault Saint Marie by midnight and you're messing with my timetable!"

They listened as Felicity's voice got louder, accompanied by the click of her high-heeled sandals as she moved from the stern to the bow, until she was standing with Gordon right over their heads.

Devon looked at Lacey, his eyes lit with mirth. "If they're both up there," he whispered, pointing up, "then who's driving the boat?"

Chapter Twenty-One

ဢ

Lacey barely suppressed a giggle. "You don't drive a sailboat, you sail it. And my guess is nobody." She cocked her head, listening to the scrabble above. "Gosh, she can really cuss when she's pissed, huh?"

Devon let out a quiet chuckle. "Yeah, she's a pistol all right."

"Did you ever sleep with her?"

His head whipped around so fast he almost lost his balance. "What?" The word came out as a strangled whisper.

She shrugged, eyes wide as she watched him. "I just wondered. She's very pretty."

"She's a rabid alley cat," he countered, still whispering. "I wouldn't fuck her with Ian's dick."

She made a face. "Okay, ew. Never say anything like that to me, ever again."

"Then don't ask me stupid questions!"

She rolled her eyes. "It's not like I'd be jealous if you had, you know. You had a life before I met you."

He had the oddest look on his face, like he was trying to keep himself from strangling her. "Thank you very much, I appreciate that. But I still never slept with her."

"Okay, fine. But just so you know, I'm not the jealous type. Which isn't to say that if I catch you flirting with some other woman I won't rip out your lungs and feed them to you, because I will. But I won't get all twitchy if we run into one of your old girlfriends."

Now he *really* looked like he wanted to strangle her. "Lacey, I get it. You're not jealous. Great, fine. Can we please stop talking about this now?"

"Sure." She remained silent for a moment, listening to the escalating argument above deck. Then she poked him in the back. "What about you?"

"What about me?" he asked, sounding like he was grinding his teeth.

"Are you the jealous type?"

He closed his eyes briefly. "Yes."

Lacey blinked in surprise. "You are?"

"Yes."

"Huh." She chewed her lip for a moment. "Jealous like, you'll kick some guy's ass if he makes a pass at me? Or jealous like if some guy looks at me you'll get all snarly? Or super jealous, like you'll never let me out of the house? 'Cause a little jealousy is okay—I mean, what girl doesn't like to be fought over? Please, it's just too fabulous. But I have to be able to come and go as I please, so if you're talking about that kind of jeal-mmph!"

She blinked wide eyes over the hand muffling her mouth. Devon closed his eyes briefly then opened them. "Yes, I will kick some guy's ass if he makes a pass at you. No, I will not get all snarly if some guy looks at you. And, yes, I will let you out of the house."

He moved his hand long enough to give her a hard kiss then covered her mouth again. "Does that answer all your questions?" She nodded. "You're sure?" She nodded again. "Then do you think we could get on with beating the bad guys and living happily ever after?"

"Mff mumph," she said.

He took his hand away. "Try it again."

"Yes, please," she said, grinning. He grinned back and hauled her in for another kiss.

When they were both suitably out of breath, he pulled back. "Later," he promised, and swung back toward the door.

He walked on silent feet down the short hall and through the salon, Lacey close on his heels. They could still hear the voices of their captors at the bow of the boat, arguing over the best way to secure the flapping sheet. They made their way past the small galley kitchen, Lacey following Devon's silent gestures to the ship-to-shore radio that sat in the small alcove just off the companionway.

He leaned down, his mouth close to her ear. "Channel sixteen is the distress channel," he said softly. "Give them the GPS coordinates I wrote down, we haven't gone too far that they won't be able to use them to find us."

"Do I tell them that you're FBI?"

He grinned. "I'm not FBI, but yeah, go ahead and tell them that. It'll make it simpler. Tell them that Felicity's armed and dangerous, and tell them she's on the most-wanted lists of most western governments."

"What about Gordon? Do I tell them he's armed and dangerous too?"

Devon smiled grimly. "Tell them she has a flunky, and that he's so stupid he's likely to get himself and anyone standing too close to him killed."

She admonished him with a look. "I'd say you were being a little hard on him, but you're probably right."

"Hopefully, by the time the Coast Guard gets here, neither of them will be a factor." He hefted the gun in his hand and pressed a swift kiss to her mouth. He pointed at the radio. "Coast Guard," he reminded her.

"Right." She dug the receipt out of her pocket and picked up the hand mike. "Devon?" she whispered as he turned to head up the steps. He turned back and she forced a smile. "Be careful. If you get hurt, it'll piss me off."

He sent her a dazzling grin and a saucy wink. "Trust me, baby," he said, and disappeared up the steps.

Lacey drew a shaky breath. "I hope he knows what the fuck he's doing," she muttered, and switching the channel to sixteen, spoke into the handset. "Come in Coast Guard, this is an emergency. Come in, Coast Guard."

Devon grinned to himself as he stepped lightly into the cockpit, ducking his head to avoid the swinging boom. He knew what he was doing, all right. Or at least, he usually did.

Night had fallen, even though it was hard to tell since Felicity had every deck light blazing, including the one at the top of the mast. He allowed himself a smirk at how un-stealth-like that was then turned his attention back to the business at hand. The temperature had dropped and it was a good ten to fifteen degrees cooler on the water than on land. He felt gooseflesh rise along his bare arms but he ignored it, turning to face the bow of the boat. At first he didn't see them, as the sail Lacey had referred to as the sheet was flapping wildly, obstructing his view. But he could still hear them.

"You idiot, you can't just hold it tighter!" Felicity was screaming at Gordon. "You have to use the thingy to tighten it!"

"What thingy? I don't know what you're talking about, and I don't like this and you promised I'd be in charge! You said my talents were being wasted in the office, that I was a born field agent, that I—"

"Oh, shut up, you little shit!"

Devon slipped off his boots and socks and stepped barefoot up onto the deck, his toes curling into the wood. He crept along the portside, one hand on the lifeline for balance. He stubbed his toe on a cleat and winced, but kept silent as he made his way to the bow. He stayed low, not wanting to cast a shadow that would alert them to his presence.

"Don't call me names! It's rude, and I'm supposed to be in charge, you said I was going to be in charge!" Gordon's voice got progressively higher until he sounded like a twelve-year-old girl.

Devon drew closer, the flapping sheet providing cover for his approach. He could see them now, facing each other in the narrow space at the very front of the vessel. Felicity's back was to him and he could see the pistol she'd tucked into her waistband. Gordon was opposite her, his hands braced on the rail behind him and a look of petulant rage on his doughy little face.

He watched Felicity shove her fist in Gordon's face. "Listen, you slimy little toad of a man, you are not going to foul this up for me. Now get this—" she waved her hand at the flapping sheet "—sail thingy back in working order, then go below and make certain our guests are still asleep. The last thing I need is for that son of a bitch to come to before I can get to Dimitri."

Devon grimaced as he recognized the name. Dimitri Ivanovich, one of Devereaux's henchmen. A former KGB torture specialist. There was little doubt as to what role he'd play in Felicity's little plan. Thankfully, he didn't intend to let things get that far.

Crouching low to stay out of Gordon's sight line, he slid forward several inches. He needed to catch Felicity by surprise—she was the dangerous one. He didn't doubt that Gordon was capable of violence—he'd kidnapped Lacey and hit her over the head, after all. But Devon was betting that once Felicity was no longer pulling his strings, the little man would be a lot easier to handle.

Gordon started to sputter a protest and Devon grinned to himself. The little toad was showing more backbone than Devon had given him credit for. He slid a little closer.

"I told you, I don't know what to do with that thing!" Gordon waved a hand at the madly flapping sheet. "I don't sail, I'm not a sailor!"

"Well, you have a brain, don't you?" Felicity practically snarled at him. "Use it, and figure it out!"

Devon slid a few inches farther along the deck, he was within four feet of Felicity now, and in another eighteen inches, he wouldn't have the flapping sheet to use as cover. He held his breath, waiting.

Gordon didn't disappoint. "You can't talk to me that way," he whined. "I'm an FBI agent! I'm important!"

Felicity leaned in, crowding little man against the rail. "You're a rogue FBI agent, you jackass. And I'll talk to you any way I want, because I'm in charge of this operation and you will *do as I say!*"

Gordon quivered, but he puffed out his chest. Voice wavering with the effort of sounding brave, he said, "And what if I don't?"

Devon figured that was his cue and rose to his feet. "My guess is she'll throw you overboard." He smiled as Felicity shrieked and spun around. "Right, Felicity? Ah-ah-ah," he warned as he saw her hand sneak around to her back. "None of that now." He cocked the pistol he was pointing at her. "Two fingers, Felicity. With your left hand. And toss it overboard."

"How did you get out?" she hissed as she complied, tossing the gun over the rail.

Devon chuckled at her. "Get out? You didn't exactly lock me in, sweetheart. You didn't even tie me up."

Felicity's face was turning red she was so pissed. "That dose of barbiturates should have kept you down for hours," she growled.

"I have a very strong constitution," he said, and smiled when she hissed at him. "Boy, you're really pissed at me, aren't you?"

"I hate you," she seethed, rage all but spilling out of her. "You are the reason why my Simon is dead!"

241

"Actually, you can probably credit a whole host of folks with that one. CIA, FBI, MI-5." He shrugged. "I'm really just a cog in the wheel of international justice."

"Justice?" She spat the word out. "You call it justice when a good, decent man is struck down by cowards? He was doing good work, noble work, but you and your government decided—"

Devon's harsh bark of laughter cut her off and had Gordon cowering behind her. "Noble work? You think the bombing of a Bosnian grammar school was noble? You see the assassination of the French prime minister as good? Lady, you are whacked."

Felicity tilted her chin up, a look of proud defiance on her face that made Devon want to drop the anchor on her chest. "There are always casualties in any revolution."

"Get real, sister. The only revolution going on is the one in your head. And guess what? It's over." He flashed his teeth in a parody of a smile. "Now, how about you and your little flunky head back to the cockpit."

"I'll get free," she boasted, tossing her hair back. Her eyes glittered at him with what he figured was part hate, part raving lunacy.

Devon nodded, eyes rolling. "And you'll avenge Simon's name, and the revolution will go on, yadda, yadda, yadda." He pointed with the gun. "Walk."

Rather than have them walk past him—and give Felicity a shot at shoving him overboard—he prodded them along the starboard side. Felicity shoved past Gordon, stomping along the deck as fast as the pitching of the boat would allow, which wasn't very fast. The wind was picking up and without the sails, which were still flapping uselessly, waves of ever-increasing size were pushing the boat around, causing it to pitch wildly.

Gordon still clung to the lifeline at the bow, not moving. Devon raised an eyebrow.

"What're you waiting for?" He gestured with the pistol. "Move it along, Aggate."

The little man swallowed, his Adam's apple bobbing wildly. His eyes were wide, and his gaze kept flicking to the waves slapping at the hull. "I can't swim," he squeaked.

Devon smiled without humor. "You probably should have thought of that before you agreed to help in a kidnap-torture-murder plot involving a sailboat."

If possible, Gordon's eyes got wider. "Torture? Murder?" He shook his head frantically. "No, no. I was just—nobody was supposed to get hurt, nobody's getting hurt. Felicity said, she said she just needed to talk to you, to talk to you about her friend Simon."

Devon felt his temper start to boil at the sheer stupidity of that statement. "She's an internationally known terrorist on the most-wanted lists of at least ten governments, including ours," he snarled, looming over the smaller man until he was all but bent over the rail. "What the fuck did you think she was going to do when she got us onboard—serve margaritas and take us on a pleasure cruise?"

"I...I didn't..."

"You didn't think, did you?" Gordon shook his head frantically. "You're a goddamn FBI agent, and I don't care if you're a paper pusher who only gets out of the file room for the annual Christmas party, you should've used your brain and fucking figured it out!"

Gordon had turned an interesting shade of green. "She wouldn't hurt Lacey, she wouldn't! She just wanted to talk to you, to tell you—"

"Were you born this stupid or do you work at it?" He leaned down until he was looming over Gordon. He bared his teeth. "The woman's a cold-blooded killer. She blew up a day care in Germany, for Christ's sake. You think she's planning on leaving witnesses—including you?"

If possible, Gordon's eyes went even wider and he latched onto Devon's shirt with pudgy hands. "You don't think she'd kill me, do you?" he whispered.

Devon leaned closer. "In a heartbeat," he whispered.

"Oh, my God, what am I going to do?"

Devon peeled Gordon's fingers off his shirt, one at a time. "You're going to walk to the cockpit, that's what. And when the authorities get here and they tell you to cooperate? You'll do it."

Gordon swiped his hands down his legs. "Right, right," he said, nodding frantically. "Okay, and you'll help me, right? You'll tell them I was secretly working with you, and I won't go to jail, right?"

"No." Gordon's face fell and Devon smiled. "But I won't kill you. Take what you can get," he advised. "Now get moving."

Gordon swallowed heavily and started to slide along the deck in tiny, mincing steps. Felicity was several feet ahead of them now, nearly to the cockpit. Devon cursed under his breath, knowing if Felicity caught Lacey by surprise, he might be forced to do something drastic.

He stepped around Gordon, ignoring the little man's grasping hands and pleas for help—as far as Devon was concerned, the little Oompa Loompa could drown. He hurried along the deck, reaching the halfway point as Felicity was stepping down into the cockpit. "That's far enough!" he shouted, cursing as the rising wind whipped the words away. He started to run, but the water made the wooden planks of the deck slick and he slipped.

He went to his knees, sliding along the deck as the boat pitched violently. He heard Gordon's thin scream from behind and ignored it. He scrambled, clutching at the grab rail, trying to keep hold of the gun while trying to keep himself from sliding into the churning waves.

By the time he managed to gain his feet, Felicity was nowhere to be seen. He cursed and moved forward, one hand on the lifeline for balance as he sped the remaining few feet to the cockpit.

He looked down and saw Felicity standing in the companionway, one foot poised to descend the steps. Breathing a sigh of relief that she hadn't yet gone down below, he levered the gun at her. "Why don't you have a seat, Felicity? Make yourself comfortable."

She glared at him from over her shoulder then spun around and plunked herself down on the cushion padding the wooden bench along the portside. She made a face. "The seat is wet," she complained, and moved to stand.

"You'll survive," he said. "Park your ass."

With one eye aimed balefully at the pistol he held, she complied with ill grace. "Anything else?" she snarled, and he grinned.

"I'll let you know," he promised. Without taking his eyes off her, he called out to Lacey. "Baby, how's it coming?"

She popped her head through the companionway. "All set," she said, slightly breathless from nerves. "The Coast Guard said it would take them about twenty minutes to get here."

"You didn't have any trouble convincing them it was urgent?"

She shook her head. "No, they said they already had a bulletin about her." She sent Felicity a dirty look. "It seems the cops picked up her partner, or at least one of them, in Sault Saint Marie."

Devon's surprise showed on his face. "Really?"

Lacey grinned. "Yeah, I guess they were doing a sting on a local forger—driver's licenses, birth certificates. Passports too—American and Canadian. Anyway, her friend Dimitri was having two Canadian passports made up with the names

245

Douglas and Maryann Freeman on them. One was obviously for him and the other had her picture on it. I guess they squeezed her real name out of him, because the second I said it they started to take me real serious."

"Well, how about that?" Devon drawled, grinning at a fuming Felicity. "Sounds like Dimitri didn't stand up too well under pressure."

Felicity's face was nearly purple with rage. "That imbecile," she hissed.

Devon chuckled. "Yeah, I guess next time you should choose your co-conspirators with a little extra care. Of course, the next time you see daylight you'll have to choose a partner based on whether or not he has his own teeth."

Felicity turned her head away and Devon chuckled again. He reached out a hand for Lacey, drawing her up into the cockpit and tucking her against his side. "You doing okay, honey?" he asked, pressing a kiss to her temple.

"Yeah," she sighed, closing her eyes and wrapping her arms around him. "But my head hurts where Gordon bonked me." She looked around with a frown. "Where is Gordon, anyway?"

"Aw, shit," Devon groaned. "I left him on the deck."

Lacey turned around, stepping up onto the bench to look along the starboard side. "Oh, he's not doing that well," she said, and Devon turned to look.

"Aw, shit," he said again, this time with a resigned sigh. "I'm going to have to go get him."

Lacey couldn't help the giggle bubbling up in her throat. Gordon was definitely in need of help. He was belly down on the deck, sprawled out like a starfish, clinging to the grab rail like a zebra mussel. As she watched, he picked up his head. She was pretty sure he was wailing for help, but the sound of the wind and the waves muffled any sound that might've reached their ears.

"Yeah, you gotta go get him." She suppressed a smile when he looked at her with pleading eyes. "You have to, Dev. You can't let him die out there."

"He probably won't die," Devon said, then sighed when she just looked at him. "Okay, okay, I'll go get him. But only so I can make sure he goes to jail for the rest of his natural life."

"Fine by me."

"Here, take this."

Lacey stared at the gun he held out to her. "Why?"

"Because if I'm going to go get fucknut, you have to keep an eye on her," Devon said, nodding at Felicity.

Lacey made a face but took the gun. "Just point it at her?"

"Yep." He dropped a quick kiss on her lips then squared his shoulders. "I'm going to go fetch Tweedle Dee. Back in a sec."

Lacey watched him go with a grin then turned her attention back to Felicity.

"You don't look like a terrorist," she mused, and drew a twist of a smile from the other woman.

"Really. And how exactly does a terrorist look?"

Lacey shrugged. "Couldn't tell you. I've never met one before tonight."

"Well, then how would you know what one looks like?"

"Good point." Lacey sat down so she faced Felicity. "So, I guess the plan was to lure Devon into investigating the rumors of Simon's counterfeiting operation so you could get even for his death."

Felicity said nothing but her eyes turned flinty at the mention of Simon's name. "It's not a bad plan," Lacey went on casually, suppressing a shudder at the icy look in the woman's eyes. Jeez, this was a scary lady. Lacey took a firmer hold of the pistol. "Except, of course, that it didn't work."

"It would have worked," Felicity hissed. "It would have worked if that insipid little troll hadn't insisted on coming along."

"Why'd you let him?" Lacey asked. "I mean, he obviously isn't the sharpest crayon in the box, and he's certainly not the strongest. You couldn't have just done this on your own?"

"I don't have to answer any of your questions."

"No, that's true. I'm just curious, anyway. It's not like anything you say can get you into hot water. Well, hotter than you're already in."

Felicity was silent for a moment then mumbled something under her breath.

"Huh?"

"I couldn't let the little bastard squeal about it," Felicity repeated. "He threatened to blow everything open unless I included him. He's got delusional ideas about being the next James Bond."

Lacey glanced over her shoulder to where Devon was dragging Gordon off the deck by the back of his shirt. The little man refused to let go of the grab rail, prompting Devon to yank harder. When that didn't work, he pressed his bare heel on the fingers Gordon had wrapped around the rail and with a yelp of pain he let loose.

Lacey turned back to Felicity with a grin. "I don't really see that happening."

Felicity glowered. "I should've killed him while I had the chance."

"Well, that's hindsight for you." She looked over her shoulder where Devon was dragging a simpering Gordon along the deck. "You need any help, baby?"

"I got it, sweetheart," he called. "How're you doing?"

"Oh, I'm fine." Lacey checked Felicity out of the corner of her eye, just to make sure she hadn't moved. She was checking her manicure, so Lacey turned her attention back to Devon just in time to see him slip on the wet deck.

She jerked a little, rising to her feet as Devon hit his knees. He let go of Gordon to put his hands out for balance but the little man clung like a barnacle, throwing his balance off even further, and they both went tumbling to the deck.

"Oh, shit," Lacey whispered, leaping up to stand on the seat. "Devon, are you okay?" she called.

Devon picked up his head, and Lacey felt her heart clutch at the sight of blood on his forehead. He touched his fingers to the cut, cursing. "Yeah, I'm fine," he assured her. He turned, shoving at Gordon's grasping hands. "You're fine, you jackass—quit pulling on me!"

Lacey grinned in relief. "Sure you don't need a hand?" she called.

He turned back to her with an answering grin. He opened his mouth to speak then his expression changed, a look of horror coming into his eyes. "Lace—look out!"

"Wha—?" Lacey started to speak, then she felt the air change behind her and realized in a flash that she'd taken her attention away from Felicity for a moment too long.

She'd think later that it all happened in slow motion, with a clarity she'd remember for the rest of her life. But truthfully, it was blindingly quick.

She whipped her head around, started to turn, to swing the gun back toward Felicity, but the other woman was already up and moving. She had a winch handle in her hand, already raised above her head, already swinging downward. Lacey knew she'd never be able to get the gun up in time.

She saw in slow motion the downward decent of Felicity's arm, the light that spilled from the companionway glinting off the chrome of the winch handle. It was coming for her head, and some fight-or-flight survival instinct made her move.

Her body flowed back, her right hand still coming up, hoping against hope that she'd be able to get a shot off before she got hit. The winch handle came down in a flash of gleaming metal and in desperation she threw herself to the side so that instead of hitting her in the head, it crashed into her forearm.

Lacey felt the snap as the bones in her arm gave way, saw her fingers relax as they went limp, the gun dropping from her fingers to clatter to the cockpit floor. She was oddly pain-free for a few brief seconds, long enough for her to wonder at it, and then it hit.

The pain was like a tidal wave that washed over her in black, greasy waves. It dimmed her vision and had bile rising up in her throat, and for a few seconds she was very much afraid she'd pass out. She dimly heard Devon's panicked shout, felt a push on her shoulder that sent her tumbling to the floor of the cockpit, but she barely felt herself hit the floor. It was taking all of her concentration not to pass out.

Devon felt his heart drop to his knees when he saw Felicity rise up over Lacey with the winch handle. He shouted out a hoarse warning and tried to gain his feet, but with Gordon clinging to him, he could only watch in horror as Felicity brought the handle down, and he could tell from where he sat, helpless on the deck, that the blow shattered Lacey's forearm.

Gordon was still clinging to his legs with the tenacity of an octopus, screaming like a two year old, and his patience was at an end. He drew back and with one, short arm punch, knocked him out. His arms immediately went slack and Devon levered himself out from under the deadweight. He didn't take the time to secure Gordon—he was on his feet and moving for the cockpit almost before Gordon's eyes had rolled fully back into his head.

He saw Felicity scrambling in the cockpit for the pistol that had fallen out of Lacey's limp hand. He was one step away from her when she finally found it, swinging it up and pointing it at him with a steady hand and a glint in her eye.

He skidded to a halt, cursing under his breath as he raised his hands. He glanced behind Felicity quickly, taking in at a glance Lacey's still form, crumpled into a little ball on the narrow cockpit floor. He thought he saw her blink, thought she was conscious, but couldn't afford to take his eyes off Felicity long enough to make sure.

"Well, well, well," Felicity sneered. "Look at how the tides have turned."

Devon was painfully aware of the edge of the boat only a few feet behind him and that if she did manage to only injure him at such close range, the shot would probably carry him over the rail and in the water. He began edging back and to his right, sliding around so that his back was to the length of the boat, rather than the vast expanse of Lake Huron.

His brain searching frantically for a way out of this mess, he said only, "This is Lake Huron, Felicity. There's no tide."

"Figure of speech, you son of a bitch." She stepped up onto the bench, leveling the gun at his chest. "This really wasn't how I planned to do this, you know. I had a very detailed plan of torture devised for you."

"Really?" he asked, his voice mild. He continued to slide backward along the deck, pulling Felicity along with him. The farther he got her out onto the deck, the better chance he had of her slipping or faltering. "I almost hate to miss it. I bet I could learn a thing or two from you."

"Oh, no doubt you could. You government-types just aren't very good at the torture game. You're too soft, too ethical. You have all these rules and regulations and people to answer to if your prisoner dies during interrogation. That's why it's so much better to freelance—you can get so much more creative."

"Yes, I've seen the results of your creativity." Devon slid back another foot. "That Russian Orthodox priest in Gstaad was especially creative. The disembowelment was a stroke of genius."

Felicity smiled. "It was such fun," she whispered, her eyes lit with a sort of fevered arousal at the memory. "He screamed so much, so much he made himself hoarse. Then he could only moan as his guts spilled onto the floor."

Devon didn't bother keeping the disgust out of his voice. "Yeah, that's something to be proud of, all right."

Felicity gave a little forlorn sigh, her eyes gone misty with sentiment. "I do miss the old days." Then she refocused on him and her eyes hardened. "I was going to have such fun with you, but it looks like I'm going to have to take care of you right here. Such a shame."

Devon stopped edging backward. He couldn't go any farther anyway, he was nearly stepping on an unconscious Gordon already. He shifted his gaze back toward the cockpit, but he was too far away now and he couldn't see Lacey any longer. He looked back at Felicity. She was up out of the cockpit now, standing on the narrow strip of decking that ran between cockpit and rail.

"I can't tell you how broken up about it I am," he said, smiling. He deliberately lowered his hands and tucked them into his pockets. Her eyes narrowed and she took a step toward him.

"I'm going to enjoy this so much," she said, and raised her arm, the gun pointed dead at his face. "Any last words?"

Devon caught a glimpse of movement from the cockpit and had to force himself not to look. He could see Lacey moving in his peripheral vision, but he didn't dare look at her. He wanted Felicity's attention focused fully on him. "Hmm...last words," he said, and pulled one hand from his pocket to tap his chin thoughtfully. "How about, 'I have not yet begun to fight'?"

Felicity laughed, the sound harsh and grating in the night air. "Oh, you're done," she said, and pulled the trigger.

Devon moved as soon as he saw her finger tighten on the trigger. He threw himself to the right, aiming for the hatch over the companionway. He heard the shot fire and almost instantaneously felt the explosion of heat in his shoulder. He grunted, registering the pain and its meaning as he hit the deck.

He landed half under the boom on his right side. His left shoulder was on fire and he knew his left arm would be useless. He risked a quick glance at his shoulder to assess the damage. Blood was seeping from the wound, the stain spreading quickly, but it wasn't pumping or spurting and he breathed a sigh of relief. Still, he knew he could bleed out fairly quickly if he didn't get some pressure on it.

Somehow, he didn't think Felicity was going to give him the chance. He rolled to his back to find her a few feet away, the gun pointing directly at his face. She sent him a fierce smile.

"This time," she snarled, "I won't miss. Go to hell, Mr. Bannion."

He grinned back at her through gritted teeth. "I'll be sure to say hello to Simon for you when I get there."

He watched her eyes go nearly black with rage as she stepped closer, closing the distance between them. She leaned over him, pushing the gun practically in his face, and he silently cursed. He'd wanted her closer so that he could kick out with his legs and catch her off guard, either by landing a full body blow or sweeping up and knocking the gun out of her hand. But she was practically on top of him now and there was no way he could get his legs tucked up before she got a shot off.

He was dead.

* * * * *

Lacey whimpered, struggling not to pass out. The pain in her arm was beyond anything she'd ever felt. It radiated out, pulsing along with the beat of her heart and permeating her whole body, until she felt like one big throb. She felt Felicity's hands under her body, and dimly realized that she was searching for the dropped weapon. She tried to push herself to her feet but Felicity gave her a little nudge and she dropped back down, fresh pain exploding in her arm.

She must have blacked out for a moment or two. When she came to, she used her good arm to push herself to her knees in the cockpit breathing hard to beat back the nausea. She could hear Felicity and Devon, but their words were faint. She had lurched to her feet and was trying to get her bearings when she heard was the sharp crack of a gunshot. The sound startled her so much that she swung around before she remembered. She gritted her teeth against the waves of agony in her arm.

She blinked tears out of her eyes and looked up, keeping her right arm tucked firmly against her side. The last thing she wanted to do was accidentally knock it against anything and blackout again. Her gut clutched as she saw Felicity, standing only a few feet away on the deck. The pistol was in her hand, an almost gentle curl of smoke twirling up from the barrel.

Her heart in her throat, she looked to where the gun was pointed. Gordon was lying on the deck, not moving, but she didn't know if he'd been shot or not, and frankly she didn't much care. She didn't see Devon and for a brief, grief-stricken moment, thought he might have been pitched overboard. Then she heard the groan, the sound lifted on the wind, carrying toward her and she saw him.

He was lying on his side, a dark stain spreading over his left shoulder, and she realized Felicity had shot him. Probably not where she'd intended—Felicity didn't strike her as a stupid woman, her questionable loyalties aside, and she doubted that an international terrorist would make the mistake of toying with an adversary as well-trained and skilled as Devon.

Which meant she'd missed or Devon was especially good at ducking and weaving. Either way, Lacey felt her heart give a little cheer. But Felicity still had the gun and she was taking a step toward Devon. Lacey saw Devon roll to his back, saw the brief flash of pain cross his face before he suppressed it. He said something but the wind had shifted and she couldn't hear it. But whatever it was had an immediate effect on Felicity.

Lacey saw the other woman lean over Devon, pushing the gun in his face, and knew there was no way—no matter how good at ducking and weaving he was—that he was going to be able to move out of the way of this bullet.

Lacey frantically searched the cockpit for something to use as a weapon, but the only things readily available were coils of rope and seat cushions. The winch handle Felicity had used to break her arm was lying on the seat but throwing it was out since she was right-handed, and if she tried to run up and hit her on the head, it wouldn't be in time to save Devon from a bullet to the face.

She felt panic start to rise up, felt tears clawing at her throat, and ruthlessly tamped them down. Her arm was a blaze of pain and nausea swam in her belly, but she ignored both of those things. She had to find a weapon or something to distract Felicity. But what, what could she use? Then her frantically searching eyes landed on the wildly swinging boom. And Felicity was standing right in its path.

Gritting her teeth against the bloom of pain that moving caused, she stepped up onto the portside bench then up the short step to the deck. The boom was loosely tethered to the winch on the portside but its starboard lines were missing, making Lacey wonder how the hell Felicity had managed to sail the boat at all.

She quickly pulled the remaining line loose with her left hand, the winch spinning madly. The wind covered the sound, whisking it away before it could be detected. Lacey glanced quickly at Felicity. She couldn't quite see her face—the other woman was standing so her back was half turned—but she could tell that Felicity wasn't changing her mind about shooting Devon.

She took a firm grip on the boom with her left hand and drew back her arm. The boom was heavy and if the wind had been pushing at her, she wouldn't have been able to manage it. But as luck would have it, the wind seemed to be swirling away at that moment, and when she saw Felicity raise her head, a look of finality on her face, she threw her weight forward and heaved the boom.

Felicity must have seen it coming out of the corner of her eye, because her head whipped up and her mouth opened on a scream. She tried to scramble out of the way but she slipped and the boom hit her just as she fell.

Lacey jerked, whipping her head away from the sight. Had Felicity stood upright, the boom would have caught her in the shoulder or upper chest. She would most likely have been knocked overboard and she certainly would have suffered a few broken bones, but she might've lived. As it was, her fall brought her head level with the oncoming column of aluminum and hardened plastic, and the impact sounded like a melon hitting the sidewalk from four stories. Lacey didn't have to look to know she was dead.

"Lacey? Honey, are you okay?"

She heard Devon's voice getting closer and opened one eye to find him walking to her in a half crouch in order to stay under the swinging boom. Seeing him moving, even though his left arm hung limply at his side, filled her with such a towering feeling of relief that she felt all the adrenaline drain out of her and she collapsed to the deck.

"I'm fine," she managed. She searched his face as he settled beside her. "How're you?"

"Oh, fine," he said breezily, a tired grin breaking out over his face. "All in a day's work." He laid gentle fingers on her cheek. "How's your arm?"

"Broken," she said, a tear escaping before she could stop it. Now that she knew he was all right, the pain was starting to leak through again. "How's your shoulder?"

"Shot," he said, and she gave a watery laugh.

"We're a pair, aren't we? Your left arm is useless, and my right arm is useless."

"For the time being," he agreed. "As long as I can still do this," he said, picking up her left hand with his right, weaving their fingers together and carrying them to his lips, "I'm a happy man."

Lacey blinked away more tears. "I love you," she whispered.

Devon pressed his lips harder to her fingers, closing his eyes. When he opened them again, they were clear and bright. "I love you too."

She sighed and leaned into his good shoulder. "Just for the record, you are quitting this job, right?"

"Absolutely."

"Good." She closed her eyes. "Because I'd really like for our next vacation to be a little bit more peaceful than this one."

Devon pressed a laughing kiss to her temple. "It's a deal."

Chapter Twenty-Two

ဢ

The Coast Guard showed up soon after that and they were bundled up and hustled off the sailboat before she could say "anchors aweigh". The ship's medic took a quick look at their injuries, proclaimed them beyond his capabilities and summoned a copter to take them to the mainland for medical treatment.

They wound up sharing a curtain area at Mackinac Straits Hospital and Health Center emergency room. Lacey had her arm in a makeshift sling, courtesy of the medic, and watched while the emergency personnel poked and prodded at Devon's shoulder. Every time they touched it, she winced.

"Doesn't that hurt?" she finally asked after watching a nurse probe the hole in his shoulder with a metal prod.

He grinned at her. She looked so adorable, sitting there on the gurney with her arm strapped to her stomach. Her hair was sticking out at all angles, there were dark circles under her eyes and her sense of humor was eroding steadily as the night went on.

He barely suppressed a wince as the nurse dug in the wound again. He'd refused all pain medication and it was more than a little uncomfortable. But he didn't want anything dulling his senses and he knew from experience that painkillers, no matter how mild, made him loopy.

"Yeah, it hurts," he told her.

"Then why don't you let her give you something? Trust me, that Demerol is the shit." She grinned.

He laughed. Apparently painkillers made her loopy too. "You a little stoned, baby?"

She giggled, surprising herself with the girlish sound. "I'm feeling no pain. Which is really cool, considering I was feeling mega pain before. My arm *hurt*."

He sobered quickly at the reminder. "I'm sorry, Lacey. It's my fault."

She frowned, blinking at him owlishly. "Huh?"

"I was supposed to protect you and I didn't do that. I'm sorry."

"You jackass."

He blinked taken aback at the vehemence in her tone. Somehow, even though he knew he'd screwed up, he had expected her to absolve him of responsibility. "I said I was sorry."

"I know—you're a jackass!" She waved her good hand at him, nearly sending the instrument tray at her elbow flying. "How big is your ego that you just assume everything is your responsibility or your fault?" She shook her head then had to grab onto the orderly who had dashed over to rescue the instrument tray. "Woo. Got a little dizzy there."

Devon choked back a laugh, schooling his face into sober lines when she turned to glare at him.

"Where was I?"

"I'm a jackass," he prompted helpfully.

"Oh, right. Thanks. It's not your fault I got hurt. I shouldn't have taken my eyes off of her. She caught me by surprise."

Then she sighed, a sad little sound as she lay back on the gurney with a thump. "I don't guess I'm cut out for this whole spy thing."

Devon ignored the interested gazes of the nurses. "No, probably not, sweetie. But it's okay."

"I told you I wasn't," she reminded him. "Remember? I said I'm a computer geek, not a Bond girl."

Hannah Murray

"You could be a Bond girl, honey. Believe me."

"Nah." She waved her hand again, this time clipping the orderly neatly in the balls. She sighed again as he crumpled to the floor with a whimper. "Don't wanna be a Bond girl. James Bond is a sissy when you think about it."

Devon watched his nurse and a second orderly rush to help their fallen colleague with sympathy. "How's that, honey?"

"Well, he's always relying on those gadgets. I mean, don't get me wrong—they're good gadgets. But Q is really the brains behind 'em. Bond doesn't actually make any of them himself."

"He's no MacGyver," Devon agreed.

"And M, she's the real brains, she's running the whole show." Lacey nodded. "Yep, they had to have a woman running things just to make it all believable."

"You know, M wasn't always a woman," he said, and she turned to frown at him.

"Whatdaya mean?" she asked, sitting up again. "She's played by Judi Dench. 'Scuse me—Dame Judi Dench. She wears skirts and everything, she's totally a woman."

"Yes, but that's not how the character was originally written…never mind."

"Thas right. And another thing about James Bond—what is that whole, 'shaken, not stirred' thing? Please. The only thing you get with a shaken martini is bruised, watery gin." She shook her head. "Stupid."

They had the orderly back on his feet—barely—and he was hobbling toward the door, mumbling something about an ice pack. Devon shook his head. His little angel packed quite a wallop.

He straightened as the doctor swept in the room, chart in hand. "Mr. Bannion, how are we feeling this evening?"

"How d'ya think he feels? He has a hole in his shoulder."

The doctor, a young man in his early thirties, looked over at Lacey. "Ah, I see you've availed yourself of the painkillers, Ms. Johnson."

"Damn skippy," she grinned sloppily at him.

He chuckled and turned his attention back to Devon. "And I understand you've refused any painkiller?" Devon nodded. "That's fine, I'm sure the very grumpy man currently pacing a rut in our tile in the great suit and bad haircut will be very pleased to hear that. He seemed concerned about it when we spoke."

Devon groaned. "Tell me he's not here."

"Who's not here?" Lacey asked.

Devon felt like kicking something. "There's no way he could have gotten here that fast. He must've been on his way."

"On whose way?"

The doctor was checking the chart. "I believe he came in from the island on helicopter."

"Shit, shit, shit!" Devon rubbed his right hand over his eyes. "I don't want to deal with this now."

"Deal with what?"

"I don't think you're going to have much of a choice," the doctor said, setting the chart aside and starting his check of Devon's vitals. "He didn't seem like the patient type."

"Tell me about it," Devon groused, blinking when the doctor flashed his penlight in his eyes. Then he cursed, ducking as a hemostat came flying past the doctor to whiz by his ear. He stared at Lacey, incredulous.

"Quit ignoring me," she said, her lower lip poking out in a pout. "Who're you talking about?"

He was still staring at her. "Did you just throw that at me?"

"You weren't paying attention to me!"

"So you throw metal at me?"

She shrugged. "It was what I had. I'm a big believer in improvising."

He laughed, and then laughed even harder when he saw the mutinous look on her face. "Okay, okay," he managed, waving his hand in surrender. "Don't throw anything else at me."

Lacey snatched a wad of gauze from the instrument tray. "I make no promises. Tell me who you we're talking about or you get the gauze."

He grinned at her, even though the doctor was now prodding his shoulder and it felt like hell on fire. "Life with you isn't going to be boring, is it?"

She may have been doped up, but she wasn't slow. One eyebrow shot up. "We're having a life together?"

The grin stayed in place but his voice went dead serious. "Oh, yeah. We may still have a few details to iron out, but we're definitely having a life together."

Lacey humphed, but she couldn't stop the smile. "Quit trying to change the subject. Who're you talking about?"

Devon opened his mouth to answer then winced as he heard the slap of cheap leather on linoleum. "I think you're about to see for yourself," he said, and turned as the curtain was flung to the side.

"Agent Bannion, report the situation."

Devon rolled his eyes. "I'm fine, Preston, thanks for asking."

"Who is this?" Lacey asked.

Devon gestured. "Preston Smythe-White, director of — well, director of an agency that isn't supposed to exist. He's my boss — technically."

"Huh. You sure he's not a Feeb? He's got Feeb shoes."

Preston ignored her less-than-complimentary reference to his footwear. "Agent Bannion, can you tell me what happened?"

"Sure. I got setup." Devon winced. "Easy, Doc."

"Sorry about that." The doctor finished his exam and began affixing a pressure bandage to Devon's shoulder. "You've got some muscle damage, but the bullet went straight through and I don't think any tendons are damaged. I want an MRI to be sure."

"Just stitch me up, Doc. I'll be fine."

"We'll get the stitches done and the MRI performed elsewhere, Doctor." Preston gave what Devon was sure he thought of as a genial smile. In reality, it made him look like a constipated goldfish.

The doctor merely shrugged and finished the dressing. He could tell something hinky was going on in his ER, but he'd been working double shifts ever since the other permanent resident on staff had crashed into a telephone pole the week before, and he just didn't have the energy to be curious.

"Suit yourself," he said, and turned to leave. "The pressure bandage should hold until you get wherever you're going, providing you keep the arm immobile. And you," he said to Lacey, "they'll be taking you up to look at that arm in a few minutes."

"We'll leave immediately," Preston said as the doctor left. "I need details and there's a civilian present." He turned his perpetually disapproving gaze on Lacey.

She stuck her tongue out at him. "Blow me, dude. I may not be on the permanent payroll, but I'm not here as a 'civilian'. Your international terrorist broke my arm and I want to know what's what."

Preston turned back to where Devon sat grinning. "What is she talking about?"

"Your information must be incomplete, Pres." Devon sent Lacey a quick wink. "This is Lacey Johnson. The FBI field office in Chicago assigned her as my partner."

"What?"

Lacey gave a mock shiver at the icy tone. "Oooh! Scary."

Devon laughed. "It might be easier if you just tell me how much you know, Pres. I can fill in the blanks."

"Treasury alerted us that some of their information may be corrupt."

Lacey snorted. "There's an understatement," she muttered.

Devon stood. He dampened a wad of gauze and started washing the orange disinfectant stain from around the bandage on his shoulder. "For starters, Simon's dead."

"How did that happen?"

"Wow," Lacey said. "It's amazing that you have like, no inflection in your voice!"

Preston didn't even glance at her but his left eye did twitch just a little. "Devon, how did Simon die?"

Devon tossed the gauze in the garbage. "In Prague eighteen months ago. He was hurt, but he got out, made it to Budapest. He died there. Felicity hid it, mainly so she could setup some elaborate revenge. They found Ivanovich waiting for her in Sault Saint Marie—from what I could get from the Coast Guard, he's already singing out names."

He opened his mouth to say more but Preston cut him off. "We can get the rest handled at the debriefing. I've got a chopper waiting to take us to Langley. We'll get your MRI and then work this out."

"Langley?" Lacey sat up, suddenly worried. "You're leaving?"

Devon shook his head at her. "No, I'm not, don't worry." To Preston he said, "Schedule the debriefing here, Pres. I'm not leaving her."

"Agent Bannion, procedure dictates—"

"Fuck procedure. Her arm is broken—was broken in the service of her country, if you want to get technical—and they may need to do surgery. I'm staying with her."

Preston looked like he was going to argue then gave a short nod. "Very well." He twitched his sleeve aside to look at his watch. "I'm expecting a call, so if you'll excuse me."

Devon watched him walk out the door. "I hate him."

"Why?"

He turned to look at her and grinned. The meds had pushed her beyond loopy into sleepy and she could barely keep her eyes open. He walked over to stand beside her. "Because he's a jackass and I don't trust him," he said.

Lacey sighed as he stroked her forehead with cool fingers. "You promise you're not going anywhere?" she asked as the nurse and orderly came in to wheel her to the surgical floor.

"I promise," he said, and leaning down, took her lips in a tender kiss.

"Love you," she sighed as they wheeled her out the door.

"I love you too," he said, and she smiled at him until he disappeared from view.

When they wheeled her back out, a fresh plaster cast on her arm, he was gone.

* * * * *

"What are you doing?"

Lacey glanced up to see Jane standing in the bedroom doorway. "Packing."

"But where're you going? Here, don't lift that." She rushed to pull a leather duffle bag off the closet shelf. "You'll hurt your arm," she admonished.

Lacey grinned and gave Jane a smacking kiss on the cheek. "Yes, Mom."

Jane watched Lacey set the duffle on the bed with a frown. "What are you packing for?"

"I'm going to Washington," Lacey said. She dug in the basket of clean laundry on the bed and came up with a fistful of panties. She tucked them into the bag and went to the dresser.

Jane frowned. "Why? Is something wrong? I thought the local office was handling your debriefing."

"They did." Lacey shrugged. "Wasn't too bad, really. They just kept me in a little room with two agents that chain-smoked and made me go over every single detail a million times."

"That sounds awful."

Lacey laughed. "It was like watching paint dry, with second-hand smoke."

"So you're all done then?"

"Yep."

Jane sat on the bed and watched Lacey go back and forth between duffle and dresser for a few minutes. Finally she blurted out, "I can't believe you never told me you were moonlighting for the FBI."

Lacey grinned. "How long have you been holding that one in?"

Jane rolled her eyes. "Since we got home and heard the whole sordid tale. It's been killing me not to ask you about it. How could you not tell me? I mean, I tell you everything."

"Yeah, I really enjoyed hearing about the honeymoon." Lacey waggled her eyebrows. "Who knew you could do that with marshmallow fluff?"

Jane snickered. "The hotel maids had a helluva time pulling the sheets apart. But seriously—why you didn't tell me?"

Lacey sat down on the bed next to her friend. "Because I couldn't, Janey." She shrugged. "I know I tell you everything. I mean, that's our rule — full disclosure. But I couldn't tell you."

Jane nodded. "Yeah, I get that. And Ian sort of read me the riot act over it, because I got kind of pissy when I first heard about it. But still, it feels weird when you don't tell me stuff."

"It felt weird for me too," she agreed.

"So, from now on, full disclosure. Right?"

"Right," Lacey agreed. "Unless it violates federal law."

"Right. So. Why're you going to Washington?"

"To see Devon, of course."

Lacey stood and stuffed one last pair of socks into her duffle then zipped it shut. She looked up to find Jane staring at her, chewing her lip. "What?"

Jane shrugged. "Nothing, I guess. It's just that you were pretty pissed at him when you first got home. I know he explained what happened, but you were *really* steamed."

"Well, after I found out what happened, I was still really steamed, but at that Preston What's-His-Nuts."

"Don't blame you there."

"I mean, what kind of jackass slips sleeping pills into someone's coffee like that?" Lacey shook her head. "Nobody was even surprised when they heard about it, apparently. The powers that be over there don't care much about individual rights, only about the big picture, so drugging an agent to get him where they wanted him is pretty mild stuff as far as they're concerned. No wonder Devon can't wait to get the hell out of Dodge."

"No kidding." Jane's face wrinkled with distaste. "By the way, did he ever tell you exactly who he works for?"

"Nope. Says I'm better off not knowing."

"I hate it when Ian says that," Jane grumbled. "He's probably right, but still. I want to *know*."

Lacey shrugged. "Since Devon won't be working for them much longer, I guess I really don't care if I know or not."

"What's the plan for when he finally makes the move here?"

"Well, he's really looking forward to working with Ian, and I think we've pretty much decided to live in my apartment until we can find a bigger place together."

"Wow, that's weird, isn't it?" Jane asked. "We've both lived in this building for so long, and now we're both going to be leaving."

"I know," Lacey said. "It's going to be strange, but things change. And it's hard to be sad when the reason behind it is so exciting." She huffed out a breath. "If I could just get him here, it'd be perfect. I know I talk to him almost every night, but I miss him."

"Has he told you what's taking so long?"

"They're working on closing down the terrorist cell, rounding up the remaining members, closing down their suppliers and whatever else they do."

"Well, I guess that's gotta take some time."

"Hell if I know," Lacey said. "I'm out of the international espionage game."

"Were you scared?" Jane asked quietly.

Lacey nodded. "Yeah, I was. I mean, not in the beginning. It all seemed like a lark, you know? Something new to do. But at the end, yeah. I was terrified."

"God, I can't even imagine. If I saw somebody trying to shoot Ian…" She shook her head.

"That right there, that's why I love you."

Jane started. "What?"

"That. You know, even though I didn't tell you, you know that the reason I was scared was because I thought I wasn't going to get there in time, that Felicity would shoot Devon before I could stop her."

"Of course," Jane said simply. "You love him."

Lacey smiled through the tears that threatened to spill. "Yes, I do."

Jane sniffed. "When did we turn into a couple of saps?"

Lacey gave a watery laugh, and grabbed a tissue from the nightstand. "I don't know, but let's not tell anybody, okay?"

Jane snagged a tissue for herself. "Okay." She blew her nose loudly. "Okay. Are you sure your arm is healed enough to make the trip? I've been helping you out a lot—I've spent more time down here than up at my own place."

Lacey shrugged. "It's okay. I'm not going to be playing third base anytime soon, but Devon can do what you've been doing, which is basically helping me wash myself so I don't get the cast wet. And frankly, it'll be a lot more fun with him."

Jane grinned. "There is that. What's your plan when you get to Washington?"

"I don't really have one, I guess." Lacey mopped her face dry. "I'm not telling him I'm coming, because he'd just tell me to stay home, and then we'd end up fighting. Better to just show up. Other than that, I don't know."

"Don't worry." Jane stood. "I know who we can ask."

They headed upstairs to Jane's apartment and found Ian in the kitchen, eating a bowl of cereal. He looked up when they trooped in. "Hey," he said. He looked from one to the other, his brow knitted in concern. "What's up?"

"We need your help," Jane said, bending down to kiss him. "Mmm, you taste like oranges."

He gestured toward his cereal bowl. "We're out of milk," he said. "I had to pour OJ on my corn flakes."

"I'll go shopping tomorrow," she said. "Do you have Devon's address in Washington?"

"Yeah," he said, eyes darting warily between the two of them. "Why?"

"Because you're going to give it to me. I'm going," Lacey said.

"Wait." Ian held up a hand. "You're going where?"

"To Washington. I'm tired of waiting."

"Lacey, he's really tied up right now," Ian said, shoving his cereal bowl aside. "I know he wanted to be back sooner than this, but they're trying to finish this Deveraux thing for good, and he's their best bet. He'll be back as soon as he's finished, I promise."

Lacey frowned at him. "What, you think I'm worried he won't be back at all? No, that's not it. He loves me, he'll be here. I'm just sick of waiting. I can't do much work because of my arm, so all I'm doing is hanging around waiting for him. It kinda sucks, so I'm going."

When Ian looked to Jane for help, she just smiled at him. "Go get the address, honey. Believe me, it'll be easier in the long run."

Ian looked distinctly uncomfortable. "He's going to kill me."

"I'll pick up some marshmallow fluff when I'm at the market tomorrow."

Ian shoved his chair back. "I'll get the address," he said, and dashed out of the room.

Jane grinned at a giggling Lacey. "Well, that was easy. Need a ride to the airport?"

Chapter Twenty-Three

ॐ

Devon let himself in to his apartment well after midnight, sighing with relief as the conditioned air hit his overheated body. Washington was in the middle of a midsummer heat wave, the humidity so high that walking two city blocks felt like walking through soup, and it wasn't much cooler at night.

Devon shut the door behind him, tossing his keys on the side table by the door. His bones felt brittle with fatigue, his mind fuzzy with it. They'd been working eighteen hours a day for the last two weeks, ever since he'd returned from Mackinac, and all he wanted to do was crawl into bed and stay there for two days.

Actually, what he wanted to do was crawl into bed with Lacey and stay there forever, but she was in Chicago. He sat down in his favorite recliner, tilting his head back and closing his eyes. He wanted to call her, to hear her voice before he went to sleep, but it was too late. Even though it was just after eleven there, he knew she hadn't been sleeping well since she got out of the hospital, and he didn't want to risk waking her.

He frowned. He'd called around dinnertime, but he'd gotten her machine. He hoped that meant she was napping, or maybe Ian and Jane had taken her out to dinner. As much as he knew she needed to rest and relax, he still missed hearing her voice.

He opened one eye and peered across the room into the kitchen. He could just see his answering machine from this angle, and the little readout was flashing the number one. He had a message waiting for him and he felt his heart lift a little, thinking it might be Lacey calling him back.

He stood and crossed the room to rewind the tape. He didn't like digital answering machines. It was too easy to accidentally erase something that he might need one day, so he always used an old analog machine with a minicassette. He reached into the refrigerator for a beer while he waited for the tape to rewind, uncapping a Sam Adams and taking a long swig. When the tape spun to a stop, he reached out and hit the play button.

Ian's voice came whispering out of the machine, the words too low to make them out. Devon frowned, unable to think of any reason why Ian would be calling. He quickly rewound the tape and turned up the volume.

"Hey buddy, it's me." Ian's voice was barely audible, even with the volume on the machine turned up all the way. "Listen, I may be taking my life into my own hands doing this—Jane's got a real vindictive streak—but I thought you should know. I tried your cell, but it was off and your voice mail was full. I hope you call to get this before you get home tonight, because—dammit!"

There was a scuffle on the other end of the line—it sounded like Ian was getting mugged—then a very loud yelp and suddenly Jane was talking. "Hello, Devon, this is Jane. Ian was just calling to say hello, and that we hope you'll be able to make it back to Chicago for our Labor Day cookout. He's just dying to try that new grill my dad got him for the wedding. Talk to you soon—bye!"

Devon stared at the machine, confused. "What the hell was that all about?" he muttered.

"It was probably about me."

Devon cursed, choking on his beer as he spun around. Through watering eyes, he saw Lacey lounging in his kitchen doorway. She was wrapped in his dark blue bathrobe, barefoot, with her hair tousled around her head, her eyes dark and smoky, and her lips pink and wet.

"What?" he managed between coughs.

"The phone call," she said, nodding at the machine. "My guess is Ian was trying to warn you that I was on my way and that he'd given me directions to your apartment and a key, and Jane was trying to stop him."

Devon blinked. "What're you doing here?"

"I missed you," she said softly, her lips curved in a smile, and suddenly it hit him in a rush that after two weeks without her, she was here.

"Baby, I missed you so much," he groaned, and with a whoop, swept her up into his arms.

She squealed, laughing as he peppered her face and neck with nibbling little kisses. "That tickles, you goof! Put me down!"

"No," he mumbled, his mouth busy attacking the sensitive skin behind her ear. "I'm never letting you go again."

"You're going to hurt your shoulder," she said.

"I don't care," he said into her neck. "It really sucked these last couple of weeks, being without you."

"I know," she moaned, shivering as he snaked his tongue into the sensitive shell of her ear. "For me too."

"I'm so sorry about leaving you in Michigan," he said, nibbling his way to her collarbone.

She gasped as he tongued the hollow of her throat. "He drugged you, Devon. It's not like you had a choice."

"I'm still sorry. And I'm so glad you're here," he said. He lifted his head to look at her face. "You're like the answer to a prayer."

"Aw," she said softly, overwhelmed by the love she saw in his eyes. "I love you too, handsome." She leaned in and kissed him, lingering over it until it threatened to get away from her then pulled back.

"Okay, put me down," she said.

"Why?" he asked. "I finally have you where I want you."

"If you don't put me down, you don't get your present."

"You're present enough."

"Aw, that deserves another kiss," she said, and gave him one. "Seriously though, put me down."

"I don't want to. I like you where you are."

"Okay," she shrugged. "I just want the record to show that I was willing to pay up, so you've got no cause to bitch."

"What do you mean, pay up?" He looked confused for a moment then his face lit up like Christmas Eve. "The bet? A night of sexual servitude?"

"I was going to," she said. "But if you don't want me to, that's fine. But like I said, no bitching later about missing out."

"Oh no," he said, and dropped her on her feet so fast she bounced. "I'm not turning this down." He gestured for her to precede him out of the room. "After you, sex slave."

"Jeez," she said, rolling her eyes. "Way to kill the romance, dude."

He snorted and propelled her out of the room. "Romance, schmomance. I got me a love slave."

She laughed and dashed down the hallway with him following close on her heels. When she darted into the bedroom, he flew in after her then came to a skidding stop.

"Whoa," he said in surprise, surveying what used to be a plain, masculine room. "How'd you do all this?"

"Do you like it?" she asked.

"It's amazing," he said. And it was. She'd turned his plain, utilitarian bedroom into a lavish paradise. His plain cotton quilt had been replaced with satin sheets in a shimmering red, his one lone pillow gone in favor of half a dozen smaller ones in a rainbow of rich silks piled high against his oak headboard. The lights were all off, but his dresser was lined with candles that lit the room with a gentle glow and gave off a faintly exotic scent.

He turned to look at her. "When did you do all this?"

"My flight got in at four," she explained. "I know you've been working late and Ian said you had something particularly tricky today, so I did a little shopping."

"A *little* shopping?" he asked, looking around the room in awe. "What else did you get?"

"Oh, just this," she said slyly, and let the robe drift to the floor.

Devon's jaw went slack, which Lacey thought was very satisfying reaction. It had taken her all afternoon to find a harem girl outfit that didn't look like either a stripper's outfit or a child's Halloween costume, but in the end she'd managed.

The gauzy pants rode low on her hips, the waist banded with a wide swath of the same fabric shot through with silver threads that just covered her pubic bone. They were a soft violet, with slits down each side that ran from hip to ankle and were banded at the ankle with the same wide band of silvery fabric as the waist. Her breasts were cradled in a bra-style top of the same fabric that pushed them up so they nearly spilled out the top. She had a golden belly chain slung around her waist and a cast on her right arm.

Devon's slack-jawed enjoyment of the outfit came to a shuddering halt when he saw the cast. He'd known her arm was broken, and she'd told him they'd had to cast it, but the robe had hidden her arm from view, and somehow he'd managed to forget all about it.

Still, there wasn't a lot of blood left in his head just then. "You...uh...your arm. Can you um...do this?"

She snickered before she could stop herself. "My arm is fine, sweetie. How about you? How's your shoulder?"

"It's fine," he said absently. He couldn't seem to take his eyes off her belly, with that shimmering chain bisecting it.

"Since we're both fine—" she took a step toward him, making the belly chain shimmy and shimmer in the light "—

why don't you take a seat?" She planted her fingertips in the center of his chest, gently prodding him backward until he bumped up against the bed. He sat automatically in response to her gentle shove, his eyes skimming up her torso to her face.

He grinned suddenly, like he'd just realized what was happening. "You've got something planned, don't you?"

"Oh, I have many things planned," she purred, sinking to her knees and shooting his blood pressure up a few notches. "First and foremost is to make you comfortable. A good love slave always makes sure her Master is comfortable."

He grinned wider. "Yeah?"

She smiled and tapped his foot with her hand as she settled on her haunches. "Put your foot up here, handsome." He placed his sneakered foot gently on her knee, and she quickly undid the laces, using her good hand to slide it off his foot, taking the sock with it. She repeated the action with the other foot then rose to her knees again.

"This might be a little difficult," she said, tapping the button fly of his jeans with a gentle finger. She didn't think she could manage them with her arm encased in plaster, but she was determined to wait on him as much as she could. A bet was a bet after all, and besides, this love slave business was kinda sexy.

"I'll undo them," he said, and started to rise to his feet.

"No wait," she said, keeping her hand firm on his fly. "I want to do it."

"Honey, you'll hurt your hand. Let me do it."

"Nuh-uh," she said. "I'm the slave, I get to do it." She studied his fly for a second, her brow furrowed in thought, then she smiled. "I know," she said, looking up at him through her lashes. "Try not to move, okay, sweetie?"

"Why?" he said, then, "Oh, my God," as she leaned her head into his lap.

She took the placket of denim covering the buttons of his fly in her teeth, holding it taut and using her good hand to work the buttons free. She heard him groan as her breath washed over him, soaking through the thin cotton of his boxer briefs as the denim parted, and couldn't resist adding a little puff of air as the last button popped free.

His hips gave a little convulsive surge and he groaned. "You're going to kill me."

She laughed and leaned back, tugging at his jeans with one hand. "Okay, I do need help with this part."

"Thank God," he said, and stood in a rush. He shucked his jeans and briefs in one swift motion then ripped his shirt over his head.

"Okay, ready," he said, and sat back down.

"Hey," she pouted. "I could've done some of it, ya know."

He looked pointedly to where his cock stood straight up like a flagpole. "Babe, it's been two weeks. I'm pretty damn tired of my own hand. I don't really need any foreplay here."

"Well tough," she said, rising to her feet. "It's been two weeks for me too, and I *do* need foreplay." She pushed him back to lie flat on the bed. "And I didn't even have the benefit of my own hand, so you're just going to have to suffer."

"What, no Raul?" he asked with a grin. He scooted up on the bed so he could lie down full-length against the pillows.

She scowled at him, holding her casted arm aloft. "I'm not supposed to get this wet, and I'm right-handed. So, no, no Raul."

"Poor baby," he said with a grin.

"Don't get sassy with me, mister. I can draw this out until Tuesday if I have to."

He arched a brow. "You know, this doesn't sound very love-slavish to me."

She grinned. "It's Lacey-style love slave," she said, unable to fully suppress a giggle.

"I don't think this is the night of sexual servitude I was promised," he groused.

"No? Okay," she shrugged and turned to leave. "If you don't want to have sex, I can always go make a sandwich." She gained half a step before she felt his big hand latch onto the back of her harem pants.

"Hold on there, sugar britches." He hauled her back until she bumped into the side of the bed. "I was promised a love slave and I want her."

She grinned at him, unable to help herself. "Then shut up and let me get on with it."

He gave an exaggerated sigh and released his grip on her pants. "Fine," he said, and lay back, tucking his hands behind his head. "But if you don't do it right, you'll have to start over."

"Oh my," Lacey said, making her eyes big and wide with mock trepidation. "I'll do my very best not to disappoint you, sir! My very best."

"Smart ass," he muttered.

She gave him a saucy wink. "You can get your hands on my ass later," she promised. "Right now, it's my turn."

She sat at his hip, bracing her weight on her good arm as she leaned over him. "I really wanted to give you a rubdown," she murmured, nuzzling his throat. "But I can't do it with the cast."

"That's okay," he said, one hand coming down to cradle her head. "It'll give me something to look forward to."

She picked up her head. "What makes you think I'm ever going to do this again?"

He snorted. "You love this."

"You'll never prove it."

"Really?" He slid his hand from her hair and delved between her thighs. His fingers stroked over her through the gauzy fabric, her pussy clenching and her breath coming out in a hiss as he unerringly found her clit.

"Oh yeah," he rumbled with a laugh. "You're immune, all right. Jesus, you're so wet I could bathe in you."

Lacey couldn't help the convulsive jerk of her hips as his fingers stroked over her sensitive flesh. "Oh, right there," she gasped, leaning into his touch. She blinked when his hand suddenly wasn't there anymore. "Hey!"

He was smirking at her as he slid his hand back behind his head. "Oh, I'm sorry," he said. "Did you want me to get you off?"

"Duh!"

"Maybe later. If you're a good love slave."

She ruthlessly choked back the laugh that wanted to escape and narrowed her eyes. "Oh, you're going to pay for that one," she growled.

He laughed at her. "Big talk. How about some action to back it up?"

"You want action, big boy? You got it." She reached behind her, unclipped the bra and let it fall to the bed. She leaned over him, supporting herself on her good arm, and lowered her head slowly. She kept her eyes on his, watching them narrow and heat as her mouth came ever closer to his cock. She saw his eyes slide closed as her breath washed over his rigid flesh, saw him tense in anticipation of that first contact, but she bypassed the tempting thrust of his cock and instead dipped her tongue in the sensitive hollow of his belly button.

He hissed, the muscles of his abdomen rippling in reaction. She did it again, this time turning her head slightly so she faced his torso and the soft waves of her hair brushed against his cock. He groaned, his hands coming down, and she quickly pulled away before he could tangle them in her hair.

His eyes flew open, and she shook her finger at him. "No, no, no," she said. "You don't lift a finger. I'm the love slave, remember? So if you want me to do something, all you have to do is tell me."

Devon's lips curved in a sensual smile. "Now, that's more like it," he murmured, his voice low and rough with arousal.

"So," she whispered, "what would you like me to do, Master?"

"I want you to suck my cock, slave," he rumbled, tucking his hands behind his head and shifting his legs farther apart. "Now."

Thank God, Lacey thought. She'd been dying to wrap her lips around him since he'd walked in the door. She scooted closer to his hip and wrapped her hand around the root of his cock. With a coy look through her lashes, she purred, "Your wish is my command," and swirled her tongue around the head.

They both moaned at the contact. She swirled her tongue over him again, feeling her cunt heat and flood with moisture at the delicious taste of him. She reveled in his groan, the twitch of his hips as he instinctively pushed closer to the wet heat of her mouth. She trailed her tongue down his length, tracing each vein and ridge with delicate precision until he was groaning continuously and driving his hips upward with every stroke of her tongue.

Lacey slid her tongue up around the head of his cock, scooping up the pre-come gathered there with a little hum of delight. Bracing herself, she climbed over his leg to settle in the V of his thighs. Still grasping the base of his cock, she laid her plaster encased arm over his left thigh for balance as she bent her head low and gently, delicately, circled one testicle with her tongue.

His breath whooshed out of his lungs and his legs fell farther apart. His eyes opened, the pupils dilated with lust, and his hands came down to clench the sheet. "Yes," he growled.

She parted her lips and with careful suction, drew one testicle into the wet cavern of her mouth. Careful to keep her teeth sheathed, she swirled her tongue in a gentle caress that had him tossing his head on the pillow and tearing at the sheet with his hands. She repeated the action with the other testicle, suckling with restrained passion until he reached down and grabbed her shoulders.

Lacey squealed as he hauled her up, dragging her over his body until they were face-to-face. "Hey," she said, careful not to whack him with her cast. "What happened to you telling me what you want instead of grabbing?"

"How do you expect me to be able to talk after something like that?" he rasped, and hauled her mouth down to his.

She whimpered in his mouth, opening eagerly for the invasion of his tongue. She shivered as he thrust firmly into her mouth in a parody of sex, his tongue sliding deep along hers. She curled her own tongue up, suckling at his and, with a hoarse shout, he tore his mouth from hers.

"I'm really sorry," he gasped. "It's a really cute outfit. I'm going to miss it."

She blinked. "What?" she gasped, trying to bring her hormones under control long enough to concentrate on what he was saying.

"Really sorry," he said, and grabbing a fistful of her pants, yanked.

Lacey let out a startled squeak as the delicate fabric tore, all but disintegrating in his hands. He yanked and pulled until it was completely off then tossed the shreds of fabric aside.

"Now," he said, "I want you to get up here."

"Where?" she panted, and squealed again as he gripped her hips and lifted her.

"Here," he said, and positioned her hips above his head. "Grab the headboard," he instructed, shifting her knees so they settled into the pillows above his shoulders.

She leaned forward and locked the fingers of her good hand around the headboard resting her cast along the top. She felt his hand dig into her buttocks, pushing her even higher, then her brain went blank at the first touch of his tongue on her eager flesh.

He didn't mess around with little teasing licks and nibbles, but instead delved deep, parting her lips with his thumbs and driving his tongue right to her core with one velvet thrust. She moaned, clenching her fingers so hard on the headboard that her knuckles turned white. She was so aroused, so ready after two weeks of abstinence, that it only took a few piercing thrusts of his tongue to send her soaring.

Her head went back as the orgasm exploded in her belly, her eyes flying open to stare blindly at the ceiling. It seemed to go on and on, the spasms racking her body and wringing whimpers from her throat. He kept his tongue moving, shifting his grip so he could attack her clit with his thumb, and she cried out as sensation began gathering anew.

It was long moments before he let the orgasm settle and fade, leaving her weak and shaking in his grip. She unwrapped bloodless fingers from the headboard and struggled to catch her breath, starting a little when he picked her up and pulled her back down his body so that they were face-to-face again.

"I thought...I was supposed...to be your love slave," she managed, still gasping for breath.

He chuckled. "Next time," he promised, and slanted his mouth over hers.

She could taste herself on his lips, and the combination of her own musk and the dark spice that was uniquely Devon had renewed desire pumping through her veins. She tore her mouth from his, panting.

"God," she moaned, diving back in to lick at his mouth. "How do you do that? I came like a firecracker not two minutes ago and with one little kiss I'm wanting you all over again."

"It's a gift," he said.

"It's a good gift," she breathed. "I really need you inside me."

Devon's eyes flared, his grip on her hips tightening convulsively. "Tell me you bought condoms today," he said through gritted teeth.

"Bedside table," she said, licking at the salty skin of his neck. She felt him reach over and heard the tear of foil. She looked up when she felt him start to slide his hands down between them.

"Let me," she said, and he handed her the condom.

She scooted down, careful not to knock her cast into him, and settled back between his legs. She grinned up at him and held up the condom, then trapped it between her lips and lowered her head.

She fitted her lips over the head of his cock, keeping her lips tight to hold the condom in place. She heard him groan as she used her mouth to slowly push the condom down his length, using her tongue to stroke and swirl and tease. She used her hands to move it the final few inches, her mouth clinging to him as she slowly drew back.

She tossed her head back and rose up on her knees, his hands sliding around to her ass to pull her toward him.

"What do you want me to do, Master?" she murmured. "Tell me what to do."

Devon lifted her up, his grip on her hips bruising, and brought her down on his cock. He arched his hips up while he pulled down, driving his cock inside her waiting warmth with one, sure stroke. When she held all of him deep inside, he slid his hands from her hips to her thighs, resting them there lightly. "Ride," he said, and she began to move.

She rose up slowly, her breath catching at the delicious friction as his cock dragged at sensitive tissues, then lowered herself just as slowly. Up and down, slow and steady, watching him through heavy-lidded eyes. He lifted his hands to her chest, taking her nipples between his fingers and rolling them, and the delicious pinch had her picking up the pace.

Her skin was slick with sweat, her breath coming heavy with the effort of keeping the rhythm steady when all she wanted to do was race to the finish. She could already feel the flutters in her belly, the coil of tension winding tighter and tighter, but she didn't want it to be over too quickly.

Devon's hips were surging up slightly on her down strokes, and his hands on her breasts were kneading firmly as his arousal grew. She moaned, loving the firm touch. Her arousal was at such a fever pitch that she wouldn't have even felt a light touch, but the hard press of his hands was perfect, making her moan out loud and clench down on him.

She began moving faster, her hips pumping wildly as he began surging beneath her. She cried out, her head going back in a hard arch as the tension inside her reached flash point. She lifted up and dropped, once, twice, then ground herself into him as she exploded around him.

She dimly heard him shout out loud, felt his hands slide to her hips and clamp down, holding her in place as he shuddered and pulsed. She collapsed on his chest in a sweaty heap, limp with exhaustion. She felt him roll her to the side and deal with the condom, but she didn't have the energy to open her eyes.

"You awake?" he asked, his voice hoarse.

She sighed a little, letting herself go boneless on his chest. "Uh-huh."

"I think we should stay here for the rest of the night," he suggested, his hand stroking up her back in a lingering caress.

"Works for me," she mumbled, cuddling into him. She could hear his heart beating against her cheek, the steady rhythm strangely comforting.

"Lacey?"

"Hmm?"

"How long are you staying in Washington?"

She picked her head up at that. "I'm staying as long as you are," she said.

"Are you sure?" he asked. "I don't know when I'm going to see daylight on this case, I could be here for a month or two."

"Ian told me," she said simply. "I have my laptop and Jane's going to send me the rest of my clothes and look after my apartment while we're gone."

"You really want to stay that long?"

"Absolutely." She frowned at him. "You don't want me to?"

"Of course I do!" He hastened to assure her. "But I wasn't sure if you'd be up for an extended stay. I'd understand if you want to get back to Chicago. You can come for the weekends, and I can always try to get away for a weekend or two."

"No," she said. "I don't want to spend the next possible few months just talking to you on the phone—I want to be with you."

He brushed a kiss over her lips. "I want to be with you too. Here, I've got something for you."

"A present?" she said, perking up a little. "I love presents!"

He snorted, rolling to his back. He stretched to reach the nightstand and opened the drawer. "I was going to give you this when I got back to Chicago, but you're here now."

Lacey felt her mouth drop open as he dropped the small, square velvet box on his chest. Her eyes flew to his. "What is that?"

Devon rolled his eyes. "It's a giraffe," he said. "What do you think it is?"

She licked suddenly dry lips, unable to take her eyes off the box. "I'm kind of afraid to speculate."

"Oh, for Christ's sake," he muttered. He picked up the box and flipped the top open, turning it so she could see the contents. "There."

"Oh *wow*," she said, awe in her tone. "Devon, it's beautiful." A single round-cut solitaire in a simple platinum setting, the ring caught the faint light from the candles and seemed to glow from within. "It's the most beautiful thing I've ever seen."

He plucked the ring from the box and tugged at her left hand. "Are you going to marry me?" he asked.

"I can't believe this," she whispered, tears clogging her throat as he slid the ring on her finger, and a look of sheer panic crossed his face.

"Why are you crying?"

She laughed, sniffling. "Because I'm happy, you goof." She molded her lips to his in a soft kiss. "Yes," she whispered. "I am going to marry you."

"Good," he muttered. "Jeez, talk about a heart attack. You shouldn't cry when a guy gives you a diamond ring."

"Sorry," she laughed. She snuggled her head on his shoulder, watching the way the diamond caught the light as her hand rested on his chest. "I like the way it feels."

"How does it feel?" he asked.

"Real," she said. "Important. Permanent."

He pulled her hand to his lips, pressing a kiss first to her palm then to her knuckles just above the ring. "It's all of those things. I love you, Lace."

"I love you too," she said.

"But I really don't think I got full payoff on that bet."

She chuckled. "Well, I've never been a love slave before," she said. "I may need to practice."

"Hallelujah!"

She dug her fingers into his ribs, laughing when he cursed, wriggling to get away from her hands. They grappled for a moment, Devon being very careful of her cast, until he finally managed to grasp her hands and pin them over her head.

"Cry uncle," he murmured, and she caught her breath at the renewed heat in his voice.

"Surrender? Never!" she said with mock ferocity.

"I can make you surrender," he warned.

"Oh yeah?" She smiled up at him and twined her legs around his. "Give it your best shot, Devil-man."

Her last thought before his mouth slammed down on hers was that life with him would never be boring.

Thank God.

Enjoy an excerpt from:
GROUNDED

∽

"I hear the boss got it on," Lenny crooned. "Did you get your kicks then?"

Rocket shook his head and pretended to sift through a pile of reports. The words on the pages became a jumble of symbols since Lenny's question brought to mind the woman from last night.

"It wasn't like that Lenny." Rocket's voice cracked. He did a lousy job of covering his elation.

"Oh." Lenny sucked in a breath and wolf-whistled. "So you got your socks knocked off then?"

Lifting his head, Rocket laughed. "You know, you don't talk like any cop I've met."

"That's 'cause I'm not a cop and don't change the subject, lover boy."

At that, Rocket threw down the pile of paper he was holding, simultaneously lowering his guard. Lenny wanted details and while Rocket had never before had the kind of friendship with a man where kiss and tell was the rule, he needed to share this with someone.

"You're wrong." He shook his head, glad they were the only two in the room. "My socks didn't get blown off. They, along with the rest of my attire, were ripped from my body by a goddess."

Lenny slapped his thigh and laughed hard. "I knew it. Who was she?"

"Some black-haired beauty who blew into my life for one night. I didn't even get her name."

"Damn." Lenny shook his head. "I need to teach you a few things about getting laid, man."

It was Rocket's turn to laugh. He learned his lesson all right, but not from any bloke. No, he'd been thoroughly taught how to *get laid*, as Lenny put it. Trouble was, one night wasn't enough.

"You know, if she's on tape, I could find her for you..." Lenny offered.

"Nah." Rocket shook his head, not wanting to abuse the surveillance system for personal reasons. "If she's the right one, she'll come back."

Not that he believed his words. Heck no. He believed the complete opposite but he wasn't about to tell his chief of security that. The sad reality for Rocket was that last night would have to suffice.

"If you don't know who she is," Lenny persisted, "then how do you know you didn't get sucked into a trap? She could be some crazed psycho after you or your money."

Rocket's head snapped to attention. He'd learned that lesson the hard way shortly after his twenty-first birthday and he wasn't about to repeat it. It probably paid to pursue the possibility but every time her face entered his thoughts, all sense of responsibility exploded.

"No." Rocket shook his head. "She didn't come across that way at all."

"No?" Lenny's eyebrows arched incredibly high. Those silk black brush strokes almost reached his hairline. "Exactly how did she come, then?"

Opening his mouth to respond, Rocket snapped it shut when he saw the mischievous twinkle in the ex-cop's eyes. "Damn you," he muttered. "I knew I shouldn't have told you about her."

Lenny laughed. "Okay, I'll lay off for now. But in my professional opinion, I'd let me take a look at the tapes if I were you."

"Your professional opinion?" Rocket asked, dropping into a nearby chair.

Lenny nodded, his expression one of exasperation. "You hired me to look after the club, yes, but you also hired me to look after your safety. Remember?"

Rocket frowned. He remembered no such thing. "I did?"

Nodding, Lenny reached across the desk and picked up the remote control. With it, he could control all the footage from every camera in the club and right now, he aimed it at the bank of television screens on the far wall.

"You didn't say it in so many words but a man of your repute needs some protection. I'm your man."

Taking a deep breath, a wave of fatigue washed over him. Rocket relented and gave Lenny a nod. "Sure, I'll buy it. Run the tapes."

Lenny grinned and hit the play button. Immediately the wall of television screens came to life, showing last night's crowd. The center screen, some seventy or so inches across, came alive with a sea of bodies dancing to the muted music.

He saw her right away, moments after she entered when she danced erotically with the men around her. It wouldn't take long for him to enter the frame and while he wanted to see how they looked together, Rocket didn't want Lenny seeing him get up close and personal the way he'd done.

"That's her," Rocket said. Lenny paused the tape. "The one in the center, long black hair."

"Jesus," Lenny gasped. "You can see right through that shirt of hers." His head spun to look at Rocket. "She's not wearing anything under it."

Rocket couldn't stop the grin forming on his face. No, she wasn't. He saw that now, though how he missed it last night was anyone's guess. On the screen before him, he got a closer look at that tattoo on her shoulder. Nothing was familiar about it but he could tell it belonged to a band, or a gang, or something of that nature. Lenny had one that he wore proudly, but his tattoo came from his days on the police force and all the members in his division had the same one.

From the camera angle, only the top of her head showed. Lenny sifted through the various angles but couldn't get a clear shot of her face. She couldn't have hidden from the cameras any better if she tried, but the frustration it caused Lenny amused Rocket.

"Don't worry," Rocket said easily. "She'll look right up into the camera in a minute."

"Say again?"

Rocket shrugged under Lenny's scrutiny. "She looked right up at me."

"See? I told you she's after you. How else would she have known you were there?"

"Luck, Lenny, woman's intuition. Don't read too much into it."

Together, Lenny and Rocket watched the scene unfold as the woman used her incredible feminine power to charm every man around her. Lenny commented that if he'd seen her first, Rocket wouldn't have stood a chance. Rocket believed him.

At the moment she looked up, Lenny paused the tape. The room fell quiet and they both stared at the screen. Rocket felt her eyes all over him again. His groin ached in remembrance of her tightness and he was suddenly glad for the cover of the table. How could a simple image of her make him hard again?

"Jesus H. Christ," Lenny cursed.

Rocket expected Lenny to comment about her gorgeous face but instead he remained tight-lipped. He said nothing, just shook his head and stopped the tape. His face paled and he looked like he might throw up. Everything about him said he recognized her, but when Rocket asked, Lenny denied it. What Lenny couldn't hide was the ghostly look of acknowledgment in his eyes, the one that told Rocket the truth.

Lenny knew her identity, which meant Rocket could get in contact with her. But Lenny wasn't telling and that had Rocket more than worried.

Why an electronic book?

We live in the Information Age—an exciting time in the history of human civilization, in which technology rules supreme and continues to progress in leaps and bounds every minute of every day. For a multitude of reasons, more and more avid literary fans are opting to purchase e-books instead of paper books. The question from those not yet initiated into the world of electronic reading is simply: *Why?*

1. ***Price.*** An electronic title at Ellora's Cave Publishing and Cerridwen Press runs anywhere from 40% to 75% less than the cover price of the exact same title in paperback format. Why? Basic mathematics and cost. It is less expensive to publish an e-book (no paper and printing, no warehousing and shipping) than it is to publish a paperback, so the savings are passed along to the consumer.

2. ***Space.*** Running out of room in your house for your books? That is one worry you will never have with electronic books. For a low one-time cost, you can purchase a handheld device specifically designed for e-reading. Many e-readers have large, convenient screens for viewing. Better yet, hundreds of titles can be stored within your new library—on a single microchip. There are a variety of e-readers from different manufacturers. You can also read e-books on your PC or laptop computer. (Please note that Ellora's Cave does not endorse any specific brands. You can check our websites at www.ellorascave.com

or www.cerridwenpress.com for information we make available to new consumers.)

3. *Mobility.* Because your new e-library consists of only a microchip within a small, easily transportable e-reader, your entire cache of books can be taken with you wherever you go.

4. *Personal Viewing Preferences.* Are the words you are currently reading too small? Too large? Too... ANNOYING? Paperback books cannot be modified according to personal preferences, but e-books can.

5. *Instant Gratification.* Is it the middle of the night and all the bookstores near you are closed? Are you tired of waiting days, sometimes weeks, for bookstores to ship the novels you bought? Ellora's Cave Publishing sells instantaneous downloads twenty-four hours a day, seven days a week, every day of the year. Our webstore is never closed. Our e-book delivery system is 100% automated, meaning your order is filled as soon as you pay for it.

Those are a few of the top reasons why electronic books are replacing paperbacks for many avid readers.

As always, Ellora's Cave and Cerridwen Press welcome your questions and comments. We invite you to email us at Comments@ellorascave.com or write to us directly at Ellora's Cave Publishing Inc., 1056 Home Avenue, Akron, OH 44310-3502.

erridwen, the Celtic Goddess of wisdom, was the muse who brought inspiration to storytellers and those in the creative arts. Cerridwen Press encompasses the best and most innovative stories in all genres of today's fiction. Visit our site and discover the newest titles by talented authors who still get inspired - much like the ancient storytellers did, once upon a time.

Discover for yourself why readers can't get enough
of the multiple award-winning publisher
Ellora's Cave.

Whether you prefer e-books or paperbacks,
be sure to visit EC on the web at
www.ellorascave.com

for an erotic reading experience that will leave you
breathless.

1356025

Made in the USA